A NEXT GENERATION NOVEL

WITH Us

J.M. WALKER

IBSN: 978-1-989782-09-5

FAMILY TREE

Angel and Genevieve "Jay" Rodriguez
(Grit, King's Harlots #1/Grim, King's Harlots #3)
Angelica "Gigi"
Ryder
Meadow

Asher and Meeka Donovan
(Stain, King's Harlots #2)
Aiden
Ashton

Coby and Brogan Porter
(Rude, King's Harlots #4/For You, King's Harlots #7)
Zachary "Zach"

Dale and Maxine "Max" Michaels
(Numb, King's Harlots #5)
Piper

Vincent "Stone" and Creena Stone
(Rust, King's Harlots #6)
Luna
Vincent Junior

Greyson and Eve Mercer
(Greyson, Hell's Harlem #1)
Jaron

Tray and Zillah Lister
(Tray, Hell's Harlem #2)
Beatrix "Bee"

John and Beatrix "Trixie" Butcher
(Hell's Harlem Series)
Cyrus
Samson "Sammy"

PROLOGUE

Meddow

I **DIDN'T WANT HIM** but at the same time I did. Although I felt that way, I still let him use my body to make us both feel good.

Ashton Donovan was a friend and a convenience. While he was good, he wasn't the best and he wasn't what I was looking for. Even though I had those thoughts, I still slept with him. But I wouldn't classify what we did as sleeping. In any way.

"This needs to end," Ashton said, taking the joint from my fingertips and bringing it up to his mouth. He stuck the end between his full lips, lips that had covered every inch of my body only an hour before. He sucked. Blowing out the sweet smoke. A low groan left him.

I appreciated his love for weed and how he never judged me when I needed it after we had sex. Even though we hadn't been sleeping together for long, what we were doing wasn't healthy. For either of us. But of course, we never talked about it.

"Getting high?" I leaned back against my headboard. I knew what he was going on about but a part of me was still hurt that it hadn't been me to say those words instead of him. "We can switch it up and get drunk instead," I offered. He was right though. I liked to let people think that I wasn't ready for a relationship when really, it had been what I wanted for a while now. But I wasn't sure what I was looking for. A guy to treat me nice. To take me on dates. To even hold the door open for me. Chivalry was few and far between, but I knew there were men who still did those small things.

"No." Ashton sat between my legs and laid back against me. "Us."

"How come?" As much as I agreed with him, a piece of my heart ached a bit to hear him say it. I should have voiced those thoughts first but for whatever reason, I could never get them out.

"Because you're not into this, Meadow. Sure, it was fun at first and you give good fucking head." Ashton puffed on the joint. "But I know it's not enough. Not for you. Not even for me."

I placed my hand on his chest, feeling his heart beat beneath my palm. "It's comfortable," I finally confessed. But it really wasn't. Ashton made me feel better because I hadn't found what I was looking for. Hell, I didn't even know what I wanted. My brain was a jumbled mess because on one hand, I wanted to be swept off my feet by Prince Charming and then on the other, I wanted to be fucked dirty against a wall. I needed to stop reading my friend's romance books. It wasn't like I had to shack up with someone right away. But I still longed to have that person to go home to.

"I know." Ashton sat up, landing those beautiful baby blue eyes on me. "But I also know that you like a challenge, Meadow. And remember." He winked. "I'm too young for you."

I laughed, wrapping my arms around him and pulling him back against me. "Maybe you're right. You need a woman who's completely into you. Not just for your hot as hell body and big dick."

He grunted, wrapping his free hand around himself. "It is quite big."

"It is." I wiggled out from behind him and moved in front of him before kneeling between his legs. Giving the tip of his cock a kiss, I moved up the length of him. "Do you think in another life, this could have worked out? Whatever this was between us?" Even though this thing with Ashton could never amount to something serious, I cared for him. I had known the guy my whole life and knew that he would never hurt me. Even though I was just one of the many notches on his bedpost, I knew everything I got with him. We had both agreed that this would be sex. Nothing more. But even I had to admit that I had some sort of feelings for him.

Ashton sat up, giving me the joint. He raked a hand through his shaggy blond hair before giving me a small smile. "I think this definitely could have worked out. In another life though. Both of us like sex too much and with other people."

I knew he had been sleeping with other women while sleeping with me. It was one reason why I wanted to end things. We had always been safe but as much as I enjoyed the casual sex, I needed someone who was committed to only me.

"We could have an open relationship." I straddled his lap, wrapping an arm around his broad shoulders. "Maybe, have a poly type thing going on."

Ashton leaned back on his elbows. "In another life, Meadow."

"Yeah. In another life." My gaze dropped to his lap. "Will you let me ride it one last time?"

"Babe." His eyes darkened. "I'll let you do whatever the fuck you want to it."

I laughed, swiping my thumb over the pre-cum dripping from the slit in his dick. A soft sigh left me. "I'm going to miss this." But I knew he was right. This wasn't healthy for either of us. As much as I didn't want to settle down, whatever Ashton and I were doing wasn't moving forward at all.

"Meadow?"

I jumped, my eyes shooting to his.

"Are you being a girl for once and letting your feelings get in the way?" Ashton raised an eyebrow.

"I…"

He flipped us over, so I was lying beneath him. "I know I said that we should stop this but it can wait until tomorrow." He leaned down, licking along the shell of my ear. "Tonight, your body is fucking mine."

ONE

Meadow

ASHTON AND I HAD broken things off and I wasn't okay. I was antsy and on the verge of calling him up and telling him that he was wrong. He wasn't. But I was bored. I had done all the baking I could for the day. I ran out of weed and didn't feel like going to get some more. Especially because it was pushing ten at night and the person I usually got the weed from didn't live in the safest of areas. My dad would kill me if he knew where I had to go to feed my addiction.

Maybe Ashton had weed.

No. I could not go there. Not again.

He was fun. A friend. That was all. He needed to move on and so did I. But God did he know his way around my body. Maybe he didn't and it had just been awhile for me and I was satisfied by anything. It wasn't the case, but it was possible. Maybe?

I pinched the bridge of my nose, clearly losing my mind.

A light knock sounded on the door to my bedroom.

I frowned, rushing to open it and finding my sister staring back at me. "What's wrong?" I asked her, stepping out into the hall.

"Are we still going out for drinks?" my sister, Gigi, asked, hope dancing in her honey colored eyes. While she got our mother's tall slender frame, I was short and curvy.

"Oh, sure. I didn't think we were still doing that." Our friend, Luna, had gotten into a fight with her boyfriend. The tension rushing through our house was thick. Everyone had gone their separate ways after said boyfriend punched the shit out of Ashton. But even in his bruised-up state, he was still hot as hell. I really needed to get it together.

I had never actually been attracted to Ashton, who was a twin. His brother, although hot as well, didn't do it for me. But when Ashton was giving Luna and her man, Zach, issues, I stepped in because, what are friends for? I had no idea in the beginning that this thing with Ashton would continue. I had assumed that we would fuck once, and he would move on to his next conquest. He did but kept me beneath him just the same.

"Ashton took Luna to the hospital." Gigi shook her head, a deep frown settling between her brows. "I can't believe Zach elbowed her."

I scoffed. "No kidding."

Although Luna shouldn't have tried to break up the fight, I probably would have done the same thing. React first and think later. And now she possibly had a broken nose because of it.

"Where's Piper?" I asked Gigi as we left the house.

"She's meeting us there. I was thinking we go to a bar that's not in our city." Gigi stopped in front of her car. "Sound good to you?"

I shrugged. Didn't matter to me either way. I just wanted to get drunk and find someone, maybe even two someones, to curb this itch.

"What's with you?" Gigi asked, narrowing her brows at me from the other side of the car.

"Nothing." I slid into the vehicle, buckled up the seat belt, and stared out the window.

She sat in the driver's side, turned on the car, and paused. Her stare burned into the side of my head.

"What?" I demanded, my head whipping around.

She laughed, putting the car in gear and backing us out of the driveway. "You know, you never should have started fucking Ashton in the first place. It's messing you up."

"No, it's not." It wasn't. I cared for him. Of course I cared for him. All of us had grown up together but Ashton couldn't give me what I wanted. I wasn't sure if anyone could.

"It really is," she insisted.

"Oh, and you know all?" I threw back at her. "So, tell me, Gigi. How's Vince doing? Did you two fuck yet? Or at least actually talk?"

She glared at me, her jaw ticking. "I have no idea what you're talking about."

"Right." I turned back around, staring out the window. "I love you but until you both get your heads out of your asses and admit your feelings for one another, don't judge me for my shit." It may have come off as harsh, but my sister needed to be told. Vince Junior had been her crush for years, but he was only nineteen. Even though he was turning twenty in the next few months, it didn't mean anything. He was still five years younger than her and that stopped her from making a move. Or so she said anyway. Something had happened before he went off to school. But none of us knew what that was.

"Fine, don't need to be a bitch about it," she mumbled.

I laughed, shaking my head. "So, where are we going?"

"Some bar in the city. It's actually near Zach's condo. I thought it would be best to go there just in case Luna needs us for anything."

I thought a moment. "Are they going to the city?" I just assumed Ashton would drive Luna home after her visit at the hospital.

"I don't know. This was more Piper's idea. I just go with the flow." Gigi shrugged.

"Interesting."

A little bit later, we were pulling into a parking lot by some bar. "This place doesn't even have a name. Are you sure we aren't going to get murdered here?" I just hoped they made my death unique. None of this boring shit that happens so much, it's overdone. Skin me alive or something and make it worthwhile. God, I needed to get a life.

"Piper mentioned it." Gigi sat forward. "But yeah, this place looks creepy. Although, it is in a safer part of town." She shrugged. "Can't be that bad."

"Right," I said slowly. "Cause that's what every victim says before they get slaughtered."

"You watch too many movies." She stepped out of the car.

"I do not." I followed her, slamming the door shut behind me. "Just because horror movies inspire me when I bake, doesn't mean I watch too many of them."

She laughed, hooking an arm around my shoulders. "Yeah, it does."

"Whatever. At least my treats turn out tasty." Baking was my calling. I lived and breathed pastries, donuts, cakes…it was also why I had a few extra pounds in my hips, ass, and tits. Although, my breasts did get me out of many speeding tickets.

Gigi and I crossed the street, heading to the bar that looked more rundown and like it didn't belong in this part of the city.

WITH US

Motorcycles sat in the alley beside the building. I paused in my steps, letting my eyes rake over the beautiful machinery. Each bike was different. In size. Color. Style.

"Meadow?"

I jumped, my cheeks burning at being caught staring. "Just looking."

Gigi nodded toward the motorcycles. "Remember, you can't touch the pretty bikes."

"I know." I sighed. I went to follow Gigi into the bar when one of the bikes caught my eye. It was bigger. With a deep blood red gas tank, it held a black skull on it. I had seen that skull before. I glanced around me, making sure that I was alone after Gigi had gone into the bar.

Once I was satisfied that I wouldn't get maimed, I ran my finger along the gorgeous artwork. What I wouldn't give to feel the rumble of the engine between my legs. I bet this bike growled like a lion.

"Careful."

My heart jumped to my throat. I slowly glanced over my shoulder, finding an older man leaning against the brick wall. His thick arms were crossed under his chest. His piercing green eyes bore into mine. A light smattering of brown scruff covered his jaw like he hadn't shaved in a few days.

"She's beautiful," was all I said.

"I agree." But he wasn't looking at the bike.

My body buzzed at the emerald orbs peering at me but as much as I wanted to play with this new stranger, I had to get inside and join the girls.

"Well, this was fun." I walked by him when a hand reached out to grab my upper arm. I met his stare, getting lost in his eyes.

He peered down at me. His tongue peeked out, licking along his bottom lip.

My eyes followed the movement, a hot shiver racing down my spine at the sight. Nothing was said but something definitely slid between us.

Clearing my throat, I pulled from his grip and headed into the bar.

(Shade)

I was going to fuck her. How I knew this, I wasn't sure but the tiny little thing that just walked past me, with heat in her eyes, was definitely going to be mine. Or ours I should say.

"Hey."

Speaking of…

Sunny Harrison took that moment to join me. He passed a glance between his bike and me, then back to his bike. "Someone touched her."

"Someone did but I promise, you won't give a shit about that when you see who that someone was." I pushed away from the wall and headed to the back of the bar. It was a shithole, but they served good beer and the owner let us do our thing without being disturbed. As long as we kept the peace of course.

"Who touched her?" Sunny asked, his voice rough like he had just gargled with broken glass. It was one of the things I liked about him. His deep voice that could make me weak in the knees every damn time, but of course, I never told him that. A bi-sexual biker wasn't the norm. Even though people were more open about sexual preferences these days, I still kept that little bit of information to myself.

Once we stepped into the bar, I nodded in the direction of the table at the other end of the room. "She did."

Sunny followed my gaze, his brows narrowing. "Which one?"

"Which one do you think?" I asked him, crossing my arms under my chest.

"The tiny one?" His nostrils flared. He looked back at me. "You talk to her?"

"Yes, the tiny one," I repeated. Even though she was small, she was curvy, and I could see the swell of her breasts pushing against her dress. She had some weight on her. Which would be perfect for when Sunny and I fucked her body at the same time. "Briefly. She's with her friends."

Sunny ran his fingers through his beard, his blue-gray eyes burning into the young woman that I wanted gagging on my dick.

"Fine." Sunny moved to the booth behind us. "I can wait."

I chuckled, sitting beside him just as another member of our club rolled in. "Right, Sunny."

He grunted, raking a hand through his hair. He repeated the movement two more times before dropping his hand on his lap. He was antsy, and I couldn't say I blamed him.

Sunny and I shared women. A lot of women. But I hadn't seen someone that sparked this newfound awareness deep inside of me in a long time. I needed to know who this woman was. I didn't even give a shit if I had her beneath me before I found out her name. I wasn't the dominant type. Never had been. I had my moments. Dominance was Sunny's job. It was why we balanced each other out so well. But there was something about this tiny little thing that had me wanting to control her and submit to her all at the same time.

"Shade?"

I jumped, finding two pairs of eyes staring back at me.

"Yeah, sorry." I rubbed the back of my neck. "I'm a bit distracted."

Jaron Mercer only grunted. He was the vice president of the Hell's Harlem motorcycle club that we were in. And while he was young, he never let that stop him from showing men twice his age who the boss really was. When his father, the president, wasn't around.

"See something you like?" he asked, his gray eyes peering into mine.

"Maybe." I nodded to the table across the room. The three women were looking back at us every so often, the one, focusing solely on Jaron himself. "You know them?"

"Yeah. Grew up with them." Jaron scratched the dark scruff on his jaw. "I'm bored." He stood, giving us a smirk. "Let's go say hi."

(Meadow)

I had walked past the three guys sitting in the booth when I went to the bathroom. Even though I never made eye contact with them, I could feel them staring at me.

Once I headed back to the table, I found the man I ran into earlier, sitting with another guy I didn't know at the same table I shared with the girls.

As I got closer, I saw Jaron Mercer sitting beside Piper.

It had been awhile since we had seen him. He looked good. Really good. He had become larger since I last saw him and while he was hot as hell, he didn't do it for me. But the two older, much older, men sparked something inside of me. I was curious and thought maybe I should test out my theory.

"Oooh. Hello, boys," I sang, waggling my eyebrows and sitting between the two older men.

"Do you come here often?" the one I hadn't met already, asked. He glanced at my mouth.

My heart jumped.

I was vaguely aware of Jaron saying something to him.

"Fuck you I don't," the man said, crossing his arms under his chest.

I shook my head, not even hearing what was said in the first place. I was so mesmerized by this guy's eyes, that I hadn't heard what was said to him.

The man leaned toward me. "How old are you?"

"Twenty-two." I grinned. "Why?"

In a quick move, he pulled me onto his lap. "Good enough for me."

I laughed, my heart jumping over the fact that this guy, a man I didn't know, took it upon himself to touch me. Desire curled deep in my belly. Looked like I enjoyed a man who took charge. "Don't get any ideas in that old brain of yours. My daddy would kick your ass if he knew you were rubbing your dick against me." A very large dick I might add.

"Your daddy doesn't scare me," he growled in my ear, his lips brushing over the soft spot beneath it. "I want to bend you over this table, hike up this sexy as fuck dress and make you beg for your daddy to come save you," he said, low enough for only me to hear.

I coughed. No one had ever talked to me like that before. It was always me doing the dirty talking. Well, this could get quite interesting.

Looking across the table, I was met by Piper's wide stare.

I gave her a wink. "You know it's rude to tell secrets in front of people." I cupped the man's face, reveling in the scratchiness of his dark beard tickling my palm. "Why don't you tell our friends here what you just said?"

He raised an eyebrow.

"Yeah, Sunny," Jaron said. "Tell us what you said."

"I'd really like to hear this," the guy beside us added.

The man I now knew as Sunny, cleared his throat. "I said to her—"

"No." I ran my thumb over his bottom lip. "Tell them what you just said. To me."

Something flashed in his dark eyes. His hand that was on my hip, tightened its hold on me.

"I said," Sunny repeated, "that I want to bend you over this table, hike up this sexy as fuck dress, and make you beg for your daddy to come save you."

I grinned, patting his cheek. "Good boy."

TWO

SUNNY

I **HAD ALWAYS BEEN** the dominant one. Whether it be in my sexual exploits, relationships, or even my damn job, I always barked out the commands. But when this little lamb made her own demand of me, I couldn't help but comply.

She had quickly given us her number when we were told by the woman sitting beside Jaron that they would be leaving alone.

Too bad. But it didn't mean that I couldn't tease this sweet little thing a bit.

While laughter sounded around the room, I cupped her knee and inched my hand higher beneath her dress.

She shifted on my lap, pushing her round ass harder against my dick, but she never stopped me. No, she continued her conversation with her friends while the big bad wolf played with his little lamb.

I passed a glance at Shade.

He moved to the empty chair beside me, placing his elbows on the table and shielding us from any onlookers. Reaching out, he cupped her knee.

She coughed and then continued her conversation.

I bit back a chuckle. "Tell me your name, Little Lamb," I murmured in her ear when there was a break in her conversation.

"Meadow," she said. Her voice was soft. Husky. But while it wasn't full-bodied and loud, it still held a hint of a confidence that I craved.

"Do you want to play with the wolves in the meadow, Little Lamb?" It was cheesy but the smile it put on her face was fucking worth it.

"Oh yeah." She pushed her ass back against me.

My cock twitched, swelling beneath her. Sliding my hand higher up her thigh, her dress now sat bunched up at the crease between her thigh and hip.

Shade kept his hand on her knee.

In a quick move, I spread my legs, forcing her knees apart.

Her breath caught.

I noticed then that Jaron and Piper had disappeared, leaving Shade and I alone with Meadow and her sister who was currently passed out on top of the table.

"She good?" I asked, pushing my hand higher up Meadow's inner thigh.

"Yeah." She hooked her arm around my shoulders and looked down at our hands on her. "She had too much to drink in a short amount of time." She glanced between us both, her dark eyes twinkling with mischief. "So, do you always pick up younger women at the bar?"

I grunted.

Shade chuckled. "No. It's been awhile. We're rusty."

"Hmm." Meadow pushed her ass into me. "By that delicious lump in your jeans, you don't seem that rusty."

A laugh rumbled through me. "That's why there's a lump. Because it's been awhile."

"Aww." She pouted. "Poor, baby. So, is this a thing? You two pick up women, bring them home and tear them apart?"

"No." Shade scratched his jaw, his eyes raking over Meadow. "But I sure wouldn't mind trying to rip you apart."

"Hmm…" Meadow leaned forward, cupping his cheek.

Shade licked his full mouth and I knew that if we were alone, he would have pushed his hand into her hair, pulled her against him, and kissed the hell out of her. I knew because it was what he did. We had fucked so many women together, that I could predict every single one of his moves. I had a feeling that with Meadow though, she would keep us both on our toes.

"I think that can be arranged," she purred.

My dick jumped. Fucking hell. This woman was something else.

But just as I was about to offer to get out of there, Jaron and the woman he had been eye-fucking, decided to take that moment to come back and join us. Jaron sat, and the woman walked right by us.

Meadow jumped off my lap. Faster than I thought possible, the three of them disappeared out of the bar.

"Well that was interesting." Shade raked a hand through his hair. "I need to take a piss." He stood, pulled back the rest of his beer, and headed to the bathroom at the back of the bar.

"What's with you guys?" Jaron asked, taking a swig of his own beer.

"I have no idea what you're talking about," I told him.

"Right." He chuckled. "Listen," he said, the smile suddenly falling from his face. "Whatever you do, don't hurt her. She has a large father and many men in her life who she considers uncles. So just be careful."

"She single?" Even though she had been sitting on my lap and flirted with us, it didn't mean shit half the time.

"Yeah, she is. As far as I know." Jaron peered at me over the rim of his glass. "Meadow isn't like most women. Hell, in a previous life, I bet she was a man with half the shit she says."

"Oh?" I raised an eyebrow, unsure as to what he meant by that.

He shrugged. "Just don't hurt her."

"I don't plan on it." But if she asked me to spank her ass and pull her hair, who was I to argue?

(Meadow)

We rented a cheap motel and helped Gigi onto one of the double beds.

"I love you girls," she slurred, rolling over onto her stomach. "Like so much."

I laughed, shaking my head and pulling off her shoes before tossing them to the floor. "We love you too, Gigi."

Piper pulled the covers up and over her when she started snoring softly.

I sighed, slumping onto the edge of the other double bed. "You can take this one. I can sleep with drunky over there."

Piper laughed lightly, sitting on the bed beside me. "Doesn't matter. At least she hasn't thrown up. Remember when we drank that really cheap wine and I got sick in my bed?" She grimaced. "That was so gross."

"I forgot about that." I giggled, shaking my head. "I think we all puked that night. It took me a long time to be able to drink red wine after that."

"It didn't take me long. I just make sure to always get the good stuff from now on." She winked.

"Good plan." I paused. "Listen." I wasn't sure if she knew about Ashton and I but I needed to tell her. "I have something to tell you."

"You've been sleeping with Ashton," she said, giving me a small smile.

"Yeah. He was giving Luna and Zach a hard time, so I thought if I distracted him, it would help." I laid back on the bed. "It was a stupid decision but I was bored."

"I'm not mad, Meadow. If that's what you're worried about." Piper had slept with Ashton and his brother, Aiden, but broke it off after her backpacking trip to Europe. Rumors went around that she met someone. I almost didn't believe it until tonight and saw the way she was looking at Jaron. Especially when shortly after, both her and Jaron had disappeared. But I wasn't sure how that had anything to do with Paris.

"I'm glad. I don't want any problems." I sat up, leaning on my elbows. "He ended things though. God, I'm making it sound like we were fucking for months. But…"

"You care for him. I get it. I care for them too, but I couldn't do it anymore."

"How did you know?" I asked, rolling over onto my stomach and leaning my chin on my palm.

She looked at me then. She sighed, turning toward me. "I heard him talking about it."

"Huh…should I be pissed that he was talking about our sex life?"

She laughed. "No. If anything, you should be proud. He was bragging, saying it was the best sex of his life."

"Oh." My face fell. "I'm sorry."

"Don't be. I wasn't into it anyway. The first time, sure, but it never should have happened again after that." She shrugged. "Live and learn I guess."

"I probably should have…I don't know. Asked you first? You know, chicks before dicks kind of thing." I laughed lightly, my heart stuttering. God, I was nervous. I never got nervous. Not about this shit. But Piper was a friend. Even though I was a few years younger than them, I was never excluded growing up. They never considered me as just Gigi's little sister.

"Girl, trust me. If they can get off my back, I'm down for it. It was fun but after Paris..." Her cheeks reddened. "And..."

"And tonight?" I added for her.

She looked away. "Yeah."

"Hey." I touched her arm gently. "I don't judge. Jaron's hot. Intense but very hot. I see the way he looks at you."

She met my gaze then. "Really? You saw something?"

"Oh yeah. It almost makes me jealous." I rose from the bed and went to the floor-length mirror that hung on the wall by the bathroom. For a rundown motel, at least they had a good-sized mirror.

"Really?" Piper scoffed. "Since when do you get jealous?" she asked, coming up beside me.

"I know. It's throwing me off too." I was only twenty-two. Was I even ready to settle down? It wasn't like I had found anything even remotely close to what I had been looking for. Ashton was fun but that was it. And it was safe with him. I wanted dangerous. I wanted more. "I think I'm going to head back to that bar." That would definitely be dangerous. I smiled to myself.

"Are you sure you want to do that? Is it even safe?"

I ran my hands down my front, smoothing out the wrinkles of my dress. "Safe is boring, Piper. That's why you let Jaron fuck you in the bathroom tonight." I turned toward her. "Isn't that right?"

She blushed, running a hand over the back of her neck. "Yeah, but..." She sighed. "Oh, who am I kidding. It was fucking amazing."

I laughed, pulling her in for a hug. "See?" I leaned back, holding her at arm's length. "Now, I'm going to go have some fun of my own."

"Fine." Piper searched my face. "Call us if something goes wrong though."

"I will. I'll text you when I get to the bar and to wherever else I end up but please don't worry. They know Jaron. So they can't be that bad."

"True." Piper chewed her bottom lip. "Be safe and have fun."

Oh, I planned on it.

THREE

SUNNY

"**I WANT HER.**" My back stiffened at the desperation in Shade's voice as he came toward me. I puffed on my smoke, not commenting on the matter at hand.

"Sunny." He took the cigarette from my hand and stuck it between his lips. "I will have her. Both of us will." He was on the verge of losing it because he had actually quit smoking a while ago. But whenever he was on edge, he grabbed a smoke, lit it up, and acted like nothing was wrong.

"How do you figure? She was probably just having some fun. Maybe she got dared by her friends to flirt with the old fuckers who couldn't stop flirting back." It wasn't like it hadn't happened before. Young women, women of all ages really, wanted bikers to have their way with them as a way of sowing their oats. We were a fantasy. Nothing more. Nothing less. Hell, I didn't even have any tattoos. It was the leather. Always the damn leather. Not that I ever cared before. But for whatever reason, it was starting to bother me. I was getting old and wanted to settle down before I met my maker.

"I don't give a shit," Shade said, continuing on his tirade. "I want her. I want to feel her choking on my cock while you're fucking her tight juicy cunt."

A shiver raced down my spine at the graphic image he put in my head. "She's young."

"That didn't stop you from pulling her onto your lap tonight."

"I was flirting. So was she. Nothing more is happening." I lit up another smoke, not even believing the words I just said.

"But that's not what you told her." Shade paused, searching my face. "I know you want her too. You told us all how much you want her. Remember?"

"Yeah. I remember," I mumbled. Anyone else and I would have been pissed that they made me voice my thoughts like that but with Meadow, I found I didn't give a shit. I realized then that we hadn't even given her our names.

"So, what are we going to do about it?" Shade asked, hope dancing in his bright green eyes.

"Nothing." I inhaled the sweet smoke, taking it down deep into my lungs and blowing it out slowly.

"Sunny." His brows narrowed.

"Shade."

"Fuck, man. Why is this only *your* decision?"

"This is both of our decisions but remember what happened last time? I let you lead. I let you pick out someone for us and do you remember what happened after that?" The memory was laughable at best. The young thing couldn't handle us.

"That was a long time ago." Shade moved to the spot beside me and leaned against the brick wall.

"Exactly but it almost tarnished our reps. You need to keep that beast of yours in check. I don't want to hurt *this* lamb."

"She needs to be ours." Shade tilted his head back, looked up at the nighttime sky, and stuck the smoke between his lips. He inhaled deeply, letting the air slowly out of his lungs.

Something stirred inside of me. Something dark. Something feral. He was mine. And I was his. But we were never physical. I wasn't even sure if he wanted to be psychical with me. I was so damn confused lately; I didn't know whether I was coming or going. But what I did know was that I knew how Shade felt. I wanted Meadow. I wanted to share her with him. My partner. My best friend. The only man I had ever let into my bed. Even though we never had sex, sharing a bed was almost just as intimate. If not more.

"You're staring again," he murmured.

"Sorry." I looked away.

"I love you, Sunny." Shade pushed away from the wall and stood in front of me. His emerald eyes searched my face. He took a step closer, the air between us becoming thick with an unknown tension I had never felt before. Not from him. Not even from a woman. Not until tonight when Meadow sat her ass on my lap.

"I know," I whispered. Normally calm and collected, it took everything in me not to shove him away. We never talked about taking our relationship to the next level. I wasn't sure why. We had agreed in the beginning after Shade had been hurt by his ex, we would just share women and that was it. But something changed tonight. And I wasn't sure if it was for the better or worse.

"We *will* have her," Shade said, his voice final.

"I know. Fuck man, I know." I raked a hand through my short hair, noticing the way it had grown in some. I needed a haircut.

"You saw the way she was with you," Shade pointed out. "With me. She's feisty as hell."

"I'd like to see her in a dominating role," I blurted. Was that what I really wanted? "See if she can handle it." Apparently so.

"I'd fucking submit to her and I don't care if it makes me look like a pussy."

"Submission does not make you look like a pussy, Shade," I snapped. "How many times do I have to remind you of that?"

"Shit. I didn't mean it like that."

"You're still so damn new." We had gone to a couple of BDSM clubs and decided to implement that lifestyle into our daily lives, but Shade was still learning.

"I've been doing this for a couple of years now," he liked to point out from time to time.

"You can do this, as you say, for your whole life and still not know everything," I reminded him.

"Sunny, I need to feel something other than my fucking palm and I know she will be what I need. What we both need."

"I know." Just as I was about to push away from the wall and head back inside the bar, the very reason Shade and I were on edge, walked up to us.

Meadow lifted her hand, giving us a small wave. Her curvy hips sashayed from side to side. Her soft curls fell down around her face. That dress, that damn white dress, hugged her curves and made me want to weep like a baby. My cock hardened, pushing against my jeans and begging to come out and play.

She tilted her head to the side, giving me a small smirk. "Are we having a party?" she asked, looking between Shade and I.

"Just out for a smoke," Shade told her, holding the pack out to her.

She shook her head. "Don't smoke but thank you. Now if you have weed, I'm down for that."

"Maybe later," he said, his eyes traveling down the length of her.

"What are you doing out this late?" I asked, interrupting my partner's eye-fucking.

Meadow raised an eyebrow. "I never did get your names," she said, not answering my question.

"What did you put us in your phone as then?" I could have sworn I gave her our names.

"I put you in as Hottie One and him as Hottie Two," Meadow said, like it was no big deal. No blush coated her skin. No hint of amusement danced in her eyes. She was straight up honest and I found I could appreciate that.

I held out my hand. "Sunny Harrison."

She grinned, slipping her small hand in mine. "Meadow Rodriguez." Her grip was firm. "Sunny? Really?"

"My parents were hippies," I explained.

"And how about you, baby boy?" she asked Shade, licking her lips.

He coughed, shifting his weight to his other foot. "Roy Allen but I go by Shade."

"Oh I like it." She looked between us both. "Sunny and Shade."

I chuckled. "It works."

"So how did you get the nickname Shade?"

Shade's eyes flicked to mine. Something flashed behind them before he looked back down at her. I couldn't make out what it was, but it was something that I wasn't ready for. That neither of us was ready for. But I had a feeling that no matter what, we would find out what that was and there would be no going back from it.

"I met Sunny when we were both prospects for Hell's Harlem. We clicked and bonded over that, so we've been best friends ever since. We were inseparable, so the guys nicknamed me Shade and it stuck." He shrugged like it was no big deal.

But it was. Because we were more than best friends. It was hard to explain to people, so that was the reason we always gave them.

"Interesting." Meadow walked between us and headed to the door of the bar. "I want a beer. You guys coming?" She disappeared inside, not waiting for us to follow.

When Shade went to walk past me, I grabbed his arm.

He staggered a bit. "What?"

"Best friends? Really?" I knew I should have kept my mouth shut but I was never known to keep my thoughts to myself.

"What did you want me to say to her, Sunny? That we have a platonic relationship and the only physical contact we have with each other is when a warm body is between us? Come on. That would scare her away and we haven't even done anything yet." He pulled from my grip and took a step away, but I grabbed his arm again.

"You know this is more than that," I told him.

"Yeah?" He raised an eyebrow. "Prove it."

"Shade." I gripped his arm tighter. How the hell was I supposed to prove anything to him when I had no idea what it was that I was supposed to prove in the first place?

Shade turned back around to face me. He pulled from my grip and in a quick move, shoved me up against the wall. "Like I said, Sunny." He leaned toward my ear, his hot breath fanning the side of my face. "Prove it." He released me roughly and stomped into the bar.

I shivered, pushed a hand through my hair, and dropped it to my side with a huff. I hated that he was right.

Heading into the bar, I found him sitting with Meadow at one of the booths. Jaron was nowhere to be found. Other patrons chatted quietly amongst themselves but all I could focus on was Shade and Meadow.

Someone new. Fresh. Young.

And someone else who I had known for over fifteen years. Shade was more than my best friend. He was my life. I just had no idea how to tell him that.

FOUR

Meadow

SUNNY AND SHADE JOINED me at the booth, but something was off with them. Sunny had a scowl on his face while Shade kept glaring daggers at him. Almost as if he were challenging him in a way. Were they an actual couple? They didn't act like it, but the way Shade looked at him made me wonder if there was something more there than they both let on. I had questions I wanted to ask but knew when to keep my mouth shut. As much as I usually voiced my opinion, I knew that this was not one of those times where I should say whatever was on my mind. No matter how much it was driving me crazy.

"Everything good?" I asked when Sunny sat beside me.

He glanced across the table, narrowing his brows at Shade. "Yup."

Shade crossed his arms under his chest. "What are you having, Meadow?"

"Just a beer please." I pulled my phone from my bag and texted Piper, letting her know that I was at the bar and I was safe. Didn't need her worrying to the point she showed up and ruined what little chances I had of having some fun.

"Want anything, Sunny?" Shade asked.

"Beer," Sunny grunted.

Shade nodded, left the booth, and headed to the bar.

"Not that it's any of my business, but what's going on?" I asked Sunny once we were alone. Looked like I didn't keep that promise to myself for long.

"It's…complicated." Sunny huffed, staring after Shade.

"Oh…well…" I turned my body toward him, lifting my knee and resting it on the bench beneath me.

Sunny peered down at me. His nostrils flared. He shook himself, averting his gaze. "You're something else, pet."

My stomach tumbled at the term of endearment. "Is that good or bad?"

He met my gaze. "Why would you think it was bad?"

I shrugged. "I know I can be a little much sometimes."

Sunny pinched my chin, tilted my head back, and searched my face. "Don't change for anyone, you hear me? I've been around long enough to know that only your true friends won't give a shit what you do, what you say, or who you're with. As long as you are fucking happy, they shouldn't care. Understand me?"

I nodded.

"I asked you a question," he said, his voice firm.

Desire coiled in the pit of my stomach at the deep vibrato of his voice. "Yes." I licked my dry lips. "Sir."

A cocky grin pulled at his lips. "I like the sound of that word on your tongue, Meadow."

I laughed. "Of course you would. I'm sure most men would like being called *Sir*."

He chuckled. "Probably."

Shade came back at that moment with a pitcher of beer and three glasses. "Jaron texted me and said that he's at the motel. He's calling it a night."

"Probably had too much sex and it wore him out," I said, pouring each of us a beer.

"How do you know he had sex?" Sunny asked, taking the glass from me after I filled it to the top.

"Both him and Piper disappeared. I put two and two together. It doesn't take a rocket scientist to know that there's something there," I explained.

"Well it's none of our business but I happen to agree." Shade took a sip of his beer.

"You do?" Sunny rested his arm across my lap, his thumb brushing back and forth over my knee.

"I do." Shade shrugged. His eyes flicked to somewhere beside Sunny. A dark shadow passed over his face. "Fuck me," he growled.

"What?" Sunny followed his gaze. "Shit." His head whipped back around. "Move beside her."

"What's going on?" I asked as Shade slid closer to me. But before he could answer, three men, large fucking men, dressed in leather cuts, joined us at the booth.

One man, with a long black ponytail, sat in the booth as another sat beside him. He was younger but had an air of authority around him. A patch saying *President* sat on the left breast of his cut. He stared at me. His sapphire orbs twinkled. The other man stood with his arms crossed, probably making sure none of us bolted.

"What do you want, Tanner?" Sunny demanded, his body stiff.

"I heard you were in the area," the man, Tanner, with the deepest blue eyes I had ever seen, said.

"It's a free country," Shade answered, inching closer to me. He rested his arm across my lap alongside Sunny's.

Under normal circumstances, I was sure anyone would feel smothered by these two big men but right now, I didn't care. I was the only female surrounded by bikers. I put on a brave face and came to the bar, hoping to run into Sunny and Shade again because I wanted them. Both of them. But even I knew when to be cautious. And clearly with the way Sunny and Shade were with me, they were protecting me as much as they could.

"Is it really?" Tanner sat back in the booth, his dark blue eyes meeting mine. "We haven't been introduced." His gaze dropped to my chest. "Are you sharing?" he asked Sunny and Shade.

My skin crawled, bile rising to my throat.

"Fuck," Shade muttered.

"Listen, whatever you came here for, take it and leave." Sunny sat forward, shielding me from the other man standing beside the table.

"Aww. No need to be rude." Tanner stuck his hand out. "Tanner Horsch. President of Satan's Rejects."

A part of me wanted to keep my hand back but another part thought it would be better to be polite. I lifted my hand and went to return the handshake when Sunny stopped me. The move had been so quick, I never even saw it coming.

"What the fuck do you want?" Sunny kept my hand in his, holding it on my lap.

Tanner chuckled. "Tell your president that I'll be stopping by." He knuckle-rapped the top of the table and motioned to his men. When he stood from the booth, he paused, staring down at us. His gaze landed directly on me. "I'm sure I'll be seeing you around, little one." He looked at Sunny. "You should bring her by the club sometime. I'm sure I could get a lot of money off of her."

Before I could think twice about it, a laugh escaped me.

Tanner raised an eyebrow. "Something funny?"

"You'd probably have a better chance of getting women to do things for you if you weren't such a domineering asshole," I blurted.

Shade softly chuckled.

Sunny's head whipped around.

I swallowed hard, but I refused to back down. I wasn't letting this fucker scare me. I was raised better than that.

"Yeah you should definitely bring her by," Tanner finally said. "Then I can show her how I shut up my girls who speak out of line."

Sunny moved to get up when I grabbed his arm, stopping him.

Tanner and his men left, their laughter following along behind them.

"What the fuck was that, Meadow?" Sunny demanded when we were finally alone.

"The guy's an asshole." I crossed my arms under my chest. "I wasn't letting him get to me."

"Fuck." Sunny raked a hand through his hair. "You need to learn not to say every damn thing that's on your mind, pet."

"You don't know me." I glared at him. "How the hell do you know that I always say what's on my mind?"

His jaw ticked.

"He's right." Shade pinched my chin, forcing me to look up at him before Sunny could answer me. "Tanner's crew isn't like ours. They don't treat their women with respect. They do anything to make a name for themselves. They want people to fear them. They get off on it."

"He doesn't scare me." But he did. And that pissed me off.

"He *should* scare you." Shade brushed his thumb along my bottom lip.

I shivered at the soft contact.

"Hmm…" His gaze dropped to my mouth. "I could get used to this."

"Used to what?" I breathed.

"Touching you." He placed a soft peck on my forehead before releasing me.

I sighed, going back to my beer. "You mad at me?" I asked Sunny, lifting the glass to my lips.

"Depends." He leaned down to my ear. "I think you should make it up to me."

"Hmm…" I turned my head, our mouths mere inches apart. "How should I make it up to you?"

"I can think of many ways, Meadow." He cupped my knee, his fingers digging into my flesh.

"Did it piss you off when he threatened me?" My hands itched to reach out to him. To cup his face. To feel him against me. To run them over every inch of him.

"More than I could ever tell you," he grumbled, pulling away from me.

My heart stuttered at his confession. "Did it piss you off too?" I asked Shade.

His jade eyes darkened but instead of answering, he slid out from the other side of the booth. "Finish your beer. We need to go."

Sunny did the same and left the bench, leaving me alone at the table. Both men looked down at me.

"We really need to go," Sunny added.

My stomach flipped. I downed the beer, finishing it quickly like they demanded.

Was this it? Would my fantasy finally come true? I still had so many questions but for now, I was going to enjoy the rest of this night and let these men do whatever it was they wanted to do to me.

FIVE

SUNNY

TANNER HORSCH PISSED ME off. Always had. Probably always would. He was your stereotypical biker and he made us good guys, look bad. I especially didn't like the way he looked at Meadow and every male instinct inside of me wanted to take it out on her. It wasn't her fault. She was beautiful. Tanner would be a fool not to notice. But it didn't mean I wanted to punish her any less.

"Does he always have that scowl on his face?" Meadow asked, pulling me from my thoughts.

As soon as she stood from the booth, I grabbed her arm and pulled her against me.

She gasped, slapping her hands against my chest.

With her body pressed up against me, my dick lengthened between us.

Her pupils dilated, no doubt feeling just how hard she made me.

Wrapping a hand around her throat, I ran my thumb along her jugular.

She swallowed hard.

I grinned, reveling in the nervous energy coming off of her.

"I'd be very careful what you say to the men you're spending the night with," I murmured, running my lips along the length of her slender throat.

"Oh?" She gripped my leather cut, pulling me harder against her. "And who says, I'm spending the night with both of you?"

Shade chuckled, pulling her from my grip. "Sunny's being nice by warning you, Meadow."

"Really?" She tugged her hands from his and headed down a long dark hallway that led to the motel at the back. Most people didn't know about it seeing as the owner never advertised the place but for bikers, our crew especially, it was a little secret he decided to share with us. "You can't make me nervous," Meadow added, stopping in front of a door at the end of the hallway. "I thought this led to outside."

Coming up behind her, I wrapped my arms around her middle and pulled her back against me. "No, pet." I kissed the side of her throat, rubbing my pelvis into the full seat of her ass. "This door leads to the motel attached to this place."

"A motel?" she breathed, pushing back into me.

Shade reached into my pocket and pulled the keys from my jeans. His gaze caught mine.

I wasn't sure if he was waiting for me to say no or that this wouldn't happen, but I didn't, and I never would.

I needed her. I needed him. I needed *us*.

This needed to happen. Tanner set my nerves on edge and ruined my mood more than it had already been. Shade and I needed to talk. Or fuck. I wasn't sure which anymore and it confused the hell out of me.

With my arm wrapped around Meadow's shoulders, we followed Shade out of the main bar area and into another long dark hallway. When we reached the end of it, he pushed open another door and let us through before he followed behind.

"I never knew this place existed," Meadow murmured under her breath.

"That's the point. It's usually for bikers but every now and again a straggler slips in." Releasing her, I held out my hand. "Last door on the right. Lead the way, pet."

Her gaze dropped to my hand. Taking a deep breath, she slipped her fingers in mine and led the way down the hall.

I glanced over my shoulder, finding Shade following us. His gaze was on her ass. He licked his lips, dropping his hands in front of him. I would put money on it that he was shielding an erection.

Stopping suddenly, I hooked my arm around Meadow's front and pulled her into my side.

"Sunny," she cried softly. "What are you doing?"

Instead of answering her, I lifted her dress up and over her ass. "Is this what you want?" I asked Shade.

His jade eyes met mine.

"Is it?" I repeated, landing a hard smack on the cheek of her ass.

She yelped, the sound shooting straight to the tip of my cock.

"Is it?" I repeated, landing another swat on her full ass.

"Yes," Shade bit out through clenched teeth.

Meadow's gaze burned into me but all I could focus on was the man staring back at me. A man I knew would be my first...everything.

"Then come here. Show me and her how much you want it." I grabbed a handful of her ass cheek and gave it a little shake. Her body fit perfectly in my hands. She was short, curvy in all the right places, and an old man's wet dream.

"Geeze," she whispered, shaking against me.

I leaned down to her ear, brushing my lips over the soft skin. "You teased us a few hours ago, pet. It took everything in me not to slip your panties to the side and shove my cock deep inside you while our friends talked amongst themselves. But as much as I love being watched, I don't think our friends are into voyeurism."

"Probably not," she said breathlessly.

I smirked, licking along the shell of her ear. "Are you into that, pet? You want to be watched?"

"As long as we're the only ones touching each other, I'm down for anything," she confessed.

I lifted my head, staring down at her. "Is that so?" I asked as Shade came up to us.

He grabbed a handful of her ass and placed a kiss on the side of her neck. "I think we can make that happen."

Meadow's grin grew. "Are you going to take me to the room and fuck me or are we doing this out here?"

Shade chuckled, pulling her back against him.

I took a step back and swiped out my arm. "Lead the way, little lamb. The wolves are hungry."

(Meadow)

Once I reached the last door on the right, I stopped and waited. I looked over my shoulder and found Sunny and Shade stalking toward me. God, I couldn't believe this was happening. My fantasy with two men that I never thought would ever take place because all the guys I had been with didn't like sharing. And not in the hot possessive way either. They were just pussies.

"You're thinking." Sunny closed the distance between us and petted his hand over my head. "Stop thinking, pet. We won't hurt you."

"I just met you tonight but somehow, for whatever reason, I believe you." I chewed my bottom lip. "But it still doesn't mean that I'm not nervous."

Shade stood beside Sunny, resting his arm on top of his shoulder. "And why are you nervous?"

"Well, both of you are big. I imagine all of you is…well…big." I let my gaze drop to their waists before meeting their gaze.

Shade chuckled. "Oh, I like you."

Sunny smirked and unlocked the door to the room. "Don't worry, Meadow. We'll make sure you're nice and wet to fit us both. And any pain we cause you, will be because you begged for it." He stepped into the room and turned toward us. "Back out now, pet. Because once you step into this room, you belong to us for the rest of the fucking night."

"What do you want, little lamb?" Shade asked, cupping my shoulders. "You want to be fucked by men?"

I swallowed hard.

"Tell me." He ran his hand to the base of my throat and leaned down to my ear. His hot breath fanned the side of my face. "Say it. Say what you want, Meadow."

I took a breath and let it all out. Everything I wanted them to do to me. "I want you both to spend the night fucking me."

Shade chuckled, the sound dark and inviting.

I knew I should have been smart and run away at that point. They were too much for me.

But I wasn't smart.

And I sure as hell didn't run.

SIX

Meadow

"**Y**OU'VE BEEN A TEASE, little lamb." Sunny stalked back and forth in front of me, his gaze not leaving mine. "You know what happens when the wolf is teased."

"Hmmm…" I tapped my chin, leaning against the wall. "Why don't you tell me? Or are you going to huff and puff and blow my house down?"

Sunny grinned, running his fingers through his beard that I had been fantasizing about since I met him only hours before. Since he pulled me onto his lap, and I felt the very large erection twitching beneath my ass.

"You've got some sass, girl."

"What can I say?" I shrugged. "I learned from the best."

"I bet you did." Sunny stopped in front of me but he was still too far away. The motel room was much larger than I imagined. It held a single king-sized bed with a door across from us that I could only assume was the bathroom.

When I took a step forward, a warm body came up behind me. I spun on my heel, finding Shade smirking down at me. I knew he had been there. His hands had been on my shoulders but the fact that there were two of them still startled me.

His brown hair was shaggy, a little long around the ears, but short enough that it had that freshly fucked style. And I couldn't wait to run my fingers through it.

"Nervous?" he asked, his tongue swiping along his full bottom lip that I would give anything to bite.

"No." I stepped up against him, placing my hand on his chest and backing him up until he hit the wall. With my six-inch wedges on, I came up to his chin. Licking along his jaw, I inched my hand down his chest to the waist of his jeans. "But *you* should be."

He grinned. "Is that so?"

"Yes." Curling my fingers in his hair, I pulled his head forward and crushed my mouth to his at the same time as I unzipped his jeans.

Shade groaned, slipping his tongue between my lips. He tasted sweet but spicy with a mix of menthol. I never found smoking attractive and it was usually a turn off but with these men, I found I no longer cared.

The kiss became frantic. Fast. Someone was desperate for more. Sliding my hand into his jeans, I wrapped my fingers around him. I never meant to take it this far and so fast, but much like the man in my hands, I was desperate. That familiar ache settled deep between my legs and I knew the only way I could get rid of it was by having these men inside me.

Shade shivered. Wrapping his arms around me, he cupped my ass and pulled me flush against his strong body. He released my mouth, trailing kisses down my jaw to my throat. "Fuck, you feel so damn perfect."

My breath caught. My fingers wrapped around him tighter. Stroking. Pulling. Getting him nice and hard. "Do you like that?" I murmured.

He lifted his head, his heated gaze burning into me. Reaching his hands beneath my dress, he gripped the sides of my panties and ripped them with a snap.

My heart jumped.

His grin grew.

I looked over my shoulder, finding Sunny with one hand on the bulge in his jeans and the other stroking his full beard. "Are you jealous?"

"Careful, little lamb. You put two wolves against each other, and you're bound to get eaten."

I shivered at Sunny's words and looked back up at Shade. "Sounds delicious." I squeezed him.

He groaned.

"Aww. Someone isn't pleasing you, sweet boy?" I kissed his chin. "What are you doing to this poor guy?" I asked Sunny.

"We haven't fucked if that's what you're implying," he said, his brows narrowing.

"No?" I looked between them both. "Too bad." I looked up at Shade, running my fingers over the light smattering of scruff on his jaw. While Sunny had a full beard, Shade didn't. "But you want to, don't you?" I asked him, my voice low enough for only him to hear.

"Careful." He pulled my dress to my waist and gave my ass a hard slap.

I jumped, a gasp escaping me. I glared up at him. "Excuse me for saying the truth."

He laughed. "Baby, you have no idea what the fuck you're talking about. If you want us to fuck you, I suggest you quit while you're ahead."

My brows narrowed but as much as I wanted to question him further, I knew when I'd overstepped. "Alright, baby boy. I'll let it go."

His body relaxed at that.

"Come for me," I said, pulling his cock free from his jeans.

"Yes," he said, even though it wasn't a question.

Interesting.

My fingers tightened around him, unable to close completely. My core clenched.

Shade ran his hands up my sides before fisting my hair and tugging my head back.

My breathing picked up at the firm grip he had on me.

"Hmm..." He brushed his nose up the length of my neck. "So young. So innocent. So fucking pure."

"There's nothing pure about me," I told him, keeping a tight grip on his cock.

"Is that so?" Sunny growled in my ear.

I squeaked not hearing him come up behind me.

"I think you *are* pure." He held out his hand.

Shade handed him my ripped panties.

"I also think that you're all talk," Sunny said, stuffing the fabric in a pocket on the inside of his leather jacket.

"Why would you think that?" I squeezed Shade's dick. "I have my hand wrapped around your boy's cock right now. Is that a problem for you? Are you wanting me all for yourself? Is that the issue?"

A wicked grin spread on Sunny's face. "Careful, little lamb. I'm not submissive like my friend here. I bite, and I bite fucking hard."

I took a breath. "Prove it."

His gaze flicked to Shade's and back to mine. "One word and we stop. If it gets to be too much for you. You say it ends and we'll end it. You hear me?"

"That won't happen." I was young, but I knew what I wanted, and I wanted these men.

"Say it, Meadow," Sunny snapped, moving behind me. "One word."

"I understand." I arched into him, reveling in the way his bulge pushed into the seat of my ass.

"Are you sure?" Shade brushed a finger down my jaw. "I may be submitting to you now but tease me again, little girl, and I'll show you just how hard *I* can bite."

"Promise?" I whispered.

He smirked, glancing over my head and nodding.

I gasped as I was pulled back and my upper half was bent forward. I grabbed onto Shade's jacket, stopping myself from falling. "What the hell?" I glared over my shoulder at Sunny.

"You're going to suck him off while I eat this sweet pussy." He lowered to his knees behind me. "Let's see who can come first."

With my hand wrapped around Shade's cock, I watched Sunny lift my dress up and over my ass. His rough, calloused hands ran up my back.

He raised an eyebrow. "I don't see you sucking." He smacked my ass. "Hurry up. Get that mouth full of cock, little lamb."

I turned my head back around.

"Look at me," Shade demanded.

A hot shiver raced down my spine. For someone who claimed to be submissive, he was dominant just the same.

Pushing his dick against his stomach, I licked up the length of him.

He groaned, petting a hand over my head. "Fuck me, it's been too long."

"Why?" I asked, kissing up the veiny ridge of him.

"I have needs, Meadow. And no woman has ever been able to handle them." His dark green eyes stared down at me.

"Interesting." I licked the tip of his cock, sliding my tongue into the slit. Pre-cum leaked from the head, the salty essence of him sliding into my senses.

"Shit." Shade dug his fingers into my hair. "So good."

As I was about to pull away, Shade's hands tightened and forced me farther down the length of him.

I gagged, gripping his leather jacket in my hands.

"You're just going to keep sucking my cock like a good little girl and let him do whatever he wants to you, aren't you?" Shade asked me, guiding me up and down the length of him.

I nodded, breathing through my nose. I had given head before, but nothing ever compared to Shade's size. These men, far more experienced than I, let me play. No other guy I had been with would let me dominate over them or let me submit at the same time. Ashton took full control. He was good. But he wasn't what I needed. It was still too vanilla for me. Although I never had a threesome before, I knew I wanted to venture into the kinky territory. I always needed more but I never knew how to broach the subject with the guys I had been with.

Something soft slid between the crack of my ass. It was warm, wet, and utterly delicious. A muffled moan fell from my lips as Shade continued to pump down my throat.

"Fuck, man, she's dripping for it." Sunny licked from my slit to the tight little hole at my ass. "I bet you're nice and tight too, little lamb. Aren't you?"

Shade pulled my head back, his cock sliding from between my lips. "Answer him."

I looked at Sunny over my shoulder, my heart jumping when he thrust his tongue inside of me. "My ass," I breathed. "Is all yours."

He winked, grabbed my hips in a rough move, and growled against my pussy.

As soon as I cried out, Shade thrust his cock back between my lips.

I gagged, taking him deeper down the back of my throat.

My legs shook, my thighs trembling. Although Shade had a hold of my head, he kept my hands free which I was thankful for. I was the one who started this, but I also needed some sort of control. I didn't mind submitting in any way, but we had to do it slowly.

"Keep your mouth locked on his cock, little lamb." Sunny ran his thumb over my soaked opening. "I want to hear your screams as he fucks your face."

Inhaling a deep breath, I wrapped my hand around the base of Shade's cock and lifted my head up and down the length of him.

"Shit." He groaned, thrusting his hips forward and back. "I'm not going to last long if you keep this up."

A sharp pinch erupted through the cheek of my ass.

I whimpered, my legs spreading even more for Sunny.

"I see someone likes a little pain." Inserting his finger into me slowly, he pumped hard and deep. He rubbed that certain spot inside of me that no man had ever been able to reach before.

My knees shook, sounds of pleasure leaving my mouth.

"Fuck, she's going to come. Yeah, little lamb, keep doing that." Shade guided me, showing me what he liked and how to please him.

Sunny slid his tongue over the tight spot at my ass while rubbing that bundle of nerves inside of me. "That's it. You're going to fucking explode for me."

A white light suddenly shot behind my eyes. My knees gave out. My nerves shattered. A scream left me, muffled by the rough thrusts of Shade's cock between my swollen lips.

"Keep going," he shouted, pumping twice before his own release followed mine. His cum shot down the back of my throat but it was hard to focus on making sure I didn't miss a drop with Sunny's fingers still deep inside of me.

My body shook and trembled, a warmth spreading from between my legs.

"Fucking beautiful." Sunny pulled me back.

Shade's cock fell from my lips.

Falling on my hands, I cried out as Sunny thrust a third finger into me. "*Fuck.*"

Sunny cupped the back of my head, pushing me face first into the carpet and picking up speed with his fingers. "Like that, baby girl?"

I whimpered. "Yes."

"Do you want more?" Sunny asked, pumping his hand against me.

"Yes," I cried out, pushing back against him. "More. Please more."

"Shade, taste her." Sunny released me and moved to a chair in the far corner of the room.

Shade moved behind me, replacing his friend and pushing my dress up my torso. His fingers brushed down the length of my spine before landing a hard swat on my ass.

I threw my head back, a low moan escaping me.

"Have you ever been with two men before, little lamb?" he asked me, landing another slap on my rear.

"No." My fingers dug into the carpet beneath me.

"But you're not a virgin," he bit out.

"No." I braved a look over my shoulder. "Does that bother you, sweet boy?"

He grinned. "It doesn't bother me but he," he pointed his thumb over his shoulder, "might be a little pissed over that."

I glanced at Sunny who currently had his cock out and his large hand wrapped around it. "I don't know."

My core throbbed. "He seems to be enjoying himself right now."

Shade chuckled and rose to his knees. Towering over me, he pushed against my upper back, lowering my chest to the floor. "He made you come. Now it's my turn, little lamb. And then you're going to come on both of our cocks."

"I like the sound of that," I panted.

"Hmm…" He smacked my ass. "What do you want?" he asked me, pushing his now rock-hard cock between the cheeks of my ass. With his jeans still around his hips, he rubbed the abrasive material against the back of my thighs. "Tell me, Meadow. What exactly do you want us to do to you?" Squeezing me, he thrust forward and back, my body leaking all over him.

I shivered. "Shade, please."

"Tell me."

"God, I need you to fuck me. Both of you." The pleasure was almost too much, and they hadn't even done anything yet. Besides the orgasm Sunny had just given me. "Shade?" My voice shook. Before I knew what was happening, he flipped me onto my back.

I gasped.

In a rough move, he spread my legs. "You see, little lamb." He kissed my knee. "While my friend may be the true dominant one between us—" He reached beneath me and lifted my hips into the air. "—This is something I won't submit for."

"What do you mean?" I asked, reaching out for him and running my fingers through his hair.

A wicked grin spread on his face before he covered me with his mouth.

I cried out, latched onto his hair, and drove my hips up against his face.

He growled, his eyes rolling into the back of his head. He sucked my clit into his mouth. It was rough, hard. So damn intense, my thighs shook the more he kept his face between my legs.

"Oh…holy shit," I whimpered, thrusting up and up. Latching onto Shade's hair, I pulled him closer. The pleasure consumed me. It was too much. Not enough. Just right.

More. Give me more.

I was greedy, hungry for the ecstasy burning through me.

Shade hummed, thrusting his tongue in and out of me.

I tugged him forward, a sob escaping me as another release crashed through my very being. His name left my lips, screaming into the air surrounding us.

He grunted his approval, released me with a wet smack, and lowered my hips back to the ground beneath me. Towering over me, he placed a soft peck on my lips.

The heady scent of my desire wafted between us. No words formed on my tongue. What could I even say?

His jade eyes twinkled in the dim lighting of the room. "Ready for more, little lamb?"

A breathless laugh left me. "Oh yeah."

He chuckled, placed one last kiss on my lips before rising to his feet. Holding his hand out, he waited.

I placed my fingers in his, letting him help me up. Turning to Sunny, I lifted my dress up and over my head before kicking off my wedges.

His nostrils flared.

I sauntered over to him and stepped between his knees. "Do you like what you see, Sunny?" I purred, straddling his lap.

His hand tightened on his cock, the tip an angry shade of purple.

"Aww." I pouted, running my finger over the slit in the head. "Little Sunny looks like he's in pain."

Sunny hissed, his hips bucking beneath me. His free hand cupped my thigh, his thumb swiping through my cream that had coated my skin after Shade gave me the second orgasm of the night.

Wrapping my fingers around Sunny's cock, I guided the swollen length through the wet folds of my pussy.

"Fuck." He shivered.

"I need more." I kissed his cheek, circling my hips against him. "Please give me more."

"You're a greedy little thing, aren't you?" Sunny released his cock and lifted me to my knees, taking my nipple into his mouth.

I moaned, digging my fingers through his hair.

A warm body came up behind me followed by fingers trailing down the length of my spine.

A breathless gasp left me. God these men and how they made me feel. It wasn't enough, but at the same time, the pleasure was almost too much to handle.

"Tell us what you want, little lamb," Shade purred in my ear, placing a soft peck on the spot beneath it.

"Hmm…" I leaned forward. "A condom."

Sunny smirked. "Patience."

I pouted. "But why?" I ran my thumb over the tip of his cock. "Doesn't this hurt?"

"No," he said through clenched teeth.

"Sunny likes holding back until he can't take it anymore." Shade kissed my shoulder before holding a condom out in front of me. "Open it and put it on him."

I did as I was told, sliding the rubber down the length of Sunny's veiny cock.

"Good girl." Shade fisted my hair, pushing his hips into the seat of my ass. "He's going to fuck your cunt and I'm going to fuck your sweet little ass."

Sunny swiped his tongue over my swollen nipple. "Fucking hell, I need this pussy wrapped around me." His fingers trailed up my inner thighs before reaching my center. He spread me open, lining up the tip of his cock with my soaked entrance.

Leaning my arms on either side of Sunny's head, I waited.

"Stick your ass out, pet," Shade demanded, running his thumb over the puckered hole.

I arched my hips, taking a deep breath as Sunny pushed inside of me. I whimpered, the size of him stretching me. "Oh God."

"Aww, little lamb." Sunny gripped my hips, holding me still. "God can't save you from the wolves now." At that moment, he dropped me onto him.

A scream shattered through me. My skin tingled. My pussy burned. I felt full but consumed. Completely and utterly...stuffed.

"Fucking hell," he gritted out through clenched teeth.

A second pair of hands grabbed hold of my waist, lifting me up the length of Sunny's cock. "Fuck man, she's soaked. I bet you're a squirter, aren't you, pet?"

I whimpered, shaking between them.

Shade pushed the tip of his cock against the hole between the cheeks of my ass.

"Breathe, little lamb." Sunny reached between us, rubbing his thumb over my clit. "This will hurt but I promise the pain will be fucking worth it."

"I...God...I can't..." I shivered, every inch of me coming alive at the sheer pleasure I felt.

"Shhh..." Shade crooned, placing a soft peck on my shoulder. "We don't want to break our little lamb." He pushed against my body. "Don't resist me, baby." He fisted my hair, pulling my head back against his shoulder and sinking his teeth into the side of my throat. With his free hand, he spit into his palm and lubed up his shaft.

Sunny kept a firm grip on my hips, running his thumb in small circles over my sensitive clit.

"Breathe out when I push in," Shade instructed.

I nodded, leaning back against him and grabbing onto Sunny's jacket for support.

Shade pushed.

I breathed out.

He pushed again.

I moaned.

He broke past the barrier of my body in one smooth thrust and I never felt so damn full in my life.

"You're doing so well, pet," Sunny crooned.

"I..." I swallowed hard. "I need you guys to move. Please move. Please fuck me. God, fuck me." I was begging, pleading for them to take me away. To take me out of my fucking skin. I didn't care how. I didn't care how damn hard they were. I just wanted more. I wanted them to devour me whole.

"Hmm..." Shade pushed me forward. "I think we should start fucking her, Sunny."

"Are you getting impatient, little lamb?" Sunny kissed my jaw.

"Yes," I breathed, attempting to move my hips but his hold on me only tightened.

"Fuck her hard," he told Shade. "I want her coming on my cock while you fuck her ass."

"With pleasure." Shade pulled out and thrust into me hard, forcing a shattered scream to leave my lips.

Sunny only smirked, reached around me, and grabbed my ass, opening me to his friend. But he never moved. While Shade fucked me, Sunny sat there.

"Oh God." I squeezed my eyes shut, the pleasure becoming almost unbearable. My ass burned but the rougher Shade became, the higher the ecstasy rose.

"So fucking tight." Shade's fingers dug into my hips. "Come for me, pet. Squirt that honey all over his cock."

"Harder," I blurted.

Sunny raised an eyebrow, a knowing glance passing between him and his friend. "Do it."

Shade towered over me, his mouth brushing along the shell of my ear. "You think you can handle me, pet? You think you can handle *us*?"

"Try me," I threw back at him. I was going to be sore tomorrow, but I didn't give a shit. I needed this. I needed them. Fuck everything else.

A wicked grin spread on his face when he pushed me forward and started thrusting into me hard and deep. His hips slammed into my ass. His fingers dug into my hips.

I couldn't breathe. The air leaving my lungs only heightened the pleasure consuming me. I heard myself beg but was that really me? Was I dreaming it?

Suddenly, spots danced in my vision. An explosion erupted through me. And I screamed.

"Fuck." Shade thrust even harder. "Keep coming, pet."

I couldn't stop if I wanted to. Warmth erupted through me.

"That's it, baby girl." Sunny gripped my inner thighs, spread me wider, and began to move.

My eyes widened. "O-Oh. Oh God."

He grinned. "Hold on, little lamb. You're about to find out what happens when you play with the big boys."

A shiver trembled through me when my head was tugged back, and a hot mouth attacked mine.

Shade swallowed my cries as both he and Sunny took control of my body. They devoured every inch of me. Thrusting hard. Thrusting deep. Ripping me into pieces and putting me back together again. They felt so damn good inside of me. So good. *Too* good. Even if this was just for fun, I refused to let them go because I knew that no matter what, no other man could ever make me feel this way.

SEVEN

SUNNY

THIS WAS NOT GOOD. Not good at fucking all. While Shade got dressed, Meadow slept in the middle of the bed with her ass pushed up against my crotch. My dick jumped, itching to delve back inside of her again.

I pulled the covers up and over her before reaching a hand beneath them and rubbing my fingers into her muscles.

She curled her arms under the pillow, letting out a soft sigh.

I chuckled, leaned over, and kissed the back of her neck.

"I'm trying to sleep," she whispered.

"Tired, baby girl?" I murmured, pressing my fingers into her shoulder blade.

"Yeah." She turned her head toward me, giving me a small smile. "You guys wore me out."

"Sleep. We got you," I said, placing a soft peck on her shoulder.

She nodded, her eyes fluttering closed.

My heart warmed. I wasn't sure what this newfound feeling was rushing through me but whatever it was, I liked it.

"I like this," Shade said, his voice low. It was as if he could read my thoughts. He moved back to the bed, leaning against the headboard. "I like this a lot. Too much."

I only looked down at Meadow's now sleeping form. After she had the intense orgasm, our own releases soon followed. Not too long after, she passed out in my arms. It was perfect. Too damn perfect and I wasn't sure how I felt about that.

"Sunny." Shade reached out for me.

When his hand cupped my shoulder, I breathed out a slow breath.

"Say something."

"What do you want me to say?" That I liked this. That I needed this. That I needed him and her. Together. That I needed to know what he felt like just as much as he needed to know as well. Things were changing. Fast. And I wasn't sure how to take it. I had never been into men before. Not that I cared if a man or even a woman was gay. It was just never *my* thing. Or I never thought it was. But truth was, I was scared. Even I was man enough to admit that to myself, but could I admit it to Shade? To the club? To Meadow?

"Sunny," Shade said gently.

"Don't." I brushed my hand between Meadow's thighs.

A soft sigh left her, but her eyes remained closed.

"What are you doing?" Shade asked, his brows narrowing.

"I'm just playing with our new toy," I told him, running my fingers back and forth over her swollen skin. "That is what you wanted, is it not? We could have had anyone but yet, you wanted her. Someone so young. So fresh. So damn innocent compared to the others."

His jaw clenched. "I don't...fuck, Sunny. Whatever shit you're thinking, stop it. It's between us. No one else."

"I have no idea what you're talking about," I said, inserting a finger inside of Meadow.

She moaned.

"She's still nice and wet," I told him. "A little swollen. Maybe we were too rough." I wasn't sure what I was doing anymore. Was I trying to make him jealous? Either way, I was fucked up. Always so damn fucked up and confused.

"Sunny," he growled.

Before I could think twice about it, I released Meadow and slid off the bed. Throwing the covers off of her, I grabbed her hips and pulled her to the edge of the bed.

Her eyes popped open then. "What the hell?"

Instead of answering, I grabbed a condom from my jeans pocket, gave my dick a few strokes and sheathed myself. "Say it."

"What's going on?" Meadow demanded. "Sunny?"

"Say it," I bit out, beating the head of my cock against her ass.

"I don't know what you want me to say." Shade glared at me.

"No?" I thrust inside of Meadow.

She cried out, her pussy clamping down around my dick.

"Fuck," I breathed, slamming into her. "Tell me."

"Sunny, I—" Shade shook his head.

"Tell me," I shouted, fucking Meadow like it was her fault Shade and I were in this mess. "Say it, Shade. Say what you want me to do." I cupped her shoulder, slamming my pelvis against her.

She white-knuckled the sheets, pushing back against me. "God. I don't know what's going on, but you feel so damn good."

"You hear that?" I threw at Shade.

"Fuck you, Sunny," Shade snapped.

"Say. It," I repeated, slower that time. "Say it," I bellowed when he didn't answer me.

"I want you to fuck me," he yelled.

Meadow gasped, her body shaking as my released poured into her.

When my heart calmed down, I towered over her and placed a soft peck on her cheek. "I'm sorry, baby. That was not meant for you. I shouldn't have taken it out on your body," I said low enough for only her to hear.

She nodded. "It's okay."

I released her, surprised that she was calm about the whole thing. Throwing the condom in the trash, I got dressed and headed to the bathroom. Slamming the door behind me, I leaned against it and blew out a slow breath.

Fuck. Fucking fuck.

(Shade)

As soon as those words came out of my mouth, I regretted them instantly. The angry eyes staring back at me as Sunny released into Meadow, forced bile to my throat. But what surprised me most was the sympathy in Meadow's dark gaze.

When Sunny shut himself in the bathroom, I slumped onto the edge of the bed.

"I take it that's never happened before?"

I looked over my shoulder, finding Meadow sitting with her legs crossed in front of her. She was holding the sheet against her body, shielding me from her nakedness.

I looked away. "Nope."

"I hardly know you guys, but can I ask what that was about? Or do you not know?"

I shrugged.

"Oh."

I turned toward her, taking in her beauty. Her dark curly hair was a mess around her face. Her deep chocolate brown eyes twinkled in the dim lighting of the room. Bags sat beneath her eyes as well, but she was absolutely perfect if you asked me. Maybe too perfect.

"I've only been with one man before," I heard myself saying.

Her gaze popped to mine.

When she didn't respond, I continued. "Sunny and I have known each other for years. We were in our early twenties when we became prospects for Hell's Harlem and have been best friends ever since." Friends. Fucking please. I hated that term when it came to what Sunny and I shared.

"What's that look for?" Meadow asked, tilting her head.

"What look?" I ground out.

She rose to her knees, hugging the sheet against her and shuffling closer to me. When she was inches away, she reached out and brushed her thumb over my face. Almost like she was tracing it to memory.

"That frown. It's almost as deep as Sunny's," she said gently.

I swallowed hard, my heart racing. What was it about this young woman that got to me? I couldn't figure it out but at the moment, I didn't want to.

"You're in love with him," she murmured.

I only nodded.

"Does he know?"

"He does but every time I say it, I feel guilty." I pulled the sheet from her hands, tugging it away from her body.

"How come?" she asked, breathlessly.

Her dark nipples pebbled in the cool air. The apex between her thighs, bare and so damn delicious, teased me. Taunting me. Begging me for another taste. But I wouldn't. No. Sunny and I needed to talk first before anything else happened with our little lamb.

The sound of the shower starting, traveled around us. Sunny had no doubt been stewing this whole time.

"Shade?" Meadow cupped the side of my neck. "Whatever shit you have going on; you guys need to talk. Go to him."

"And do what?" Her pretty little clit peaked out at me. I licked my lips.

She laughed. "I think you both need to talk before we do *that* again."

My gaze snapped to hers.

She gave me a cocky grin. "As much as I would love to have your face between my legs, right now, you need to talk to him."

I nodded, blowing out a slow breath. But although I agreed with her, I still inched forward. Brushing the back of my hand over her lower stomach, I reveled in the way her skin erupted into tiny goosebumps.

"Shade."

"Hmm…" I leaned toward her, giving her ear a gentle nip.

She jumped.

"I will fuck you again, little lamb. And I will taste you. I'll suck your clit between my teeth so damn hard, your pussy will squirt all over my face."

"I'm sure you will." She shivered, leaning away from me. "Talk to him before I change my mind and let you do whatever it is you want to do to me."

"Haven't you already done that?" I asked, raising an eyebrow.

She winked. "Not everything, baby boy." She placed a quick kiss on my mouth before jumping off the bed.

I bit back a groan at the sight before me.

As Meadow pulled her dress down over her head, the door to the bathroom opened.

Sunny peaked his head out, his gaze finding mine. "We need to talk."

My heart jumped.

I glanced back at Meadow. She nodded which gave me the push I needed to get off the bed and go to him. She jumped on the bed, leaned against the headboard, and turned on the TV.

"Shade."

Turning back around, I headed into the bathroom. I walked past Sunny but couldn't meet his gaze. It wasn't like I had any intention of saying those words.

When the door shut, my heart jumped.

"What did you tell her?"

I looked at him then.

His dark hair shone from the shower. The scent of soap wafted around us, invading every sense I had.

Sitting on the toilet seat, I rubbed the back of my neck. "I told her that I've only been with one man before."

"Did you tell her more about him?"

I shook my head. "It's way too soon for that shit and we would need a lot of alcohol too."

Sunny grunted.

My ex fucked me up. And that was putting it mildly.

"What else did you tell her?"

"That I'm in love with you but she figured it out on her own." I looked away, hating the guilt that resonated in him because he didn't feel the same.

"What did she say to that?"

"Nothing." I rubbed the back of my neck again, trying to ease the ache that had settled on my muscles since the beginning of the night. I wasn't sure why, but something was changing and fast. Maybe it was because both of us were sick of this shit. We needed more. But I wasn't sure if that was together or apart and I didn't know if I wanted to find out.

"She didn't say anything at all?" Sunny scoffed. "Come on, Shade. Everyone has something to say. Everyone comments about this shit."

I frowned, meeting his dark stare. "Jaron told us that Meadow isn't like most people. Or did you forget that. She may be young but there's something about her. Something we both need."

"I know." He huffed. "Fuck. This shit between us is new. I need you to have patience, Shade. You know how I feel about you. But our friendship comes first."

I stood, closing the distance between us. Before I knew what was happening, I pressed my body up against his.

His dark eyes widened. "Shade."

"I won't pressure you," I said, my voice low. "I promise to God that I won't pressure you into anything you aren't ready for. But I won't hide how I feel about you."

He searched my face, his jaw ticking. "I'm not gay. I have nothing wrong with people who are but I'm not..."

"Gay." I brushed a thumb along his jawline. "I know. Neither am I."

"But you've been with a man." He grabbed onto my hips, pulling me closer.

A shot of electricity rippled down my spine at the contact, but I ignored it. Sunny needed slow.

"You know how that shit ended," I murmured, glancing down at his mouth. "I'd rather be with you and not fuck you, than go through that again."

"He hurt you."

I went to pull away when he tightened his hold on me. "You know he hurt me. I was a kid. Experimenting. I was attracted to you, but I didn't want to ruin our friendship, so I hid my feelings. And then…" I swallowed hard. I couldn't talk about *him* without going back to that dark place in my mind. That place I had hidden from for the past fifteen years. That part of my mind was hell. Even for me.

Sunny cupped my nape, leaning his forehead against mine. "I'm sorry."

"Don't." I wrapped my arms around his thick shoulders, holding him against me.

"I am and I'm sorry for what I did earlier. I shouldn't have brought Meadow into this."

"I don't think she minded so much."

He grunted.

I smirked, staring at him. My best friend. My partner…in…everything.

"What?" he whispered.

"I'll make you want me as much as I want you." I released him and left the bathroom before he could respond.

(Sunny)

"I'll make you want me as much as I want you."
Fucking hell.

Scrubbing a hand down my face, I took a breath and followed Shade out of the bathroom. Meadow was sitting on the bed with a phone to her ear. Shade joined her, resting his arm across her lap.

She caught my gaze, giving me a wide smile. She pulled the phone from her ear. "I'm ordering pizza. You good with that?"

My stomach rumbled. I chuckled. "Yup. Definitely good with that."

Her smile grew. She placed the phone back up to her ear. "Yes, sorry. I'm still here."

While she placed the order, I sat on the bed and leaned against the headboard.

"Don't make this weird," Shade mumbled.

I bit back a sigh. We never used to have issues talking but this, this was different, and it was something on a whole other level that neither of us were used to. I wasn't even sure if we were ready for it.

EIGHT

Meadow

"**H**OLY FUCK." SHADE GROANED. "This pizza is amazing."

I grinned. "I can't believe you've never had it before."

"No." Shade glanced at Sunny. "Why is that?"

Sunny shrugged, crossing his legs at his ankles. "You have an obsession with sandwiches. That's why we've never had this pizza before."

"Fuck me." Shade groaned again. "I've been missing out."

I laughed. "It's the only pizza I'll order." After it had been delivered, Sunny, Shade, and I grabbed the two pizza boxes and sat on the bed. I couldn't remember ever spending time with the guys I slept with, but this was nice. My stomach twisted. Nope. Not going there. Things with Ashton had just ended. It wasn't like we were serious but neither of us could deny that something was starting. I wasn't stupid. I *could* fall in love with him but he could also break my heart at the same time. It was one reason why I was thankful he had ended it. He was far from ready to settle down. He liked variety and had a hard time being a one-woman man.

"Meadow?"

I jumped, not realizing I had zoned out. "Yeah?"

"You good?" Sunny asked, searching my face. For what, I wasn't sure. It wasn't like I showed my feelings. Ever. Not since *he* ripped my heart to shreds and stomped on it in the process.

I cleared my throat, grabbed another slice of pizza and moved farther up the bed. Leaning against the headboard, I took a bite of what was delicious just a moment ago but now tasted like cardboard. I choked down the bite before I answered. "I'm fine. Why?"

"Because I've been around long enough to know when a woman says that she's fine, she's actually not fine." Sunny moved closer to me, dropping his arm between us and running the back of his hand along my outer thigh. His fingers pushed the fabric of my dress higher, but he never took it further. He didn't have to. That small touch alone was enough to shove me over the edge and beg for him to fuck me again.

My skin erupted into goosebumps, but no matter the effect these men had on me, I wouldn't reveal all of my dark and dirty secrets. Although, I was sure they could figure them out all on their own. It wasn't like I hadn't begged for them to rip me apart earlier that evening.

"What's going on?" Sunny asked softly.

"Nothing." I finished the slice, wiped my mouth with a napkin and drank the rest of my beer. Shade had quickly gone to the bar, grabbed a few bottles and came back shortly after. I wasn't sure how many times they had been to this motel but clearly it had been enough for him to just randomly grab beer whenever he wanted.

Shade stood from the bed and walked around it until he was standing directly in front of me. "I think something *is* wrong." He lifted his hand when I went to speak. "I don't expect you to tell us everything. It's not like we've known you for long. But you will tell us. How do I know that? Because it's how you're wired. As soon as you let someone in, they know every single thing there is to know about you. But you don't have many people you've let in, do you, little lamb?"

I swallowed hard, not liking the turn of events taking place before me.

"Answer him," Sunny said, his deep voice rumbling through me.

"I...I have best friends." How the hell could Shade pick me apart like that? And so soon.

"Best friends?" Shade knelt on the bed and crawled toward me. "Do they know you? Truly know you? How about the men you've fucked? Did *they* know you, Meadow?"

Everything inside of me was telling me to run and hide. To get away. To shove Shade to the ground and scream how wrong he was.

But instead of running, I did the opposite. I glared up at him. "What are you getting at? Is this your thing? Both of you fuck a girl and then dig into their head? Find out all their dark and dirty secrets. Secrets that are *not* your business. You're a biker. Are you a damn shrink too?"

Much to my surprise, Shade wrapped his hands around my ankles and pulled me toward him.

I gasped, slapping my hands against his chest. "What the hell are you doing?"

"You see." Shade cupped my jaw and turned my head toward Sunny. "He fucked you in front of me. Just the two of you." His nose brushed up the length of my neck. "Now it's *my* turn."

WITH US

(Sunny)

Maybe I should have stopped it. Maybe I should have shoved Shade off of Meadow and demanded to know what the hell he was doing. I knew things were rocky between us. They had been for the last little while. That's what happened when you spent so much time with the same person and never talked about what the issue at hand really was. It was like we had fallen into a rut and I had no idea how the hell to get out of it. Although that little piece of shit voice in my head told me what I had to do, I wasn't sure if either of us were ready for that just yet.

I needed slow. I loved him. I loved him like he was a part of me. But I still needed slow. So instead of pushing him away from Meadow, I sat there and watched.

"Shade," she whispered, looking up at him and then at me. "I don't...this isn't a good idea."

"No?" He leaned down to her ear, muttering something that only she could hear but kept his gaze locked on me.

She swallowed hard, her slender throat working at the rough movement. "You wouldn't be mad?" she asked me.

My heart jumped.

Lying on my stomach, my fingers itched to touch her, but I wanted to see what happened next. I wanted to see just how far Shade would take it and what he planned on doing with her. He had always been dominant, even though he wouldn't agree. When it came to Meadow, he submitted in ways I never thought I'd ever see in him. But this was something else. This was on a whole other level that made every fiber in my being, tingle.

"No." I reached out and brushed my finger along her jawline. "I fucked you and he wasn't mad. Not at you anyway."

"I wasn't mad at you," Shade said, pulling Meadow farther under him and inching his hands up her thighs. He pushed her dress to her waist, slipping his hand between her legs.

Her breath caught.

"I was wondering what the hell was going on but mad?" He kissed her cheek. "No, I wasn't mad."

He was lying but who was I to argue. I moved behind Meadow, leaning against the headboard and watching the show taking place in front of me.

Shade chuckled, towering over Meadow. "He doesn't believe me."

"Neither do I," she told him.

I grinned, crossing my arms under my chest.

Shade looked at me then. He cupped her tits, pulling the fabric of her dress lower. Without taking his gaze from mine, he latched onto a nipple, sucking it between his teeth.

Meadow hissed, the sound shooting straight to my dick.

He released her with a pop, flicking his tongue back and forth over the swollen nub.

"Geeze," she whispered, arching beneath him. "You know, I don't mind if Sunny joins."

"I got a better idea." He placed a hard peck on her mouth. "Sunny, grab her hands."

Before she could protest, I did as he said and held her arms above her head.

Her chest rose and fell.

"Hmm..." He inched down the length of her body. "I like this. You restrained. Being held down by Sunny." He pushed her dress to below her chest and sunk his teeth into her hip. "It's hot as fuck."

My dick twitched at the rasp in his voice, all the blood rushing from my head to the tip of my cock.

"I agree," Meadow murmured. She tilted her head back, her gaze meeting mine. "Do you like it, Sunny?"

I linked my fingers in hers, bringing her hand up to my mouth. "Yes, pet." I kissed the tips of her fingers before dropping her hands to the bed. "I like it a lot." Holding her hands on either side of her head, I glanced at Shade. I nodded once.

He smirked, pushed her thighs open, and held her down. When he shoved his head between her legs, she cried out, bucking beneath him. He groaned, his eyes rolling into the back of his head. He covered her sex, thrusting his tongue deep inside her.

I licked my lips, my mouth salivating for a taste. I would. In time. But right now, she was all his.

Meadow squirmed, trying to close her legs but Shade only gripped her inner thighs harder.

My cock lengthened, threatening to burst at the display before me.

Shade released her with a smack, licking his glossy lips. "Fucking perfect."

"Please," Meadow begged. "I need you or both of you to fuck me. I don't give a shit right now. I just need you inside me."

Laughter fell between us.

"You wanna join, Sunny?" Shade asked, kissing her inner thigh.

"I do but I'm actually enjoying this at the moment." As much as I wanted to play with our new little toy, this was hot as fuck. Something neither of us had ever done before. We shared and that was it. But we never fucked a woman in front of each other before. Not until I did it an hour ago. And now it was Shade's turn.

I released her at the same time Shade flipped her onto her stomach.

"Hmm…" He landed a hard swat on her ass.

She whimpered, gripping the blankets beneath her.

"I haven't felt this pussy squeezing my cock yet." He undid his jeans, lowering the zipper. Pulling a condom out of his pocket, he tore it open. "Ready, baby?"

Meadow lifted her head, meeting my gaze. "Oh yeah."

I brushed my thumb over her bottom lip. "You're perfect."

She opened her mouth to say something when Shade thrust inside of her. "Fucking hell."

A dark chuckle left him. "Fuck me. I've never felt something so damn wet."

"Sunny." Meadow rose on shaky arms. "Kiss me."

I glanced at Shade.

He nodded once, releasing her.

It was all the encouragement I needed. I cupped Meadow's cheek. "Crawl to me, pet."

And she did.

NINE

SHADE

"**YOU THINK WE'LL SEE** her again?" I asked, watching Meadow run up the driveway to her house. She said that she lived in it with her sister and two other friends. It made me feel better knowing that she wasn't alone in such a big place.

"Yeah, I do," Sunny answered.

When Meadow hit the steps of the porch, she turned and gave us a wave before blowing a kiss our way.

I chuckled, waving back.

"She's something else," Sunny murmured.

Once Meadow was safe inside, Sunny straddled his bike.

As many times as we used Meadow, I was still itching for more. I was on the verge of snapping. Needing that connection with another human being, constantly. I wasn't sure what the hell was wrong with me, but I knew I needed something more. Something else. Something…*raw*.

"Shade."

The abrupt use of my name pulled me from my thoughts. I took a chance and glanced at Sunny. He stared out ahead of us. His jaw was set. Firm and rigid. Much like the rest of him.

"What?"

His gray eyes flicked to mine before putting his bike into gear. "Nothing."

"What are we doing?" I blurted.

"How the hell should I know? You've done this before. I haven't," he reminded me.

I scoffed. "I haven't done this shit since I was a kid. That was fifteen fucking years ago, Sunny. You know that."

When he didn't respond, I glanced his way.

"I need to go for a run," he mumbled.

I turned back around, unsure as to what to do from here. We had spent the night with Meadow. Let her sleep and then took turns with her. But we never fucked her at the same time again. I wasn't sure why. Maybe my confession bothered Sunny in ways I didn't think would ever happen. But what I did know was that something had changed, and it changed fast.

"I wonder how sore Meadow is going to be today," Sunny said, breaking the silence.

My body stirred, an ache settling deep in my balls. "Probably the same as me."

He grunted. "Likewise, my man. I've never fucked something so damn hard before."

I shivered, scrubbing a hand down my face. I wondered what it would feel like to be fucked by him like that. To feel him truly let go. Although he had given Meadow everything she had asked for, something told me that he still hadn't unleashed his full wrath. I had seen him with other women. Hell, I had fucked other women *with* him, but he still held back. Every damn time. And I wasn't sure why.

"Shade."

Much to my surprise, Sunny reached for my hand. He took it in his, brushing his thumb over the back of it. "I care about you. I hope you know that. I know our shit is fucked up and we shouldn't have brought Meadow into it. We hardly know her but I..."

"I *want* to get to know her," I added, this newfound revelation not sitting well with me. Sunny wasn't a talker. I was the one who did the talking. I pulled my hand from his and crossed my arms under my chest. My muscles twitched. A run sounded like a good idea at the moment.

He sighed. "I want to get to know her too. I'll meet you at home."

I watched him drive away, his bike kicking up dust behind him.

I sighed, getting on my own bike and following him.

An hour later and I pulled up in front of our house. Sunny was still straddling his bike in the middle of the driveway.

I parked, shut mine off, and joined Sunny.

He never looked my way. Instead, he sat there.

Silent and unmoving.

What could we even say?

I loved him. He loved me. Even though he never told me, I knew he loved me in his own way. But we never had sex before. I never even hinted at it. I was fine with him just wanting to share women. It never even crossed my mind to ask for more. And now...it was all I could think about. And my confession last night didn't help.

"Shade."

"What?" But I wouldn't meet his gaze. How could I? I had been with the guy for years and I never touched him. Never kissed him. Never even held him. We shared a hug every now and again but that was it. I wasn't sure what I needed anymore but I knew that I needed something.

"Look at me," he demanded, that deep voice of his rumbling right to the marrow of my bones.

I may have been submissive when it came to Meadow but there was no way in hell that I was letting—

"Look at me," he repeated, his voice firmer.

Much to my dismay, I looked at him. Like a good little boy, I did as I was fucking told. All because I couldn't help it.

"What's that look for?" Sunny asked, cocking his head to the side.

"I have no idea what you're talking about," I murmured, heading up the sidewalk to the house. The small bungalow held so many memories. Happy times along with the sad. I could only hope that one day it would also have a woman living there with us. And maybe a kid or two.

When I went to open the door, a heavy hand cupped my shoulder.

"Shade, submitting is not a bad thing."

My eyes snapped to his. "I know that. But I refuse to submit to you. I've submitted to a man before and look what happened."

Sunny flinched like I had slapped him. "Are you comparing me to that fucker?"

"Shit." I shook my head. "No. You're not him."

"But submitting to me makes you feel like you're with him again. And yet, you submit to Meadow." Sunny chuckled softly. "Wow, Shade. I knew we had issues, but this is…this is something else."

"You know that's not what I meant." I followed him into the house, wishing he would talk to me.

Sunny continued walking down the hall, kicking off his shoes in the process, and tugging off his leather cut. But he didn't say anything. No. Instead he closed up.

Because that was what he did. Sunny Harrison didn't say shit when he was backed into a corner.

"Sunny."

Nothing.

"Talk to me." I was pressing him, and I knew that eventually my pressing would make him blow but I needed something. Anything from him. Even if it was his full wrath.

"What do you want me to say?" he finally asked, throwing his keys into the wooden bowl our nephew had made us when he was a kid. Jaron, although not blood related, had insisted on making all of his uncles something when he had taken woodworking class in school. I wondered if he remembered that.

"I want you to say something. Anything. I don't give a shit what," I told Sunny, focusing back on the issue at hand.

"I'm going to take a shower." Sunny shoved past me but not before I grabbed his arm.

"What are we doing? We've never fought over this shit before." I released his arm and placed my hand against his chest. His heart beat hard beneath my palm.

Sunny's brows narrowed. "Something changed last night, and I can't figure out if it was for the better or for fucking worse." In a quick move, he wrapped a hand around my throat and pushed me up against the wall.

My breath caught.

"You told me you want me to fuck you." His eyes dropped to my mouth. "But I don't know if I can. Can you be with me, knowing that this might not become physical?"

"It's never been physical," I reminded him. I took a chance and grabbed onto his hips, pulling him against me. His cock pushed against mine, igniting a burn I had never felt before. Not since fucking Meadow the night before and this morning. Over and over again.

"If we're going to see Meadow again, we have to lay some ground rules," he said, his voice raspy. "If we make this a thing and want to include her in on it, we have to talk to her."

"Communication is key," I murmured, using the words he had told me so long ago.

"Exactly." Sunny inched forward, his mouth so close but yet so damn far away at the same time.

"This is getting pretty physical," I told him, pulling his shirt from his jeans. "Are you...are you good?"

Sunny leaned a hand against the wall by my head. "I care about you, Shade. I've always cared about you. Our club brothers have been nothing but supportive of whatever it is that we have but you know it won't go further than that."

"I don't give a shit what anyone thinks."

He sighed, leaning his forehead against mine. "Yeah, you do. That's why you've only ever been with one man."

"No." I pushed away from him. "That's because he fucking raped me. That's why I've only been with one man, Sunny." Not letting him get another word in, I stormed down the hall to my own bedroom.

Both of us had rooms across from each other and one that was meant for whoever we decided to include in our duo. We had fucked random women in it from time to time, but it wasn't the same. We needed someone else. Someone who lived with us. Someone who could put up with our issues and keep us in line. Someone who balanced us out. Someone who was the glue to our broken mess that we called a relationship.

Instead of going to my own room like I had originally planned, I pushed open the door to the room at the end of the hall. My gaze landed on the large bed that had been custom-made. It was a little bigger than a king-sized bed. Perfect for three people.

"Hey." Sunny came up behind me. "I didn't mean to bring that shit up."

"I know." I shut the door and went to walk past him when he stepped in front of me.

"I didn't. I'm confused. This whole thing confuses me."

"Yeah, Sunny." I sighed. "I get that."

"No." He cupped my shoulders, pushing me against the wall. "I don't think you do."

Much to my surprise, his mouth came down on mine.

Hard.

(Sunny)

I had no idea what the hell I was doing. Did I want to fuck Shade? Did I want to take our friendship, hell, our relationship, to the next level? I wasn't sure but what I *did* know, was that I wanted him. In some way, shape, or form. Maybe sex would eventually happen. I wasn't sure, but I needed slow. As impatient as we both were, slow was how we were going to take this. Because his friendship came first and foremost.

When my mouth landed on Shade's, his body stiffened and I thought I had fucked up. I went to pull away but his hand cupped my nape, tugging me against him.

Taking a chance, I licked along his bottom lip before closing my teeth and giving it a gentle nip.

He jumped, pulling me closer.

The kiss deepened, a groan falling between us. Maybe even a growl. I wasn't sure. I didn't care. This was...nice. Needed in a way.

"Sunny," he whispered before the kiss could turn into anything more.

I leaned back, brushing my thumb along his swollen bottom lip. "I don't know what I'm doing but whatever it is, I'm glad I'm doing it with you."

He gave me a small smile. "Same."

Stepping away from him, I cleared my throat and rubbed the back of my neck. "I need slow though. I can't lose you and I'd rather be friends than for me to fuck this up and lose you completely."

Shade rolled his eyes. "We've been through hell together, Sunny. Remember? And I know you're an asshole, so I can't see you fucking this up."

I chuckled, punching his arm.

"Ow, fucker." He rubbed the spot I hit. "You can't kiss me and then hit me."

"Try me." I stepped up to him, hooked my arm around his shoulders and kissed his cheek. "Thank you for being patient with me."

"Always." Shade wrapped his arms around my shoulders, pulling me against him. "You will never have to worry about not being able to take things slow with me. I get it." He released me and started walking down the hall. "I'm going to call Greyson and check in. See if he needs us for anything today."

"Okay." I gave myself a shake, thankful that turned out better than I thought it would.

While Shade called Greyson Mercer, the president of Hell's Harlem, I took a long, hot shower. As much as I didn't want to wash Meadow off of me, I needed the scalding liquid to ease my aching bones. I had no idea why she liked older men. I was grumpy, mean as fuck, and my bones hurt. All the damn time.

Once I finished my shower, I quickly got dressed and joined Shade out in the living room. He was sitting on the couch on the phone, with his head in his hands.

"Yeah...No. He never said anything more than that." Shade looked up then. "Hold on." He set the phone on the coffee table in front of him and pressed a button. "Sunny's here and you're on speaker."

"Good. Sunny, I was just filling Shade in on the fact that Tanner decided to make an appearance last night," Greyson explained. "It seems Meadow riled him up."

My back stiffened. "What?" I knew what that meant too. It meant that Tanner had taken a liking to her. Well over my dead fucking body.

"What did he say?" Shade asked, his voice coming out rough.

I sat beside him. When our knees touched, a spark of need shot through me. It was unexpected. I almost pulled away when Shade's hand landed on my knee.

He glanced at me then, but I refused to meet his gaze. I didn't know what I was doing, and I didn't need his questioning stares making it worse.

"He said that he ran into the both of you and met this tiny little thing that had a mouth on her." Greyson paused. "Listen, I can't control what you do outside of the club. Hell, I can't control you within the club either but when it comes to Meadow, I can't protect you if something happens to her."

"We won't hurt her," I told him.

"I know *you* won't, but you also know Tanner and his sick fucking ways."

I grunted. "We'll watch out for her."

"We will," Shade said, leaning back against the couch. "Have you heard anything else?"

"Jaron's supposed to be meeting up with—hey, beautiful. What's wrong?"

"Sorry to interrupt," came his wife's reply in the background. Their voices became muffled when Greyson covered the phone. "Guys," Grey said, coming back a moment later. "I have to go. Eve got food poisoning after eating some bad meat."

"Shit. That's the worst. Hope she feels better," Shade said, grimacing.

"Grey, you should really learn how to clean yourself and maybe that won't happen to her again," I threw at him.

"Ha. Fucking. Ha." Greyson chuckled. "See you this weekend?"

"Of course," Shade and I said in unison.

We said our goodbyes and Shade disconnected the call.

"What do you think Tanner wants with Meadow?" he asked, stretching his long legs out in front of him.

"I have no idea, but I don't like it. At all." I scrubbed a hand down my face. "Maybe we should talk to her."

"Or we wait and see if he actually does anything? He could have said more to Grey last night but…"

"We'll wait so he can take care of his wife." I had always liked Eve. She kept Greyson on his toes and never gave him a hard time whenever he went on a ride with us. Although he was retiring as president soon, she had supported his club life ever since we met her so many years ago.

"Yeah," Shade said.

A moment of silence fell between us.

Was this how it was going to be? We shared a kiss and now it was…weird.

"You're making it weird again," Shade said, nudging me in the shoulder.

"I know." He was so damned in tune to me, it was like he could hear what I was thinking before I even said anything. Another sigh left me.

"Hey." Shade linked his fingers in mine, holding my hand between us. "I'm good with slow, Sunny."

"Fifteen years is more than fucking slow. It's not even a snail's pace."

"I don't give a shit about that." He lifted my hand. "Look at this."

I looked. I looked fucking hard.

Both of our hands were calloused from work. I was a mechanic, so my hands were always dirty no matter how many times I cleaned them. They had become stained from years of working on cars, bikes, and even rigs.

"Meadow never pointed out my dirty hands," I mumbled.

"She probably doesn't care. They aren't even dirty. They're stained." Shade turned his body toward me, dropping our hands on his lap. "I liked seeing you with her."

My body stirred at the memories of the night before. So much pleasure erupted between the three of us. It had never been like that with any of the other women we had shared.

"What's different about her?" I asked, pulling my hand from his. "We just met her, but it was so damn perfect, I want more. And I don't know why."

"I don't know either, Sunny."

I rested my arm across his lap, wanting more but scared to even hint for something.

"You know you're the only person I've ever opened up to. Even though we've never had sex, you still know more about me than...than..."

I met his gaze. "I know."

Shade stood from the couch. "Beer?"

"Sure."

He nodded, headed to the kitchen, and came back a moment later with two beers. He twisted the caps off of both and handed me one before sitting beside me.

He turned on the TV, flipped through a couple of channels until settling on an old horror movie that we had seen countless times thanks to another club brother and his wife having an obsession with them.

"I like this one," Shade said, taking a swig of his beer.

I liked the movie too, but I couldn't concentrate on it. No, instead, all I could think about was his lips pressed up against the head of the bottle. Or how the cords in his thick neck worked with each swallow. Or how a drop of liquid leaked out from the corner of his mouth. He wiped it away and was about to stick his finger between his lips when I stopped him.

The move had been so quick, I surprised myself.

Shade's eyes widened. "What are you doing?"

Instead of answering him, I brought his hand to my mouth and stuck his finger between my lips. Licking the drop off of his finger, I kept my eyes locked on his. I didn't know what had possessed me to make such a move but when Shade's pupils dilated, and his nostrils flared, I knew I had made the right choice.

(Shade)

This was new. For him and for me. Although I had been with a man, that had been years ago, and it didn't turn out well.

Sunny released my hand, sitting back. "I...I'm not—"

Before he could close up on me, I grabbed the collar of his shirt and pulled him against me.

"Shade," he said, his voice raspy.

"Just shut up and kiss me." I cupped his nape, pulling him forward.

"Slow," he ground out before he covered my mouth with his. Although he had insisted on taking things slow, he pushed me back, deepening the kiss.

I groaned, sliding my hands down his broad back.

Sunny pushed his way between my knees, rubbing his pelvis against mine. A growl sounded, I wasn't sure if it had come from him or me.

Wrapping a hand around my jaw, he tilted my head and split my lips apart with his tongue.

"Sunny," I whispered against his mouth.

He released me, staring down at me with eyes that had never been hungry for me before. "I'm sorry."

"Why are you sorry?" I asked, licking my lips.

"I want slow, but I also want..." He sat back on his ankles, pushing a hand through his hair.

"Hey." I sat up, my gaze falling to the large bulge in his gray sweatpants. I swallowed hard, knowing that if we ever took it further, he would hurt. And it would hurt so fucking good. "I don't know how Meadow did it. Taking both of us."

Sunny stood and sat behind me. Pulling me back against him, he wrapped his arm around my middle. "I could feel you inside her."

I smirked. Sitting up and taking a chance, I looked at him. "I want..."

"What?" Sunny cupped himself. "This? Because as hard as I am, I don't know if I can do that. Not tonight."

"I know. I can wait. I just..." I took a chance and reached out to him. I placed my hand on his knee, sliding it up to his inner thigh.

His breath hitched but when he didn't push me away, I continued. I could feel his gaze burning into the top of my head, but I refused to meet his stare, knowing that I would lose this moment of bravery if I did.

His cock jumped beneath the fabric of his pants, hardening the higher my hand went.

"I want to touch you," I told him, licking my lips.

"Do it," he growled, laying back against the arm of the couch.

My heart hammered in my ears, knowing this would be the next step and we wouldn't be able to go back from this.

My fingers brushed over the hem of his shirt, slipping beneath the fabric and running along the waist of his pants. Moving to my knees, I towered over him, lifted the hem of his shirt, and reveled in the way his abs jumped under my scrutiny.

Lowering my mouth to his hip, I licked along the hard edges. When he didn't stop me, I continued.

His breathing picked up, his fingers tightening on the cushion beneath us.

Pushing my hand beneath his shirt, I splayed it across his heart.

I licked and bit. Sucked and nibbled. My mouth traced every inch of his lower stomach. My tongue dipped between the creases of his abs, dove into his belly button and devoured every inch of his torso.

Taking a chance, I looked up the length of his body.

His eyes were on fire as they seared into my soul.

Hooking my fingers into the waist of his pants, I lowered them, revealing his thick cock. I licked up the length, the scent of him forcing pre-cum from my own dick.

His nostrils flared. Throwing his head back, he arched beneath me.

I took that as my hint and closed my lips around the tip.

"Fuck," he whispered, his chest rising and falling with ragged breaths.

Taking him farther, the length of him slid down the back of my tongue when suddenly his phone rang.

"Shit." He reached into his pocket and pulled out his phone. "Fucking hell."

When I was about to pull off of him, he cupped the back of my head and began to thrust.

The ringing stopped but quickly started back up as soon as it ended.

He ignored it and began fucking my throat.

The hold on the back of my head tightened.

I released him, kissing his hip. "Who is it?" I asked him, wrapping my hand around him.

He groaned, his hips bucking. "I don't give a shit who it is."

My hand tightened around him, picking up speed.

"Fuck." He covered my hand, stopping me but never removing my hand from his cock.

"Sunny?" I squeezed him. "Who's on the phone?"

Sunny muttered a curse. "My ex-wife."

TEN

SUNNY

I **WAS YOUNG AND** stupid once. After Shade and I had drifted apart for a year or so in the beginning, I met someone and he did the same. Although she didn't do it for me like Meadow had last night, Roxanne Wilson had been convenient.

"Roxanne," I greeted. "It's been awhile."

She snorted. "It has. You keep missing your payments."

I rolled my eyes. "Those kids aren't mine. They were never mine." I stuffed my aching cock back into my pants and leaned forward. I gave Shade a smirk.

He chuckled softly, shaking his head.

"They should be," she said, sniffing.

I bit back a heavy sigh. Although I had loved her kids, she confessed they weren't mine after I demanded a DNA test. Add on the fact that I found her fucking her yoga instructor. It was so damn cliché, it made me twitch. And she had been trying to get me to pay child support ever since. I used to pay it. I used to *want* to pay it. But after finding out that the kids weren't mine, I got my name removed from their birth certificates and cleared up by the courts, so I didn't have to continue supporting kids who weren't mine. I helped when I could but that was it.

"You promised," she reminded me.

"No. I only promised to help you before I caught you cheating on me. And even after that, I still continued helping you like a damn sucker. Remember what happened after that, Roxanne? You kept the money for yourself."

Her breath hitched.

"I also told you that I would help them through school when the time came. But they're not even out of high school yet." Even though everything inside of me told me they weren't mine in the beginning, I still believed her and had claimed them as such. Twins also didn't run in my family, so that was a big indicator, but I was still hopeful. I had always wanted a family of my own. When the tests came back saying they belonged to someone else, I left her. I still loved them, but I couldn't stay with their mother. No matter how hard I tried in the beginning. And now they were the ones who suffered but thanks to social media, I still kept in contact with them.

"Sunny," Roxanne said gently. "I need your help."

"No, you don't. You need my money. That's it."

"It's more than that."

"Really? What is it then? You know, you haven't contacted me in quite a while. Did your current boyfriend, husband, fuck-buddy throw your ass out? Is that the problem, Roxanne?"

"You were actually nice once."

I grunted. "I was a lot of things once."

"Something…something has come up. I need your help."

Years ago, I would have caved and heard her out but not anymore. "We keep having the same conversation each month, Roxanne." I covered Shade's hand and locked my fingers between his. "I'm not doing this shit with you again and again. Take care of yourself and leave me the fuck alone." I hung up and put my phone on silent, knowing she would call right back. For the third time.

"She's still trying to suck money out of you?"

I nodded. "I have no idea why I married her in the first place." I had felt sorry for her. I was also hurting when Shade and I weren't talking at the time. As much as it made me look like an asshole, I used her as a distraction. It worked. For a little bit. Even after I had left her, I wanted to help in any way that I could, but cheating was a deal breaker for me. I could be a domineering dick, but cheating was unacceptable. Although it was a normal thing in the biker life, it wasn't me.

"You were bored, and you didn't have me around." Shade winked.

I chuckled. "Yeah." I released his hand and stared at my best friend. My partner. A man I loved. Also a man who had started giving me a blow job only seconds before. It had grown from a friendship to something more rather quickly, but it still never became physical until today. "Why have you waited?"

Shade crossed his ankle over his opposite knee. "Because I would rather be with you and not fuck you, than to not be with you at all."

"But why? There are other men and women out there who could make you happy."

"Nope." Shade turned toward me. "I don't want them. *You* make me happy. Even when you're grumpy, old man." He leaned toward me and placed a soft peck on my forehead before pulling away from me. "I'm going to take a nap and dream of that sweet little thing we spent the night with." He headed to the hall leading to our bedrooms. "If you want anything, Sunny, anything at all, you know where to find me." Instead of waiting for me to respond, he headed down the hall, the sound of a door closing a moment later.

My body stirred, my mind conjuring up images of what would happen if I *did* follow him. But I didn't. I couldn't. I wasn't sure why but a part of me was scared. And I didn't know if that fear would ever go away.

(Meadow)

"Hey, Meadow."

I glanced up from the newspaper I was reading and saw Gigi coming toward me. "Hey."

She placed a mug of coffee on the table and sat beside me. "How'd you get home? I thought you were coming back to the motel."

"I was supposed to." I had every intention of driving back home with Gigi and Piper but Sunny drove me on his bike while Shade followed us. "You got home early."

"Yeah." Gigi slumped in a chair across from me, holding her mug of coffee like her life depended on it. "I woke up hungover and needed some grease. So Piper and I stopped off at McDonald's on the way home."

I was a little jealous that she could eat her weight in crappy food, and it wouldn't affect her at all.

"Meadow."

I placed the paper down and waited. Something was off with her. She usually spent some time each morning giving me a hard time about reading the paper. I liked reading the paper. It was more reliable than technology was. And if I was cold, I could burn it. It was a win-win if you asked me.

"Where did you go last night?"

"Why?" I bit back a smirk. After Shade and Sunny made sure I was okay, they dropped me off at home this morning. I was able to slip into the front door without anyone seeing me.

"You went to see those men," Gigi said, taking a sip of her coffee. "Was I that drunk that I never noticed?"

"Are you going to sit there and judge me if I say that I *did* go see them?" I asked, waiting for an answer.

"I don't judge."

I laughed. "I love you, Gigi, but yeah, you do. You get that trait from our wonderful father."

She huffed. "I don't mean to judge."

"It's human nature." I paused. "Don't worry about it."

"How can my younger sister have more of a sex life than me?" She scowled. "It doesn't make sense."

"You know there's ways around that, right?" Hell, if it were me, I would have been all over that. Vincent Junior was hot, and he didn't act like your typical nineteen-year-old. I'd also bet my life savings on it that he was a dirty fucker.

"What's that look for?" Gigi asked, narrowing her brows.

"Just wondering what it would be like to fuck a guy younger than me." I tapped my chin.

She coughed, her cheeks reddening.

I raised an eyebrow. "Wait…" I pointed at her. "Why are you blushing?" My eyes widened. "Did you fuck him already?"

She stood from the table and started stretching. She did that whenever she was stressed or backed into a corner.

"Gigi, it's not a big deal if you did." I didn't know what their deal was, but I had seen the way Vince looked at her. Something was definitely up between them.

"Yeah, I know." Gigi rose her arms up and over her head. "The twins are coming by sometime today."

Before I met Sunny and Shade, my body would have reacted in some way to the fact that Ashton was coming over. But now, there was nothing.

Interesting.

"Is everything okay?" Gigi asked, frowning.

"Yeah. Why?"

"Because you usually go to your room when I tell you the twins are coming over. Even when they're not coming over until hours later."

"I guess...I don't know. Ashton and I aren't sleeping together anymore anyway." It had been short and fun. So much fun but now that I found the two men who did everything for me and more, I was addicted. I should call them. Or text them at least.

"I'll have to meet these two guys. Again. When I'm sober." Gigi laughed. "If they were able to get you off of Ashton's dick, that's saying something."

I coughed. "Who are you and what have you done with my sister?" Gigi normally didn't swear or do anything that would be considered bad for her. She had wine every now and again or beer, like the night before.

"Yeah, yeah." She finished stretching. "So, tell me about them." She waggled her eyebrows.

I laughed. "They're nice. They took care of me and were gentlemen." Until I got them in bed that is.

"Good. I'm glad." Gigi grabbed her mug from the table and headed to the sink. "I'll be going to the center if you want to join me."

"Sure." The Dove Project had been created by all of our moms when they were our ages. It was to help human trafficking victims. It helped them get jobs, schooling, shelter, and family. No one was turned away. No matter the gender or age, everyone was welcome. The center had grown so quickly, our fathers ended up expanding the place. It sat on the outskirts of town and was well-known by the surrounding cities and towns.

As Gigi and I stepped out of the house and into the late morning sun, my phone rang.

Gigi paused in her steps. "Who is it?"

I glanced at the display, frowning. "Hey," I said, answering the phone.

"You free, babe?" Ashton asked. "Aiden wants some of that weed we smoked a week ago. Or maybe it was longer. I can't remember."

"I don't have any on me." Truth was, I hadn't smoked weed in a few days. And I hadn't even thought of it. "And besides, my contact won't take money from me anymore."

"The fuck? Meadow, you selling your body for that shit?"

I rolled my eyes. "Listen, I appreciate you getting all protective but no. I'm not selling my body." As much as I loved weed, I would never stoop to that level just to get it.

Gigi raised an eyebrow.

"My dad would kick my ass if I did that." I continued walking to Gigi's car with her following beside me. "But listen, Gigi and I are heading to The Dove Project. Aren't you guys doing some work there?"

"We just finished," Ashton said. "We were going to come over."

"Gigi told me. You guys are done working already?" I stopped at the passenger side to Gigi's little beater of a car.

"Yeah, we're fast, baby."

I laughed. "I've known you guys my whole life. You're not fast at anything. Especially if you're getting paid by the hour."

Ashton chuckled. "True. Listen, you can come over and we can have a little party of our own."

"Sorry, handsome. I'm not Piper. I don't want you both."

Ashton's laugh deepened. "Aiden has shit to do. And I wouldn't invite him anyway."

"You want me all to yourself?" My thoughts traveled back to the night before and this morning. "Listen," I said before Ashton could respond. "You know this is over. You said so yourself."

"Yeah." He sighed. "I know. I'm not the brightest it seems."

"You'll find someone. I know you will."

"And so will you, Meadow."

My body heated at the two someones who had invaded every inch of me only hours before. "We'll see you guys later. You are still coming over right?"

"When do we not come over?"

"True. See you tonight." I disconnected the call before I could get anymore flirting from him.

"Is it weird now?" Gigi asked when I sat beside her.

"It wasn't but I also hadn't slept with Sunny and Shade at the time." I scrubbed a hand down my face. "I don't know what I'm doing but I know that Ashton is not who I'm meant to be with."

"Has any of the guys you've been with ever been who you're supposed to be with?"

I glanced at my sister. "No."

"Listen, you're young, Meadow. We all are. You have years to decide who you should be with. Hell, I don't even..." She stopped herself, shaking her head. "Doesn't matter. Anyway, just don't rush into anything."

"Yes, mom." I crossed my arms under my chest and stared out the window. "I'm not rushing shit. I'm having fun. Which you should do too."

Gigi scoffed. "Right. And who am I going to have fun with exactly?"

"Vince of course."

"I'm too busy to have fun," she grumbled.

"You're never too busy. Sometimes you need a moment to yourself or with a hot, young thing that could help you get your head out of your ass."

Her head whipped around. "My head is not in my ass."

I laughed.

She sighed, a smile tugging at her lips. "I don't want to talk about it anymore."

"Fine." I smirked. "But you know it's true."

"Will you stop?" She laughed, shaking her head.

I giggled.

"It's difficult. Ever since Vince went off to school…it became…I don't know. Weird I guess." She only shrugged but didn't elaborate.

I remembered the first time he came home. It was Thanksgiving. We hardly saw him. He had made some excuse that he was visiting friends. The pain etched on my sister's face at the time would forever be burned into my memory. For that, he deserved his ass kicked but I had a feeling that my sister was doing that all on her own.

Once we pulled up to The Dove Project, my heart skipped a beat. Every damn time. It was like the large compound had a life of its own. It had amazed me as a kid and still amazed me to this very day.

"This place keeps getting bigger and bigger," Gigi said, pulling the car into an empty parking space.

"And I think it's only going to get bigger." Once she put the car into park, I stepped out of the vehicle. A ding sounded on my phone, indicating an incoming text.

Sunny: You free this week?

I grinned, my body heating.

Me: Depends.

Sunny: On?

I thought a moment, my grin widening.

Me: Am I getting both of you or just one?

The dots moved on the screen. Stopped. Continued moving. And stopped again.

I laughed to myself, leaning against Gigi's car.

"You coming?" she asked, heading toward the large building.

"In a moment," I called after her.

My phone dinged, startling me.

Sunny: Depends.

Me: On?

Sunny: Think you can handle both of us again?

My body lit up.

My phone rang that time.

"Sick of texting, old man?" I laughed.

Sunny chuckled. "This is easier and then I can jerk off to the sound of your voice."

I coughed. "Well, that's an image."

"A good one I hope."

I laughed. "Yeah, a very good one."

"Good. What? Yes, I know." A muffled voice sounded in the background. "I'm about to ask her if you untwist those panties, Shade. You're worse than a woman. Ow. Fucker."

"What are you wanting to ask me that has your boy riled up?" I jumped up onto the hood of Gigi's car.

"We want you to come over for dinner," Sunny finally said.

My stomach tumbled when I realized he never commented about me referring to Shade as *his boy*. Maybe things were finally looking up for them. Or they had talked. Or fucked. I was betting on the former. I wasn't sure Sunny was ready to take that next step yet.

"I can do that," I told him. "I'm free Thursday night."

"That works for us, pet."

I shivered. God, I loved when he called me that.

"We'll see you then. Oh and, Meadow?"

"Yeah?"

"I suggest bringing an overnight bag, but you won't be needing any clothes."

I smirked. "Do I get a say in this?"

"Nope." And with that, Sunny hung up.

I shook my head, stuffed my phone into my bag, and headed into The Dove Project. I was greeted by the receptionist. Giving her a small wave, I hiked the strap of my bag up onto my shoulder and made my way to the kitchen. I needed some therapy and baking would be the only way to do it.

While most people worked out, went for a run, or even did art, I baked. And I baked a lot. But it never amounted to anything more than me just baking for local delis and restaurants. I had been told several times that I could sell my baked goods in grocery stores and mass produce them, but I believed that it would ruin the product. Unless I could teach people to bake like me, there was no way I was selling my goods. Hell, I didn't even know what half the recipes called for. I just guessed most of the time and if the final product turned out great, then that was an added bonus.

Once I reached the large kitchen, a sense of calm washed over me. This was my happy place. It didn't matter where the kitchen was. Any and all kitchens just made me…happy. At peace. It was where I belonged.

Not in a sexist way either but because I actually wanted to be there.

"You'll make a man happy one day, kiddo."

My mom smacked Dad playfully. "Even if she didn't bake or spend most of her time in the kitchen, she'd make a man happy."

Dad scowled. "That's not what I meant, princess."

I laughed quietly at the memory.

"Meadow."

I spun around, finding Luna coming toward me. "Hey, girl. How are you?"

"Not too bad. I ran into Clara. Literally." She rubbed her shoulder. "She's small but man, that hurt."

I laughed.

Clara Blanco had been volunteering at the center for a few months. I never really talked to her. Just said *hi* in passing but she had always been nice to me. It was all I could ask for. Most of the women I had come across, no matter the age, were catty and out for blood. They thought of themselves first and didn't give a shit who they hurt in the process.

"You good?"

"What?" I shook my head, giving Luna a smile for reassurance. "Oh yeah."

"Good. Listen…" She paused.

"Hey." I knew she was going to mention something about Ashton. "Don't worry about it. It's what friends are for."

"Well, I've never had a friend sleep with a guy for me."

I shrugged, pulling some bowls off the top metal shelf. "Like I said, don't worry about it. I was bored. He was bored. And it got him off your ass, did it not?"

"Yeah." She sighed, chewing her bottom lip. "I guess."

"What is it?" I turned to her, leaning my hip against the edge of the table.

"I just don't want you to get hurt. Ashton isn't ready to settle down no matter how much he thinks he is. That's all."

I laughed harder. "Trust me, Luna. I don't want a relationship." Not with him anyway. "So I'm no more ready to settle down than he is."

"Okay." Luna gave me a soft smile. "Well then…" She turned toward the bowls I had laid out before me. "What are you working on today?"

"I have some pies to make. I'm thinking of mixing as many fruits as I can together."

"Whatever you make, it will be amazing. I don't know how you do it, but I've never had watermelon in a pie until you accidentally made it that one time."

"I was high and bored. I should not be in the kitchen after smoking a fatty." Although the pie turned out delicious. There had been other times where I mixed veggies and fruit together and that should not have happened. I served it to the twins, and they ate it just to be polite. But Ashton actually loved it.

"Either way, it was still good."

"Thank you." A sense of pride washed over me. I wondered if Sunny and Shade would like my baking. I made a mental note to make them something for Thursday. God, I still couldn't believe I was going to their place for dinner and spending the night. My body heated, remembering the demanding tone when Sunny told me that I would be staying over and that I wouldn't need any clothes.

"Did you meet someone?" Luna asked.

I jumped, forgetting she was still there. "Uh…"

"Gigi said that you ended up going back to that bar you guys went to and didn't come home until this morning."

"I have no idea what you're talking about." I winked and headed to the large walk-in freezer to grab some baked goods.

"Well, be safe." Luna laughed, the door shutting behind her a moment later.

I sighed. My friends had never been interested in the guys I slept with before. It was why they never knew about...*him*.

Shoving those memories to the back of my mind, I grabbed the ingredients I needed and put myself to work. Several hours later, I had five pies, two cakes, six dozen chocolate chip cookies and three dozen cream-filled donuts all spread out before me.

My hands hurt. My back hurt. My everything hurt. But I was proud of the work I had done today and was also happy that this would be going to good use. Although everyone who lived at this center had come from shitty situations, man, could they ever eat. And if they were happy, I was happy.

When I finished cleaning up, I was making my way out of the building when I found Ashton coming toward me. Not too long ago and my body would have lit up but now...nothing. No reaction. At all. I wasn't sure how I felt about that either.

"Hey, babe." He gave me his gorgeous smile and wrapped me up in a hug.

"Hey." I returned the embrace. "I didn't think you were coming back."

"Yeah, my mom needed some help. One of the pipes burst in the basement, so my dad sent me to check it out."

I released him. "Oh, well good luck." I went to walk past him when he grabbed my upper arm. "Ashton."

"I know I ended this..." He pulled me back into his arms. He leaned down to my ear, his hot breath washing over the side of my face. "But I'm down for picking this up again."

My phone took that moment to ring. I pulled it from my bag, my heart stuttering when I saw that it was Sunny calling.

"Who's that?" Ashton asked, keeping his arms around me.

I pulled from his grip, ignoring his question and answering the phone. "Hey, Sunny."

"Who the *fuck* is *he*?"

My eyes widened, my head whipping around. I scanned the vicinity around me but there was nothing out of the ordinary. "What, are you stalking me now?"

He chuckled, the sound deep and delicious. "Oh, pet. I'm not there. But I have eyes. I have eyes every fucking where."

"Meadow?"

I glanced back at Ashton.

A deep frown had settled between his brows.

"I'm good," I told him.

"Answer my question, pet," Sunny growled.

"Listen, being told what to do while you're fucking me is hot and all but that's the *only* time you get to control me." I hung up the phone, shoved it back in my bag and started walking toward the sidewalk.

"Where are you going?" Ashton called.

"Home. Alone," I called out over my shoulder. I needed to bake and get these damn men off my ass. Who the hell did Sunny think he was? Thinking he could control me. In bed, sure. I submitted like the best submissive out there. But when it came to my day-to-day activities and life outside of the bedroom, *I* was in control. And if he thought any differently, he could fuck right off.

When I reached the sidewalk, I started walking the few blocks home. The afternoon sun was warm to the skin but cool enough that you wouldn't sweat your balls off.

My phone dinged, rang, dinged again, and rang some more. Everything inside of me told me that it was Sunny. Didn't matter. Just because the sex was the best I ever had; it didn't mean shit.

The hair on the back of my neck tingled. I stopped suddenly, glancing around me.

"Follow your gut, kiddo. Your gut is always right."

My dad told us over and over again how our conscience was in our gut. It was that clenching feeling, almost like you ate a bad plate of tacos. And right now, that feeling was there.

My phone rang again. Fishing it out of my bag, I lifted it to my ear without looking at who was calling.

"Yeah," I greeted.

"Pet, I—"

"Can you come pick me up?" I asked, thankful that it was Sunny, even though he pissed me off. "Please."

"You still at The Dove Project?"

"Should I even bother asking how you know where I am?"

"One of our club brothers was in the area and I asked him to check up on you to make sure that you were safe."

"Really?" My heart swelled that he had cared enough to have someone to watch over me. "Oh, well...thank you. I'm just walking home now and I...I just..." I hated sounding paranoid, but something was off.

"We're on our way, Meadow. Stay on the phone with me."

"Okay," I said, blowing out a breath of relief.

"Are you out in the open?"

"Yeah, there's not much here though. The compound is big, so our parents had it built outside of town. But I always walk home. It's good exercise and I've never had issues before." I was rambling. I never rambled. I wasn't that kind of girl but this unease coursing through me, threw me off.

"Alright, baby girl. I promise we're coming for you."

"Okay." I continued walking, not liking this feeling of being watched.

"Listen." Sunny cleared his throat. "I'm sorry."

My heart jumped. "You are?"

"Yeah. I'm an old fucker. Set in my ways and shit. Shade is constantly reminding me to…well…"

"What?"

"Loosen the purse strings I guess you could say."

"I've done this before. Being controlled. I don't like it, Sunny, and I sure as hell don't find it sexy. If you want me to do something, just ask me, but don't get pissed off if I say no." I paused, wondering where the hell that confession came from.

"Alright, pet. But you have to remember that I'm used to being in control. So, we'll need to work together on this. Yeah?"

I sighed. I could work with that. "Okay."

"We're about two minutes away."

A vehicle came toward me. "Uh…Sunny, what are you guys driving in?"

"It's a black '67 Mustang." He paused. "Why?"

The vehicle slowed down, coming to a complete stop a few feet away. The windows of the black SUV were tinted, so I couldn't make out who was actually in the large beast of a vehicle.

The passenger door opened, a large man stepping out of it. He shut the door, looked up to the sky and turned my way.

I swallowed hard. "Sunny, I suggest driving faster."

"What's going on, Meadow?"

I gripped the phone tight in my hand.

The man who I recognized from last night, started walking toward me.

"It seems we meet again," Tanner said, his deep voice sending a sliver of fear racing down my spine.

Once he stood directly in front of me, I had to lean back to look up at him. The guy was tall. Why were all these guys so damn huge?

"Fucking hell," Sunny growled in my ear. "Shade, drive faster."

Much to my surprise, Tanner took the phone from me and put it up to his ear. "Sorry, Meadow can't come to the phone right now."

I looked around him, seeing two other men leave the SUV and lean against the hood. One lit up a smoke while the other crossed his arms under his chest and kept his gaze locked our way.

I looked back at Tanner. "What do you want?"

"Like your little toy said, I suggest driving faster," he told Sunny and pressed a button on the phone. Handing it back to me, he nodded toward his guys. "Be a good little girl and nothing will happen. My guys are hungry. They haven't been fed in a while."

"What do you want?" I repeated, my stomach twisting at what he was suggesting.

"To chat. But it doesn't look like we have a lot of time." He reached into his leather jacket and pulled out a small white business card. "Come to my club."

I laughed. "Yeah, because Sunny will approve of that." Although I didn't like being told what to do in any way, when it came to Tanner, I listened.

"I don't give a shit if he approves or not. I have questions and I know you're a curious little thing, so I don't suggest making me wait." Tanner turned on his heel and started walking away. He stopped, glancing at me over his shoulder. "Also, that little compound fascinates me. Be a good girl, do as I say, and I won't make an appearance."

My blood boiled through me. Fucking fucker. My hands clenched into fists at my sides. Before I could stop myself, I stomped toward him. "You leave those people alone. They've been through enough without having you breathing down their necks or doing whatever it is you want to do to them."

He chuckled but continued walking away from me.

I rushed to him and shoved him forward a step. "What are you even doing here? Isn't it against some rule that you shouldn't be in Hell's Harlem territory?"

He spun on me, forcing me back. "Careful, Meadow. I'm not Sunny or Shade. If I say I'm going to rip you apart, I mean it. And to answer your question, this isn't Hell's Harlem territory. I think you've seen too many movies."

I scoffed, rolling my eyes. "I know how it works. They would know that you're here. Wouldn't that cause more issues for you?"

Tanner's brows narrowed. "You ask too many questions. Now be a good girl and go play with your Barbies."

"You don't scare me," I said as the sound of a car screeched to a stop behind me.

Tanner cocked his head to the side, a slow grin spreading on his face. "You're lying."

I scoffed, waving my hand between us. "You act all big and tough to make up for other shit you're lacking." I turned on my heel. "Go crawl back to your hole, Tanner."

My head snapped up, finding Sunny and Shade coming toward me. Shade's eyes zeroed in on me while Sunny looked over my head.

"Bring her to the car," Sunny demanded, his voice rough, as he walked past me.

"Sunny." I stepped in front of him. "Hey." I placed my hands on his chest, expecting to feel his heart racing beneath my palm. But when it was calm, a shiver trembled through me.

A deep chuckle sounded from behind us.

"Looks like your little toy calls the shots."

I glared at Tanner. Just when I was about to storm back up to him, arms wrapped around my middle. They pulled me back against a hard body.

Sunny took a step forward.

"Sunny, don't," I said, my voice as firm as I could make it.

Sunny stopped, glancing down at me and then back at Tanner.

Tanner lifted his chin, a slow smirk spreading on his face. "Looks like I'll be making another stop to see your president tonight," he said, heading to the passenger side of the SUV.

When all three men were tucked away in the vehicle and drove off, a breath I didn't realize I had been holding, left me.

Sunny closed the distance between us, grabbed my hand, and pulled me away from Shade. Faster than I thought possible, his hand connected with my ass.

I yelped, the burn of his palm sending a wave of heat rushing through me.

He did it again.

Swat. Swat.

I opened my mouth to object, to scream, to yell, to demand for him to leave me the hell alone but something in his dark gray eyes stopped me. I wasn't sure what all was going on in his head but what I did notice was that he was scared. For me. For him. For Shade. I wasn't sure. But the fear that hid behind his eyes made all the words die on my tongue and give in to his punishment.

ELEVEN

SUNNY

SPANKING MEADOW LIKE THAT was not something I had intended to do. But hearing the fear in her voice when she asked us to come pick her up and then Tanner being there when we arrived, set something inside of me on edge. It was like that beast had been dormant for so damn long, he didn't know what the hell to do now that he was unleashed. Spanking Meadow seemed to be the only way to put him at ease.

Giving her ass one final slap, I ran my palm over it, easing the sting I was sure she felt.

But she never said anything. No complaints. No pushing me away. Nothing. I was almost expecting her to at least glare at me or demand to know what I was thinking. When she didn't, I leaned my forehead against hers and blew out a slow breath.

"I'm sorry, pet."

A heavy hand cupped my nape. Knowing it was Shade, sent my nerves at ease.

Meadow ran her hands inside my leather jacket. "I won't demand answers now, but you *will* tell me what that was about."

"That was for scaring the shit out of us. That was for calling Tanner out when you have no idea who the fuck he is." I lifted my head. "That was for walking home instead of calling us. I know your dad is alive and well and would probably give you shit for being out here by yourself. I don't care that you've done it so many times, you probably know these roads like the back of your own hand. But times have changed, baby girl. Tanner is only one of many monsters lurking in the dark corners."

Meadow's eyes searched my face. "I didn't mean to scare you, but he pisses me off. I dated a fucker like him. Luckily, I got out rather quickly before it got really bad, but it still messed me up." Her mouth snapped shut. She pulled away from me but only because I let her. "Anyway. That doesn't matter. Will you drive me home now?" She headed to the car and slipped into the front seat, not waiting for us to follow.

"Sunny," Shade said gently.

"Don't." I walked past him but not before I saw the confusion in his eyes. Well, welcome to the club. Because I had no idea what the fuck I was doing.

"Sunny." Shade rushed to my side. "She's not like the others. You can't control her because it's in your nature. You have to work with her."

"I know that," I snapped at him.

He flinched.

"Fuck." Pulling at the collar of my jacket, I started pacing. "She needs to be careful and I want to protect her. I want..." I had never been into the whole Daddy Dom/baby girl thing but with Meadow...I stopped, looking back at the car.

She sat in the passenger seat, her dark eyes locking with mine.

Every fiber of my being called out to her. To protect her. To provide for her. To make her ours.

"Whatever it is that you want, I'll help you get it." Shade cupped my shoulder, giving it a light squeeze. He leaned toward me, his hot breath fanning the side of my face. "I know she wants it too."

"She already has a daddy," I blurted.

Shade chuckled. "Yeah, but she's not fucking that one."

I let out a huff. Even though he was right, it still didn't mean I liked hearing it. "What am I supposed to do now?"

"We need to talk to her, remember? Communication is key and all."

I grunted and headed to the car. "Whatever happens, don't you dare fucking leave me."

Shade rolled his eyes. "I've been with your grumpy ass for years. If I haven't left you already, I sure as hell am not going to leave you now."

"Thanks, asshole," I muttered.

He blew me a kiss and slipped into the back of the car.

I sighed, shaking my head and joined them in the vehicle. "Meadow, I—"

"I don't have daddy issues," she blurted.

I frowned, passing a glance at Shade.

He only shrugged.

"I mean…" Meadow bit her bottom lip. "I don't know what I mean. I know that I don't have daddy issues though, but I liked what happened out there."

"You mean when I spanked you for scaring me?" I asked, turning toward her.

"Yeah." She ran her hands down her thighs. Up. Down. A shaky laugh left her. "I've never been nervous about talking before." She cleared her throat, taking a deep breath. "I like that you want to take care of me and protect me from the monsters lurking under my bed."

My body stirred. "I'm not into the Daddy Dom/baby girl dynamic but calling you *baby girl* seems natural. Taking care of you. Touching you. Keeping you safe. It's all natural. I don't know why, when we hardly know you. But I want to get to know you, Meadow. I want more."

"And so do I," Shade said, sitting forward. He reached out and brushed his hand down her arm.

Meadow turned her body toward us, lifting her knee onto the seat. "I want that too. I like that you talk to me and you don't treat me like a kid. I know I'm younger than you. I get that. And I don't have a lot of life experience yet, but I will. My parents raised us to be able to take care of ourselves if something ever happened to them. I can even change a flat tire by myself and stop a leak. My brother taught me that part."

"Good." I chuckled. "I don't want you to have to depend on us, but I do like being there for you when you need it."

She gave me a small smile. "I know. That's why I called you when Tanner showed up. He creeps me out."

"It's funny because he actually does some decent stuff." I started up the car.

"What do you mean?" she asked.

"He loves animals. His crew actually stopped a dog fighting ring. But I think that was more his call and his crew just went along with it. It fucks with your head though. Because on one hand, he'd do anything to bring those who hurt animals to justice but then on the other, he'd have no issues killing a human." Shade sat back. "It's fucked up."

"He hates humans basically," Meadow added.

"Something like that. Animals have never crossed him." I didn't know Tanner's whole history, but I *did* know that something happened, and he lost all faith in humanity. I wasn't even sure he trusted his crew half the time. He probably just kept them at his side so he knew where they were at all times.

"He wants me to stop by his clubhouse."

My head whipped around. "Excuse me?"

Meadow shrugged like it was no big deal. "Oh, come on, Sunny. I'm not actually going to go. I have nothing that he wants."

"What did he say to you?" Shade asked, his voice calm while I was wired up tight. Always the calm one.

I put the car into gear and drove us home. Needing to keep my mind occupied for fear I would lash out, drive over to Tanner's, and knock him the fuck out.

"He just said that he wanted me to stop by his club and that if I didn't, he would show up at the center. Do you think he would make good on his threat? Because I really don't want to go to his club." She shivered. "He bothers me."

I cupped her inner thigh. "You won't be going to his club. Not without us at least."

"Okay." Meadow covered my hand. "Are you guys good?"

I met Shade's gaze in the rearview mirror.

He winked.

I coughed.

"What? Tell me," she demanded. "I want all the dirty details."

Somehow, I knew she wasn't kidding.

(Shade)

Sunny and I had a lot to work through, but he was right. I enjoyed taking care of Meadow too. When she called, needing us, it stirred something inside of me I had never felt before. It made the alpha in me roar. Although I submitted to her in every sense of the word, I reveled in dominating her just the same.

"Did you two talk at least?" Meadow asked.

"Kind of." I brushed my hand down her arm, watching it erupt into tiny goosebumps. I covered Sunny's hand that was on her thigh and pushed it higher.

Her breath caught.

I could feel Sunny looking at me. Even though he was driving, I could still sense that he glanced my way every chance he got. I didn't know what I was doing. But I enjoyed seeing his hands on her.

"Shade," Meadow whispered. "Tell me what happened."

"We talked. This thing is new for us. Sunny's never been with a man before." I pushed their hands higher up her thigh. "But I know he wants to be with me."

"Is that what you want?" she asked, her voice taking on that husky tone I had come to crave whenever she was turned on.

"Yes. I want him to know that it's meant to be. Whatever happens between us, it'll be perfect. It's ours. It'll always be ours. And now that you're…"

"What?" Meadow lifted our hands off of her thigh and pushed them beneath the hem of her dress. When our joined hands came into contact with her skin, Sunny let out a soft growl. I only grinned, knowing it was taking everything in him not to pull the car over and devour every inch of Meadow.

"Ours, Meadow. You're ours." I pushed our hands higher up her thigh until we came into contact with her… "Fucking hell."

She laughed.

"Christ." Sunny groaned. "You're not wearing any panties."

"They get in the way. Besides, I was hoping I'd run into you today. And you were just going to rip them—"

Before she could finish her sentence, I pushed Sunny's index finger into her.

She sighed, spreading her legs and giving me what I wanted.

Full control.

TWELVE

Meadow

WHILE SHADE CONTROLLED THE actions between my legs, I couldn't help but look at Sunny. His jaw was clenched tight. His gaze wouldn't meet mine. He was focused. Determined. But for the little time that I knew him, I knew that he was also on the verge of snapping.

"Turn toward me," he demanded, his voice gruff.

And there it was.

I did as I was told. "Is this what you wanted, Sunny?" I purred, spreading my legs.

Shade chuckled, keeping his hand on ours and helping Sunny finger me.

"Fuck yes." Sunny shook himself. "You're killing me here, Shade."

"I think you need to drive faster," I told him. I gave Shade a wink before unbuckling my seat belt and crawling over the console to Sunny.

"What are you doing?" he demanded. "Put your seat belt back on."

I giggled, licking up the length of his ear. "Will you spank me if I don't?" I nipped his ear lobe. "*Daddy*."

"Fucking hell." He blew out a slow breath, pulling his finger from my body and giving my inner thigh a light pinch.

I squirmed but it still didn't stop me from teasing him. "I like your hands between my legs, Sunny. Also, I can't wait to watch you fuck Shade." I glanced at his lap, the large erection jumping beneath his jeans. "Hmmm…looks like you can't wait either."

Sunny stepped harder on the gas, knocking me back.

He chuckled, sticking his finger that had just been inside me, between his lips.

I sat down and put my seat belt back on. Kicking off my shoes, I placed my foot in his lap and rubbed it over his swollen length. "Did anything else happen besides you two talking?"

Sunny glanced at Shade in the mirror.

"We kissed," Shade answered for both of them. His hand moved back to my thigh.

"And?" I knew something else had to happen. You didn't spend fifteen years with the same person for it not to. "Did you almost have sex?"

"You're asking us like we're just talking about the weather." Sunny shook his head, cupping my foot and running his thumb back and forth over my ankle. "You're something else, baby girl."

I shrugged. "Not really. I came into this after you'd been together for a long time. I don't expect you to just dote on me but on each other as well. You can clearly tell you're in love."

Sunny coughed.

Shade only grinned. "She already knows us well."

Sunny rubbed the back of his neck. "I'm new to this. Do I love Shade? You bet your beautiful ass I do. But it's harder for us. We're bikers and people aren't always accepting of it."

"But your crew is, are they not? They have to know that there's something there besides just friendship." I sat forward. "Have they said anything? Because I'll kick their asses if they have."

Sunny's gaze flicked my way before a laugh boomed through him. "You would to, wouldn't you?"

"Of course." I sat back, leaning against the door. "I'm a firm believer that love is love. I don't care what you're into as long as it's completely consensual between all adult parties."

"I think I just fell in love with you," Shade muttered.

I laughed. "I mean it though. If you want help getting to know each other physically, I can help. Or if you want to do it on your own first, that's fine with me too. I don't have to be there." I lifted my hand when they went to talk. "And don't think I would be jealous, because I wouldn't be. I'm not that type of woman."

"No, you're not. You're better." Sunny shook his head. "I think I just fell in love with you too."

A laugh burst through me harder than before. "Awww, shucks." I blew him a kiss. "Are you taking me home?"

"Did you want to go home?" Sunny asked.

"Hmm…" I tapped my chin. "Not really."

"Good because I wasn't taking you home anyway, baby girl."

I laughed, grabbing his hand and placing it on my lap. "I love it when you take control."

I yawned, pulling the arm tighter around me and spreading my legs out on Shade's lap. We had decided to go back to my place instead of theirs and just watch some movies. The girls weren't home, so I didn't have to worry about answering any questions they might have. Bringing a new guy home was hard but bringing home two and the questions would never end. But we couldn't stay out in the living room for long, knowing that at any moment, someone could show up. Not that I cared but Sunny had enough problems with his relationship with Shade, I didn't want to add any more stress by them having to deal with strangers badgering them with God only knew what.

Shade gave me a smirk, resting his arms on my bare legs. I had changed out of the dress I was wearing earlier. Not that the outfit I had on currently was any less revealing. The tiny shorts I wore, rode up some but surprisingly, the guys were gentlemen and didn't hint for more.

"Tired, little lamb," Sunny purred in my ear.

"Yeah." I kissed his cheek, his beard tickling my lips. "I've been baking a lot."

"You bake?" Shade asked me, tilting his head.

"Uh...just a bit." I giggled. "It's also why I can't keep the weight off." I shrugged. "I like food."

"Weight." Sunny lifted my tank top and ran his hand over my stomach. "What weight?"

"Stop." I pulled it down. Although they had already seen me naked, that was different. I was out of my element. I felt sexy the night I spent with them. Also, the shot of tequila beforehand had helped as well.

Sunny began tickling me. "There's no weight. At fucking all. You're damn near perfect."

I laughed, smacking his hands away.

Shade chuckled, pulling me onto his lap away from his friend.

"You think I'm damn near perfect?" I asked Sunny, hooking an arm around Shade's neck.

"I do." Sunny rubbed his mouth, the movement sending a flutter racing through my lower belly.

"I happen to agree with him." Shade kissed my chin, letting his lips slide down my jaw. "Absolutely perfect."

"You guys sure know how to make a girl feel good about herself," I said when I suddenly remembered I had some dessert left over. "Oh." I jumped off of Shade's lap. "I have a surprise for both of you."

"You better come back here naked, pet," Shade called after me.

"Yeah, yeah, hold your horses." I ran into the kitchen and opened the freezer.

"Hold your horses?"

I squeaked, spinning on my heel and slipped. Faster than I thought possible, Shade caught me and stopped me from falling on my ass.

"You scared me," I murmured, running my finger over the dark scruff on his strong jaw.

"I'm sorry, little lamb. You need to be careful."

"You startled me," I breathed, taking in his dark eyes.

He smirked.

"I could have hurt myself," I told him.

"I'd never let you fall." He pulled me tighter against him until I felt every line of his hard body.

Wrapping my arms around his neck, I brushed my lips along his ear, causing a shiver to ripple through him.

"Will you kiss my booboo?" I whispered, holding out my finger.

A wicked grin spread on his face. He grabbed hold of my hand, licked his lips, and slid my finger into his mouth.

My breath caught in my throat.

His tongue licked along it, sucking hard, sucking deep before releasing it with a pop.

"Holy hell," I breathed.

"Now get me my surprise, woman." He gave me a wink and smacked my ass.

"Yes, Sir." I saluted him. "You know, if you sucked my finger like that, I bet you could suck—"

"Not happening, pet." He chuckled, shaking his head.

"Not yet," I corrected.

"What's not happening?" Sunny asked, coming into the kitchen that suddenly felt really small with both of them in there with me.

"It's not my fault that it's a fantasy but I won't pressure you." I smiled sweetly at them and batted my eyes.

Sunny raised an eyebrow. "You still going on about us fucking?"

"Who me?" I gasped. "I would never do such a thing."

A look passed between them before they glanced back at me.

"What?" I asked, my heart picking up speed.

And then they were on me.

(Sunny)

Meadow was comfortable with Shade and I taking it to the next level. Although it hadn't happened yet, not completely anyway, we had kissed and touched. And I knew that in time, maybe even soon, it would turn into more.

With Meadow thrown over my shoulder, I slapped her ass and carried her down the hall.

"Where are you tak—" She moaned.

I chuckled.

Her question was cut short by Shade kissing her.

"Holy shit," she breathed. "If you never fuck me again, just kissing me would bring me to an orgasm."

"Woman, you say the sweetest things."

I threw him a grin and smacked her ass again, needing her to focus. "Where's your bedroom, little lamb? I don't want your roommates coming home and seeing their friend getting shredded by two hungry wolves."

"Put me down and I'll show my hungry wolves where my bedroom is."

I placed her on her feet, captured her face, and covered her mouth with mine.

She moaned, snaking her arms around my neck. "God." She pushed me back. "I can't with you. With both of you. Just your kisses have me melting."

I chuckled, running my fingers along my mouth. "Show us where your bedroom is, baby girl. *Now.*"

"Yes, Daddy." She winked, turned on her heel, and led the way.

"She's something else," Shade murmured.

"Fucking right she is." Just her calling me *Daddy* could bring me to my knees.

Meadow stopped at the end of the hallway. "Coming, boys?"

THIRTEEN

SUNNY

AFTER BOTH OF US used Meadow good and hard, we got a call from Greyson that we had to meet at the clubhouse. We didn't want to leave her but getting a call from the boss became a priority when the guy would send a search party just to prove a point and embarrass us.

But now that we were on the way home, both of us were on edge. I needed my bike and to ride her good and hard since what I really wanted to do was currently passed out in her bed. I wished we would have brought her back to our place.

"I wish we would have brought Meadow to our place instead of leaving her at home. I could use another good fucking," Shade said, taking the thought right out of my head.

I rubbed the back of my neck, trying to ease the strain that had set up permanent residence ever since Greyson told us what he wanted to meet with us for.

Tanner Fucking Bones.

The guy had taken a liking to our new little toy.

"He's fucking with our heads," Shade said, checking his cell. He frowned and put it away. "I don't like this."

"Neither do I," I finally said. "I need to go for a ride. Or a run."

"A run sounds good." Shade sighed, pushing a hand through his short brown hair. I noticed then that it had grown in some on the sides. I also noticed how wrinkles sat at the corners of his eyes. Did I put them there? Was he stressed because of me?

We were now on our way home after leaving the clubhouse and both of us were wired. Shade was right. We should have brought Meadow home with us. But as much as we wanted that to happen, we needed to give her space just the same.

Shade's phone dinged then. "We won't see her for the rest of the week. She has an emergency job for the center."

"Baking I hope."

"Yeah."

I breathed a sigh of relief. I didn't like that she worked at The Dove Project. Not with Tanner sniffing around the place. I didn't know what his obsession was with it but if his threat rang true, those innocent victims would be worse off once he got ahold of them.

Tanner was a sick fuck and I wouldn't put it past him to be worse than the people who ran the human trafficking rings themselves. They ran from monsters only to fall into bed with the Devil himself. I just hoped it never got that far.

My chest constricted. "We need to make sure we have guys watching the center."

"Greyson's on it." Shade's gaze flicked to mine. "You know that. You were in the meeting. Remember?"

"Right." My jaw clenched. I looked away. Once we finally pulled up to our house, I swerved the car into the driveway, turned it off, and rushed from the vehicle.

"Sunny."

Ignoring Shade, I ran up the steps, unlocked the door, and barged inside.

"Sunny, what the hell?" He kicked the door closed, following me farther into the house. Our house. A house we had moved into together so many years ago. A house that held so many memories. Us sharing women. Fights. Laughter. So much damn happiness but most of that was fake. We weren't happy. At all.

"Sunny."

I spun on him, forcing him back a step. "Why?"

"Why what?" His eyebrow rose. "What's going on?"

I closed the distance between us. In a quick move, I had my hand around his throat and his big body up against the wall.

"Why are you with me?" I finally asked. "It can't be because you're happy." My voice was low, rough. "You want to continue sharing women for the rest of your life?"

"No." His brows narrowed. "I want to continue sharing one woman. Meadow. That's it. She's all I want."

"She's young. She won't stay with us forever." I released my hold on his throat. "She'll find someone younger. Someone who can give her what she wants."

"We are what she wants. She needed help and she called us. Remember?" Shade searched my face. "Where's this shit coming from?"

I pushed away from him. I didn't answer because I didn't know. I was too old for this but at the same time, I was fucking terrified that it would be a repeat of the hell my ex-wife put me through.

"Sunny." Shade stepped in front of me. "Talk to me."

"I don't want to fucking talk."

He placed a hand on my arm, letting it travel up to my shoulder before cupping my nape. "Tell me."

"Shade." My body vibrated. I reached out and touched the scruff on his jaw. "No." I shoved away from him and sat on the couch. "I can't do this."

"Fine. Keep telling yourself that, Sunny." Shade headed down the hall to the bathroom, the sound of the shower starting a moment later.

"Fucking hell." I pulled my phone from my pocket and opened my last text to Meadow.

Me: I don't know what I'm doing.

I hit send before I could think twice about how desperate I sounded.

My phone rang.

I jumped, not expecting Meadow to actually call me. "Hey."

"I'm here, Sunny. Whatever you need. I don't care that we just met a few days ago."

I sighed. "You're something else, pet."

"You keep telling me that and I'm going to get a big head." She paused. "Listen though. Whatever you want to do, he'll let you. He's patient. Shade loves you."

"I know." I dropped my head in my hands.

"I won't be jealous, if that's what you're also worried about, but I would like to join eventually."

My body stirred at the thought. "I'd like that too."

"Good. Now get off the phone with me. Take it slow. Kiss. Touch. Fuck. Drink a couple of beers. Watch a movie. Whatever you want. Just know that he's not going to leave you."

"How do you know all this when you only just met us?"

"Call it women's intuition. You guys seemed to figure me out rather quickly. Remember?"

My cock hardened as the memories of Shade calling her out on feelings she wasn't ready to reveal and then fucking her in front of me.

"Now hang up, Sunny," Meadow continued, pulling me from my thoughts, "and I'll see you in a few days. Oh, and I expect you to tell me all the dirty delicious details." She hung up before I had a chance to respond.

The shower ended, sparking a need to rush through me. Meadow was right about one thing. I needed more. Maybe not full on sex but I needed to let Shade know that I was in this for the long run. When he had given me a blow job, not that it lasted long, no fear had rushed through me. Taking it slow then was what I needed but I enjoyed when he touched me. And now I wanted to touch him and return the favor in a way.

I only wished we would have met Meadow long ago so she could give me the strength from the very beginning to take this to the next step.

"Sunny, listen, I'm sorry about before," Shade said, coming down the hall and into the living room. "I shouldn't press you and I need to be patient. This shit with Tanner is fucking with my head and then Meadow being so damn delicious is also messing with me."

I shot to my feet and closed the distance between us in two long strides.

"What's going on?" he asked, his eyes wide.

In a quick move, I had my hand back around his throat and shoved him up against the wall.

"Sunny," he said, his voice deep.

I stared at him. My best friend. My partner. The only person I had ever let into my heart. But I knew that Meadow could join him. She would be the only one besides him that could crack the icy walls that I had built up around the beating muscle so long ago.

"What are you going to do?" he asked, his voice low.

I let my gaze travel down his naked torso. Although he was in a towel, it did nothing to hide the growing bulge beneath it. I licked my lips, a shiver trembling through me at what it would be like to take our relationship to the next level. I had never been with a man before. Shade had. I knew he would be patient with me. Hell, we had been together for fifteen years and he never pressed for more.

Faint scars sat on his torso from years of fighting. Being a biker was hard, but I wouldn't change it for anything.

"Why haven't you hinted for more?" I asked him, reaching out and running my thumb over his hip bone.

A notable shiver trembled through him. "Because I didn't want to pressure you. I knew being with a man wasn't your thing."

"I want it to be." I took a step closer to him. "With you anyway. But it's different. I don't look at you as a man but as someone I care about. Someone who knows me and puts up with my shit. I look at you as my partner and not as…"

"A man," Shade whispered.

I nodded. We were just two people who depended on each other. He completed me in ways I never thought possible. I never had this with Roxanne, and I knew that he didn't have this with his ex.

Pushing my hand to the back of Shade's neck, I hooked my fingers into the towel and ripped it free from his body before letting it drop to the floor at our feet.

His breath caught. Shade submitted to Meadow the other night and now here we were.

"I like Meadow," I told him, brushing the back of my knuckles over his lower stomach, his cock jumping at the soft touch.

"Oh, I know."

I smirked. "I like her a lot."

"I know that too and so do I." Shade grabbed onto my hips but didn't hint for more. I was in control. He was giving that to me, and I could never thank him enough for it. "I want her again."

I met his green eyes then. "So do I."

"But I..." He pulled me closer, but our hips still didn't touch. "I want you too."

"I talked to her."

His gaze locked with mine. "When?"

"Before you got out of the shower. She told me to take it slow and that you wouldn't pressure me. I told her I didn't know what I was doing."

"I don't know what I'm doing either," he confessed. "Sure, I've been with a guy but we both know how that turned out."

"Yeah, you ended up with a man who didn't want more."

"Until now." His eyes became darker, greener even.

"Meadow also said that she wants to join next time," I said, pressing up against him.

"Fuck," he breathed.

"She would enjoy this," I murmured, glancing down at his full mouth. There was a light pink scar on his bottom lip.

"I bet you can't hit me harder than I can hit you," Shade slurred.

I chuckled.

Greyson paced back and forth in front of him. "How much you wanna bet?"

The memory brought a smile to my face. Greyson had hit him. Hard. And won five hundred bucks because of it. He never kept the money though and gave it back to everyone who had placed bets against his drunk ass.

"What's that smile for?" Shade asked, searching my face.

"I was remembering how you got this scar." I reached up and brushed my thumb over his bottom lip. "Feels like forever ago."

He laughed lightly. "Apparently I thought I was more sober than I actually was."

I smirked.

"I wish Meadow was here," he finally confessed.

My gaze snapped to his. "Yeah?"

He nodded. "We could strap her to our bed and make her watch."

A sly grin spread on my face. "What would we do while our little lamb watched?"

He swallowed hard, tightening his hold on my hips. "Kiss."

"Hmmm..." Cupping his jaw, I turned his head to the side in a rough move and leaned toward him. Licking along the length of his throat, the scruff of his beard scratched at my tongue. "I think we would do more than kiss." I wrapped my other hand around his cock.

He jumped, bucking his hips into my touch.

"First, I would tie her up. Her pupils would dilate because she's a kinky little thing. And then I would kiss her. Get her nice and hot. Make her fucking squirm."

Shade's chest rose and fell, his cock hardening even more in my hand.

"And then." I pushed my thumb along the tip of him. "I would lower my mouth to her pussy."

His breath hitched.

"I would eat the fuck out of her, get her to the point where she's begging and then I would stop." I pushed my hips against his, rubbing against him.

"Sunny," he whispered.

"Ask me what I would do next?" I pinched the tip of his dick when he didn't respond.

He jumped.

"Ask me," I demanded, pushing into him hard.

"What would you do next?" he finally asked.

"I wouldn't tell her what we were doing. It would be our present for our little lamb. A treat for her. And then when we're good and ready, we would untie her and let her join us." I turned Shade's head toward mine. "Would you like that?"

"Fuck yes."

"Good." I released his jaw, glancing down between us. "I never thought I'd be touching you."

"I'm a patient man, Sunny." He ran his hands up my sides before cupping my nape. "I won't pressure you into anything you don't want to do."

Knowing he was speaking from personal experience, my chest tightened.

"I want you to come for me," I murmured, stroking my hand up and down his thick length. I imagined Meadow on her knees, licking him, holding my hand and helping me.

"Sunny." His lips found the side of my neck. "I've waited fifteen years for this."

A surge of anger rushed through me. In a quick move, I spun him around and slammed him up against the wall, all the while keeping my hand on his cock. "You trying to make me feel guilty?"

"Fuck." He groaned, arching against me. "No. I'm just stating a fact."

Pushing my arm against the back of his head, I picked up speed with my hand. Rubbing my pelvis into his ass, I wondered what it would be like to be with him. Truly with him.

"Keep your hands against the wall," I demanded, my voice firm.

His cock swelled in my hand.

Inching my arm around him, I placed my hand on his chest. His heart thumped hard beneath my palm.

Kicking his legs apart, I kept a firm grip on his cock. Inching my hand up and down the length of him, I placed a soft peck on his shoulder. "When you come, I want you to call out Meadow's name."

She was going to have a field day with this one. I could already hear the questions leaving her mouth.

"Sunny," Shade groaned, dropping his head on his shoulders. "Fuck."

I chuckled, lowering my hand and squeezing him. Wrapping my free hand around his jaw, I pulled his head back and sunk my teeth into the side of his neck. "Nice and hard, baby boy."

He shivered at the term I had used, knowing he liked it when Meadow called him that.

"You going to submit to me like you do for our little lamb?"

"Yes," he murmured, his hips thrusting forward and back.

"Good. Wrap your hand around mine. Help me make you come. And don't forget to say her fucking name."

He did as he was told, circling his fingers around mine and guiding me up the length of him.

This was the next step.

It moved us forward.

I just hoped that neither of us would end up regretting it.

FOURTEEN

Meadow

ROLLING AROUND IN GARBAGE was not my idea of fun. But after bringing out a couple of bags from the country diner, I accidentally dropped my phone in the large bin and now I was knee deep in goo.

Oh God, something just slithered by my feet.

I shivered, my stomach rolling. "You have got to be fucking kidding me."

When something else brushed against my calf, I screamed, jumped, and hit my head on the edge of the bin.

"Meadow?"

I rubbed my head, stood up, and found Sunny and Shade staring at me. "Oh, hey guys."

"Care to tell us what you're doing?" Sunny chuckled.

"I dropped my phone and can't find it, and I think something's alive in here with me."

Sunny's laugh deepened.

"I'm glad you find this funny, asshole." I scowled.

"Let me help you out of there, baby girl." He reached into the garbage bin for me.

"Fine." I wrapped my arms around his thick neck. When he went to pull me out, my sandals slipped off my feet. "Oh God."

"I think you lost your shoes," Shade said, glancing into the bin.

Sunny held me against him, cradling me like a child.

"I think so too." I wiggled my toes. "I liked those sandals too. They were comfy."

"I'll buy you new ones but I'm not going in there after them." Sunny laughed, shaking his head.

I couldn't help it. I laughed along with him. "Okay, you can put me down now."

"Nope." Sunny held me tighter. "Not happening."

"But you'll get garbage goo on you and I'm sure I smell." I wrinkled my nose for added effect.

"I don't give a shit." Sunny nodded toward the back door.

Shade opened it. "Do you work here?"

"I bake for the owner from time to time. I can't believe I lost my phone." I let out a heavy sigh.

"It probably wouldn't work now anyway if it fell into that goo you keep talking about." Shade poked my ribs.

"Probably not." I laughed, making a mental note to get a new phone.

Sunny carried me over to a large sink.

Shade turned on the tap and ran a cloth under the water before cleaning off the muck that covered my feet.

My heart swelled at the sweet gesture.

"Better?" he asked, his jade eyes meeting mine.

"Oh yeah." I winked.

He grinned, shaking his head. He rinsed the cloth and turned off the water.

"Stand watch?" Sunny said, ignoring the fact that I was mentally fucking his friend.

"Of course." Shade went to walk away but spun around quickly and came back toward us. "One thing first." He cupped my cheek and covered my mouth in a hard, bruising kiss.

I sighed, taking his tongue deep between my lips.

"Hmm…" He released me, giving my bottom lip a gentle bite. The sharp pain shot right to my clit. "Until later."

"Geeze, Shade." I shivered, circling my arms tighter around Sunny.

Shade chuckled, gave me a wink, and headed back outside.

Sunny grinned down at me but didn't say anything as he carried me into the dining area of the restaurant. Luckily, it was slower than usual and I wouldn't have a bunch of questioning stares wondering what the hell was going on. Except for…

"Meadow, please tell me why you're being carried around like a damsel in distress when we both know that you are definitely no damsel."

I laughed. "Kimmy, this is Sunny. Sunny, Kimmy. I lost my phone in the garbage bin and then I lost my shoes."

"Did you go in after it?" Kimmy Renaud asked, placing her hands on her curvy hips. Her graying eyebrows narrowed in the center, but a hint of amusement flashed in her green eyes.

"I did." I squirmed against Sunny. "You can put me down."

"Not happening, pet," he grumbled.

"I'm probably getting heavy," I told him, my body heating at the mere intensity rolling off of him in waves.

"Nope. You aren't."

I sighed and continued squirming. "Put me in one of the booths then."

"Fine." He carried me to the nearest booth and placed me on the bench, sliding in after me.

"Better?" I asked him, cupping his arm.

"No." He wrapped an arm around my middle, pulled me into his side, and snuggled his face into the crook of my neck. "Now it's better."

I giggled, his beard tickling my skin.

He leaned back, giving me a goofy grin.

"Why do you have Shade outside and not in here with us?" I asked, resting my arm across his lap.

"Because we had a meeting a couple of days ago with Greyson and the rest of the guys," Sunny said but he didn't elaborate.

"That's it? That doesn't seem like a good enough reason."

A deep rumble shook the walls of the restaurant. I glanced outside, finding several other bikers I didn't know, pulling up to where Shade sat on his bike. Even from there, I could see the deep frown set between his brows. "What's wrong with him?" I asked, noticing the smoke between his lips.

He sat up straighter, looking my way over his shoulder. Shade winked, blowing me a kiss.

I waved.

"Tanner's taken a liking to you and we're trying to figure out why," Sunny murmured in my ear.

But before I could ask any more questions, Kimmy came back with two glasses of water and placed them on the table in front of us.

"Care to tell me what this is about?" she demanded, nodding toward the crowd outside her restaurant.

"Nothing's going on," Sunny told her.

Her eyes flicked between him and I. Her brows furrowed. She crossed her arms under her chest, jutting her chin forward. "If something happens, I'll call my old man who will then call his buddy, Greyson. Neither of them will like that."

"You know Greyson?" Sunny shifted beside me.

"Of course I know him. I also happen to know Meadow. So if something happens to her, I don't think Greyson would like an appearance from my—"

"Old man. I got it," Sunny mumbled.

"What's going on?" I asked her. Kimmy had always been polite, nice, never demanding answers, or sticking her nose in where it didn't belong. Something sparked this new side of her, but I had no idea what it could be.

"Meadow." Kimmy headed behind the counter. "I need to talk to you."

I gently pushed Sunny, but he wouldn't budge. "Let me out."

"You're not wearing any sandals."

"The floors are clean," I told him. "Trust me. Kimmy is like Monica from *Friends*. She's constantly cleaning." I pushed him again. "Sunny, move please."

"Fine." He slid out of the booth and paused. "Fucking hell."

"What's wrong?" I followed his gaze, glancing out the large window and found the guys circling Shade. "Who are they?"

"Some of Tanner's crew," Sunny grumbled.

"Go." I latched onto his jacket when he went to pull away. "Wait." I pulled him toward me, placing a hard peck on his mouth. "Take care of our boy."

He grunted, kissed me one last time, and left the restaurant, the sound of the door dinging behind him.

Even though I hadn't known the guys for long, I knew that Shade was the calm one and Sunny was the one with the temper. But as the guys approached Shade, the anxiety inside of me rose. Shade's brows were narrowed and before I knew what was happening, his fist landed against a younger guy's face.

I gasped.

Before it could turn into more, Sunny pulled Shade away from him.

"Meadow."

I jumped, forgetting that Kimmy was near.

"Sorry about this," I said, swiping my arm out.

"You need to be careful," she told me, crossing her arms under her chest. She nodded toward the scene in the parking lot. "I've spent many years around bikers. They find a new shiny toy, play with it for a bit and then once they're bored or that toy becomes used up, they move on to something else."

I frowned, no longer interested in the scene outside. "Are you referring to me as a toy? As *their* toy?" I asked, sitting back in the booth.

Kimmy moved to the booth across from me. "Not exactly, no. I just don't want to see you get hurt is all."

Could she be right? It wasn't like I wanted to settle down or anything, but I enjoyed the way the guys made me feel. I also liked that they treated me as an equal and not someone who was younger than them.

"Just be careful," she said, patting my hand and leaving the booth. "And tell your guys to clean up their mess after."

"I will." I stewed over her words, not liking the anxiety they caused. Maybe I wanted more than a fling after all.

(Sunny)

Shade had always been the calm and collected one. It was me who acted first before thinking but whatever the fucker said to him, pissed him off enough to hit him and in turn, sent rage coursing through me.

"What's going on?"

I bristled at the new voice.

"Fucking hell," Shade mumbled, pulling away from me.

"I asked a question," Tanner demanded, joining the fuckface who said whatever it was to Shade to set him off.

I stiffened, getting ready for a fight but much to my surprise, Tanner got in the prospect's face.

"You causing issues, Rat?"

"Nope." The fucker, Rat, crossed his arms under his chest. He glared at both Shade and I.

"What did he say to you?" I looked at Shade when he didn't answer. I had caught the tail end of their conversation when I left Meadow inside, but it wasn't enough to send Shade's fists flying. "Tell me."

"Yeah," Tanner cupped Rat's nape, giving it a hard squeeze. "Tell us what you said."

Rat winced. "I said that he should be shot and pissed on for being gay."

"The fuck?" Fury burned through me. I went to take a step forward when Shade grabbed my arm, stopping me.

"Did you?" Tanner leaned his elbow on Rat's shoulder. Which was funny in a way seeing as Rat was shorter than him. "Is that true?" he asked Shade.

"Yeah," he grumbled.

"Interesting." In a quick move, Tanner had Rat to the ground with his knee pressing into his back. Rat yelled out, trying to shove Tanner of off him but he was too small. "You see. I have an issue. I despise the fuck out of homophobic assholes like yourself." Tanner grabbed Rat's arm, twisting it behind his back until a pop sounded.

Rat screamed.

Tanner chuckled. "My favorite sound."

Shade and I passed a glance.

"Did you know that my brother is gay? You saying he's fucked up for where he sticks his dick? At least he's happy and healthy. I've seen the sick snatch you stick your dick in, you might want to get a check-up." He twisted Rat's arm farther behind his back. "I need to wash my damn hands," he muttered.

Rat sobbed, still attempting to push Tanner off of his back even with the broken arm.

"He has a brother?" Shade murmured, low enough for only me to hear.

Tanner caught our gaze, giving us a wink. "I think you should apologize." He whispered something in Rat's ear, something that made his eyes go wide and his face pale. I almost asked what was said when the sound of the door leading to the restaurant chimed.

"Everything okay?"

My body stirred. I spun around just as Meadow came toward us.

"Get back inside," I told her.

"Why?" She frowned, looking around me. "What happened?"

"My prospect disrespected your boys." Tanner pushed off of Rat. "Take him to the clubhouse," he told the two large fuckers who had been watching the whole thing all along. He brushed the dirt off his knees and came toward us. "I'd apologize on his behalf, but I've never been known to be a morally decent human being. So, I'm not about to start now."

"Meadow," I said, ignoring him. "You're not wearing any shoes."

She shrugged. "I need to take a shower anyway. What did he say to Shade?" She walked by me when I didn't answer, and went up to him. Grabbing his hand, she ran her thumb over his knuckles. "What did he say to you?"

He stared down at her, a notable shiver trembling through him. "He said I should be shot and pissed on for being gay."

Meadow snorted. "Fucking please. You're not even gay." She rolled her eyes and turned around to face Tanner. "You stuck up for them?"

"I wouldn't call it sticking up for them." Tanner yawned. "But that shit pisses me off."

"His brother's gay," I told her.

"You have a brother?" she asked him, keeping Shade's hand in hers.

"Yeah, little one. Something like that." Tanner met my stare. "Listen, I asked Meadow to come to my clubhouse—"

"I wouldn't consider it asking," she mumbled.

"Anyway, I asked her to come but I think the three of you should." Tanner looked over his shoulder, watching Rat being shoved into the SUV. "He'll probably die before he patches in." He sighed. "It's hard to find good prospects these days."

"Why are you wanting us to come to the club? Is it club business? You don't need Meadow there if it is." I didn't trust the guy. Respect him yes but that was as far as it went.

"Look." When Tanner looked at me then, it took everything in me not to step in front of Meadow and shield her from whatever monsters hid inside of him. I was man enough to admit it, he made me nervous as hell. "I need you both there because yes, as you said, it's club business. Your president is retiring soon. I've called Jaron but he's busy apparently. And the rest of the club couldn't care what I have to say. Which, I'm kind of sad about."

I rolled my eyes then. "Right."

"Point is, come to the club, bring her with you because she's nice to look at and then my girls won't be so damn twitchy around a bunch of men. It'll be nice having some fresh meat inside those walls." He laughed at some inside joke that only he knew the punchline to.

"And if we don't?" Shade said, pulling Meadow behind him.

"Oh, you don't have to. But like I told her, that compound looks rather delicious and I'm sure it holds some tasty treats that my men would love to devour." Tanner lifted a hand before either of us could say anything. "You show up. Those victims stay unharmed."

"I'm sure whatever it is you think you could do to those poor people is nothing compared to what they've already been through," Meadow told him.

A wicked grin spread on Tanner's face. "You're willing to take that chance, Meadow?"

Her jaw clenched, her cheeks reddening but she stayed quiet.

Good girl.

"Didn't think so." Tanner clapped his hands together. "Well, kids. It's been fun. Too-da-loo," he said, waggling his fingers and heading back to his bike. The SUV drove off, followed by Tanner and the rest of the guys. The rumble of the bikes disappeared, the farther away they got.

Once we could no longer hear them, I breathed a sigh of relief.

"You don't think he would actually go after the center, do you?" Meadow asked, her voice soft and unsure. I didn't like this side of her. I was becoming used to her confidence and when Tanner knocked her down a peg or two, it pissed me off.

"What the hell was that?" Shade spun on her, gripping her shoulders.

"Whoa there." She shoved him back. "Don't you dare put your hands on me like that."

Shade stiffened, gave me a look, and stomped off toward his bike.

A shaky sigh left Meadow.

I grabbed her hand. "Come with me."

She didn't say anything and let me lead her toward Shade. "He needs some time, baby girl. Tanner is not a man to be messed with or pushed." I stopped, forcing Meadow to look up at me. "He could rip you apart." I cupped her cheek.

"I don't like seeing him lose his temper," she murmured, nodding toward Shade.

He sat on his bike, glancing our way.

"That's your job," Meadow continued.

I smirked, placing a soft peck on her nose and leading her the rest of the way to Shade. "You good?" I asked him.

He huffed, scrubbing a hand down his face. "I'm sorry," he told Meadow. "I know what it's like to be touched when you don't want to be. It's not cool. And I shouldn't have done that."

Meadow's face softened. She moved around to the other side of him and placed a hard peck on his mouth. "I like it when you touch me. I like it when both of you touch me but not like that. Angry sex is one thing but that…"

"What?" he murmured.

I grabbed his hand, holding it in mine as he spoke to her.

Meadow caught the movement, a small smile splaying on her beautiful face. "I was with a guy who tried controlling me. Physically. Mentally. I don't mind submitting but on my terms only."

Shade nodded. "I was with a guy who forced my…He forced me to…" He coughed, cleared his throat, and squeezed my hand.

"I'm sorry, baby boy." Meadow stood taller, her gaze falling to our joined hands. "So, is this finally a thing now?"

"It's always been a thing and now you're a part of it," I told her.

Her smile grew, an unknown energy passing between all of us. "Good." She clapped her hands together. "I'm glad. Now I need to go home and take a shower." She grimaced, looking down at herself.

"Come over to our place," Shade suggested.

"Really?" She looked between us. "Okay. I'll run home quickly, take a shower and come over." She backed up. "Text me your address." She ran toward her car, giving us a wave over her shoulder.

I chuckled, shaking my head.

"Sunny."

I met Shade's gaze then, all previous humor gone.

"We have to protect her. And that center."

"You don't have to tell me that, Shade."

"I know." He looked around us.

"If this bothers you…" I pulled from his grip.

"No." He mumbled a curse. "Listen, we need to talk to Greyson."

I rolled my eyes. "Come on, we both know that Catch had a thing for Greyson and Tray. And besides, Greyson doesn't care who we fuck as long as it's consensual."

"And no animals or children are involved," Shade added, using Eve's quote she liked to ingrain in our brains from time to time. "I know he doesn't, but this is new for you. I don't need you getting scared and leaving me."

"Since when do I give a fuck what anyone thinks?" I cupped his face and placed a hard peck on his mouth.

He stiffened, pulling away. "Sunny."

"Shut the fuck up. I'll kiss you in front of our crew. In front of the whole damn world. I don't give a shit who is near. As long as Meadow is fine with this, that's all I care about." I kissed him again before he could say anything more and stole the very breath from his lungs and made it my own.

FIFTEEN

Meddow

I CHECKED THE ADDRESS on my phone, looked back at the house before me, and back again to my phone. After losing my cell in the garbage bin, I remembered I had an old one I could use until I was able to get a new phone. Maybe this one was broken. I typed the address into Google again and this location came up. Again. But this couldn't be the right address. For one, the house was huge and second, it almost looked too fancy for men like Sunny and Shade. I rolled my eyes. Now *I* was being judgy.

"You gonna stand out here all night?"

I jumped, spun around, and found Shade coming up the driveway with a few bags in his hands.

"Sorry, I'm late. I had to head back to the center. We're expanding it and it's taking all of us to make that happen," I blurted out in one breath. Why I felt the need to tell him all of that, was beyond me. Truth was, these guys had me unraveled and I didn't know how to deal with it half the time. Okay, most of the time.

Shade chuckled.

My cheeks burned. "What?"

"Nothing, little lamb." He kissed my cheek. "Nothing at all."

The scruff on his jaw tickled, sending a wave of heat rushing through me.

"I was just admiring your house," I told him, taking a bag from his hands.

"It is pretty amazing. Sunny had it built about ten years ago. We love the crew but sometimes you just need time away from them."

"I get that. I love my best friends but there are always people over. And the kitchen is small as hell." I followed Shade up the path to the large house. "One of these days, I'm going to have a kitchen so damn big, I won't even know what to do with it." It was unlikely but a girl could dream.

"Wait until you see our kitchen." He winked.

My stomach flipped. God, these men and what they did to me.

"Are you good? I mean, with this whole Tanner thing."

My stomach twisted. "Since he demanded that I go to his club and then he made an appearance and one of his boys made you lose your shit? Oh yeah. I'm fine and fucking dandy." I grabbed Shade's arm. "Are *you* good?"

"Listen." Shade raked a hand through his short brown hair. "What Sunny and I have or what's going on..." He scowled. "I'm confused as fuck and I hate it. But Tanner...we'll protect you from him."

My heart swelled. "I think Tanner needs a hobby," I muttered, looking back at the house that sat before us. "Sunny called me," I said more to myself. Even though I didn't know exactly what was going on with them, it did something funny to me that Sunny would call me, needing advice over what to do about him and Shade.

"I know." Shade looked at the house. "He told me. Whatever you said to him, thank you."

"Of course." I continued walking up the path, the hairs on the back of my neck tingling. I stopped, glancing back at Shade.

"I gave him a blow job," he said, his eyes on my ass. "But it didn't last long because we were interrupted."

My stomach tumbled. "Really?"

He met my gaze. "Yeah. It would have probably turned into more but Sunny got a phone call and..." His cheeks reddened. "Anyway, it was intense. He's intense. But I guess you know that already."

"Yeah. I do. But you're just as bad."

He closed the distance between us. "I am?"

"You are. You may submit to me, but I know that if needed, you could dominate me too." I stood on tiptoes and kissed his cheek. "I can't wait for that to happen, by the way."

A wicked grin spread on his face.

"Come on, baby boy." I laughed, making my way up the steps. "You can play with your toy later." Once I reached the porch, the door opened, revealing Sunny.

"Hey, pet." His eyes raked over me. "Have a good shower?"

"Yes." I smiled. "I washed all of that garbage goo off of me." I grimaced. "So gross."

He chuckled, taking the bags from me and bringing them into the house. "I know you like baking," he called out. "So I brought out a bunch of ingredients for you to play with."

I passed a glance at Shade before I kicked off my flip-flops and headed into the kitchen. "You did..." My eyes widened. The kitchen was the biggest I had ever stepped foot inside. "Oh God, I..."

Shade laughed, coming up behind me. "I think she's speechless."

Sunny smirked, leaning against the granite countertop. "It's all yours to play with, pet."

"I've never been in a kitchen this big." Everything was black. It was definitely a man's kitchen, but it was perfect if you asked me. "I think I just came a little."

The guys laughed.

There was a large island sitting in the center of it. With blood red appliances, a deep gray granite countertop, and black marble flooring, this kitchen was a baker's wet dream.

I ran my hand along the top of the island, letting out a soft sigh. "Do you cook?" I asked both of them, hoping this kitchen got at least a little bit of use out of it.

"I do," Sunny said. "But I don't bake. I have no self-control when it comes to sweets, so I stay far away from them."

"You want *me* to bake though?" I wasn't a cook. But I could make a mean cherry pie.

"I do. For you, I'll eat anything." He waggled his eyebrows.

I giggled, coming around the other side of the island. "Thank you. My kitchen at home is tiny. I'm the only one who uses it really but it's still not big enough. So this..." I let out another sigh.

Shade chuckled, sat at the island, and rested his elbows on the countertop. "Feel free to use this kitchen whenever you want."

"Really?" I stared at both of them. "You would do that for me?"

"Of course." Sunny grabbed my hand and pulled me into his arms, wrapping them around my shoulders. He kissed the side of my neck.

"I like this," I murmured, leaning into him. I felt safe with them. It was like it was just meant to be. I never believed in love at first sight, but I realized that I now understood.

Before I could let my brain think more on that subject, I pulled myself from Sunny's arms and went to the ingredients spread out on the counter behind him.

"I'm not even sure where to start." I tapped my mouth.

"Well, I'll make supper and you make dessert. Whatever you want, pet." Sunny kissed my head and started pulling items from the fridge.

"Are either of you allergic to anything?" I asked, still staring at the spread laid out before me.

"Nope," they both answered in unison.

Coming up with an idea, I started baking what I knew they would both love. My friends loved it, especially Ashton, and I could never make enough of it.

My chest tightened. Knowing I had brushed Ashton off since he ended things between us, then met Sunny and Shade, I felt a little guilty. This had never happened before and I wasn't sure how to take it.

"What did you decide to make?" Shade asked a half an hour later as he came up beside me. He handed me a beer before taking a swig of his own.

"Donuts. But they're super messy, filling, and absolutely delicious." I shrugged. "I love them. My friends love them. And I think you guys will too."

"Probably." Sunny pulled his own beer from the fridge and leaned against the counter beside Shade. "But we'll have to figure out a way to work off all of those calories."

Shade chuckled, giving me a wink.

I laughed, sitting on the stool by the island. "Thank you for this."

"For what?" Sunny tipped his beer toward me. "We haven't done anything. That's all you."

"You've done more than you think. I don't usually do this type of stuff with a guy, let alone two of them." I picked at the paper label on the beer bottle, my thoughts taking me back to *him* and everything he tried to take from me. Maybe he succeeded.

"We're not like the boys you've been with, Meadow." Sunny moved to the stool beside me, pulling me closer between his spread knees. "You *do* know that right?"

I nodded, chewing my bottom lip.

"Hey." He pinched my chin, tilting my head back. "Say it. Say that you know we're not like him. The fucker who hurt you."

"It's funny because I wasn't even with him for long. But I fell for him fast. After that, I started sleeping with anyone…" God, I sounded like a slut. Truth was, I felt like I didn't deserve anything more than sex. He had used me for his own personal gain, and I didn't know how to pull myself back from that.

"What?" Sunny frowned.

I shoved my head from his grip and pulled back the rest of the beer.

"I'm assuming that conversation needs some more alcohol," Shade said, handing me another beer.

"Yeah but you guys don't want to hear about that shit." I suddenly felt like a little girl and vulnerable. So damn vulnerable.

"We want to hear whatever it is you have to say." Sunny placed his hands on my knees and ran them up my thighs.

My skin tingled beneath his touch. I could feel the heat coming from him even though my jeans were in the way. "When's supper done?" The donuts would be about an hour. They had to bake on a low temperature to get that perfect taste.

"About an hour." Sunny's gaze dropped to my mouth.

I stood, wrapped my arms around his neck, and straddled his lap. "Think we could do something to pass the time?" I asked Shade.

Shade rubbed his mouth. "I'm sure we can come up with something."

I looked down at Sunny. "Do you think so?"

His hands ran down my back. "Oh yeah."

"Tell me something first. How far have you two gone?" I asked, rubbing myself over Sunny's crotch.

"Not far enough," Sunny growled in my ear, giving it a gentle bite. The sharp pain shot through every inch of me.

"Really?" I cupped his cheek, running my fingers through his beard. "Do you think you'll go farther?"

Shade stood from the stool he was sitting on and came around the island before sitting behind me. "What are you getting at, little lamb?"

"I mean, do you think you'll have sex?" As much as it would be hot, I got it if they didn't. Their friendship was important to them. It didn't take a rocket scientist to figure that out. I also knew and understood their fears. After sleeping with Ashton, things became weird. Not for him but for me, but that was only because I knew I could fall for him. I was thankful when he ended things. We weren't right for each other. I only knew that because I had found out he had slept with other women while sleeping with me. It would take a special kind of person to make him become a one-woman man.

"Where did you go?" Shade asked, pulling me off of Sunny's lap and onto his. "You disappeared."

I swallowed hard. "Nowhere."

"Meadow." Shade frowned.

I pulled out of his grip and went to check the oven, making sure the donuts didn't burn. They didn't and they were starting to smell delicious.

"Pet."

I spun on them. "Listen, you don't want to know my shit. It's in the past. And we hardly know each other anyway, so let's keep this for what it is."

"And what's that, Meadow?" Sunny crossed his arms under his broad chest, staring me down.

"Sex obviously because I don't know about you but it's all I can handle right now." I went to take another beer from the fridge when a firm hand grabbed my upper arm. Sunny pulled me back against him.

"I'm sorry, Meadow." He kissed my temple. "I didn't mean to press."

"It's fine." I turned in his arms, wrapping my hands around his thick neck. "We still have a bit before the donuts are cooked and supper is ready. I think you should give me a tour of your bed."

Sunny grinned. He crouched low and threw me over his shoulder.

I gasped, a bubble of laughter escaping me.

Shade chuckled from behind us.

While Sunny carried me to the bedroom, I couldn't help but wonder what would come of this. I had never thought about it before. I usually went into it wanting sex and sex alone but these men, they latched onto something inside of me that I needed and made it theirs. I wasn't sure how or even why, but I knew that I could fall for them.

For both of them.

(Shade)

I could read Meadow like the back of my own hand already. She liked for those around her to think she didn't wear her heart on her sleeve, as cliché as it sounded, but she did. And I was willing to accept it with open arms.

While she slept between Sunny and I, I ran my hand in small circles over her upper back.

"This feels way too comfortable," Sunny murmured, sitting back against the headboard. We had taken her to the room we shared whenever we brought a woman home. I hated sleeping by myself, but I didn't want to put any more pressure on Sunny than he was already putting on himself. So we always went to our separate rooms. Until now.

"Yeah but it feels good."

"It does." Sunny pulled the blankets higher on Meadow, petting a hand over her head. Her breathing was even, her back rising and falling. When we had brought her into the bedroom, things escalated quickly. An hour had past and the food was cooked. But instead of eating, Sunny went and shut off the oven before rejoining us and two hours after that, Meadow passed out.

"Shade."

I met my best friend's gray eyes. My fingers itched to reach out to him. To run along the hard lines of his naked body. To just feel him while we waited for Meadow to wake up.

Sunny ran a hand down his hard stomach and beneath the blanket.

My throat went dry, my cock jumping at what was possibly happening beneath the covers.

Moving higher up the bed, I pulled Meadow away from Sunny and sat beside him.

She stirred and rolled over onto her side.

Taking that as a sign, I met Sunny's gaze.

He glanced at my mouth, licking his lips. Pulling his hand from beneath the cover, he placed it on my chest, running it slowly down my stomach until he reached the part that throbbed for him. When he came into contact with my cock, a hiss escaped me.

"You're hard," he whispered, watching me.

I kicked the covers off me and stared.

His big hand was wrapped firmly around the shaft of my cock. It stroked from base to tip. Slow. Agonizing. And so fucking good.

"Shade."

My gaze flicked to his at the barked demand of my name.

He smirked. "Kiss me."

(Meadow)

With my eyes still closed, I was vaguely aware of the sounds in the room. Heavy breathing. Deep groans. Shade and Sunny were doing something but I didn't know what. Should I open my eyes and find out? Should I reach out a hand, hinting for them to let me join their private moment?

"Fuck." That was Sunny. I knew because I quickly came to realize that he liked that word and used it whenever he had a chance.

"Meadow."

My eyes popped open then, finding both men looking at me.

A wicked grin spread on Sunny's face. He licked up the length of Shade's neck.

I swallowed hard, glancing down the hard ridges of their naked bodies.

Sunny's hand was wrapped around Shade's cock, giving it slow but firm strokes.

Shade's chest rose and fell but his eyes wouldn't move away from mine. "More."

"You going to give him what he wants, pet?" Sunny asked, his voice husky.

"I'm rather enjoying the show actually." I rolled over onto my stomach.

"Don't give a shit," Shade bit out. "I need to touch you."

I moved toward him, placing a soft peck on his mouth. "Do you like having his hand wrapped around your cock, Shade? Does it feel good? I know I like it when he's inside me." I kissed the corner of his mouth. "So good."

"Fucking hell," he groaned.

I giggled, sitting behind his head.

He lifted his back off the bed and leaned against me. He reached a hand out for me, circling our fingers. "I can smell how wet you are."

"I have two hot guys touching each other in front of me. How can a girl not get wet over that?" I cupped Sunny's cheek. "Right?"

He chuckled, shaking his head.

"I want to taste him," I whispered, placing a soft peck on Sunny's mouth.

He brought his thumb up to my mouth, slipping it between my lips. Shade's pre-cum dripped onto my tongue.

A breathless gasp left me.

"Fuck." Shade's body shook, his hand stroked his cock, pumping hard and fast until his release shot onto his stomach.

"You two are something else." I couldn't believe I just witnessed that.

Shade sat up.

"I like this," I told them, pulling him back against me. "I like this a lot."

"So do we, pet." Sunny sat back against the headboard, hooking his arm around my shoulders.

Shade turned onto his stomach, resting his head against my chest and curling an arm around Sunny's middle. "I like this a lot too."

I smiled, running my hand over his back. "My sister's throwing a party this weekend if you guys want to come with me."

"We would love to, but we have to make an appearance at the clubhouse before our president hunts us down." Shade lifted his head. "If you want to come over, we can pick you up after though."

"Okay." I ran my thumb along his bottom lip, earning me a soft growl. I grinned. "We should eat something." As if on cue, my stomach rumbled.

We laughed.

"We should probably feed our girl." Sunny kissed the side of my head. "Need to feed this sweet little body so you can get more energy."

"Hmm…" I cupped his cheek. "And what does this little body need energy for exactly?"

Shade slid down the length of me, hooking my leg over his shoulder. "For this."

When his mouth covered my core, I cried out and rode that delicious high until he gave me permission to fall.

SIXTEEN

SUNNY

I HALF EXPECTED TO fuck Shade but after the hand job I had given him, he never hinted for more. I appreciated that because as much as I wanted to take it further, I still wasn't ready. I didn't know why either. It didn't make sense. None of this did. But while I watched him devour every inch of Meadow, I couldn't help but just lay there and watch.

Her screams slid into my ears. Her begging for more, trembled through every inch of me. I wanted to join and yet, I was mesmerized by the control he had on her body. So instead, I did nothing.

After she came for the third time, he released her, placed a soft peck on her mouth and left the bed.

"God, you guys are going to be the death of me." She laughed, pulling her messy hair up into a bun on top of her head.

Sliding from the bed myself, I grabbed her hand and pulled her toward me and into my arms. "We're going to take a shower." I pinched her chin, forcing her head back to meet my mouth. "And then we'll feed you."

"Okay," she whispered against my lips.

I chuckled, giving her ass a light swat. "Meet us in there."

She stood on tiptoes and gave me a final kiss on the cheek before doing as she was told and slipped into the bathroom.

"Sunny."

"Yeah?" I met my best friend's dark stare.

"That…" He cleared his throat.

"Was hot as fuck?" I answered for him.

He laughed, rubbing the back of his neck. "Yeah, it really was."

I wrapped an arm around his shoulders and kissed his cheek, breathing in the scent of Meadow on his lips. "I want more but I also need time."

"I know." He met my gaze. "Just let me know when and I'll take care of you. Every inch. I don't expect you to let me fuck you because I'm not a top at all. You know that. But I want…" His gaze dropped to my waist. Reaching out, he ran a finger down the shaft of my cock.

I hissed, my hips bucking toward him.

He smirked, swiping his thumb through the slit and bringing it up to his mouth. "Just say the word, Sunny." He stuck his thumb between his lips, gave me a wink, and followed Meadow into the bathroom.

I blew out a slow breath.

Holy. Fucking. Hell.

"Meadow." I groaned around a mouthful of dough. "This thing is fucking amazing."

She giggled, her cheeks reddening. "Thank you. Everyone I know, loves them. Haven't had any complaints yet." She patted her back. "I'm so proud of myself right now."

Shade chuckled, wrapping his arm around her middle. "It is really good."

"Good." She kissed his cheek, meeting my stare from across the table. "What?"

"You look good in our home," I said, leaning back in my chair.

"Oh." Her cheeks reddened. "Thank you. I've never...I've never actually done this before." Her cheeks darkened even more.

I raised an eyebrow, leaning forward. "Why, Meadow. Is our little lamb all of a sudden becoming shy?"

She snorted. "Hardly. I just feel comfortable with you guys and I'm not sure why. I just..."

"What?" Shade asked her, resting his chin on her shoulder.

"I like you." She placed a soft peck on his mouth. "Both of you."

"We like you too, pet." My phone rang, interrupting our little moment. I fished it out of my pocket, biting back a curse when I saw who was calling me. "Yeah," I barked into the phone.

"Well don't you sound cheery?" Roxanne mumbled.

"What do you want?" I demanded, locking eyes with Shade.

His jaw clenched, knowing who it was I was talking to. A woman who made my life a living hell and more.

"I want you back." Roxanne sniffed for added effect.

I rolled my eyes, pinching the bridge of my nose. I could feel Meadow staring at me, no doubt wondering who it was that made me even grumpier. "Not happening, Roxanne."

"Roxanne?" Meadow whispered.

Shade mumbled something to her.

Her head whipped around. "You were married?"

Fucking hell. "Rox—"

"Please, baby. We were good together," she slurred.

"Have you been drinking?"

"No." She hiccupped which was followed by a round of laughter.

"Woman. Put yourself together." I wasn't opposed to people drinking, hell, I did it myself. But when her drinking became a problem, that's when I didn't agree with it.

"You've gotten judgmental, Sunny." Her laughter subsided.

"Listen, I'm busy. Have a good night, Roxanne." I hung up the phone, put it on silent, and shoved it back in my pocket. Ignoring the stares coming from both Shade and Meadow, I rose from the chair and headed into the kitchen. I needed a drink myself. I also needed to get Roxanne off my ass. Years ago, I would have caved. I would have given her all the money in the world to help her and her kids. But when I found out that she was keeping the money for herself and letting her kids go without, I stopped.

"Sunny?" Meadow came up behind me, placing a gentle hand on my back. "Want to talk about it?"

"Not really." I pushed away from her and pulled three beers from the fridge. Popping off the caps, I handed her one. "I met her when I was twenty-two."

"I thought you and Shade have been together since then," Meadow said, taking a swig from her bottle.

Shade took that moment to join us. He leaned a hip against the counter, crossing his arms under his chest. He nodded once, giving me all the encouragement I needed to go on.

"We were but we hit a rough patch. I knew even at that time that Shade had feelings for me." I remembered back to the first time he told me that he was in love with me and the way I had responded. It could have been better, but he never commented on it.

"Is that when you met your ex?" Meadow asked Shade, jumping up onto the countertop.

"No, I met my ex in school. We went to college together. I was taking every course I could that had to do with auto repair." Shade chuckled, his thoughts clearly going back to a time when things were...easier.

"What's so funny?" Meadow looked between us.

"I was trying to impress him." Shade nodded toward me. "But it didn't work, and he had already met Roxanne."

"It was stupid," I grumbled, leaning against the counter beside Meadow. "And you never had to impress me, Shade."

"So you were with Roxanne, and Shade, you were alone?" Meadow leaned her arm on my shoulder. "Or was that around the same time you were with your ex."

"Same time," Shade mumbled.

"Was he good to you?" Meadow asked softly.

A dark shadow passed over Shade's face, the humorous glint in his eyes, no longer there. "No, little lamb. He was not. He was the bastard I told you who forced me to do stuff when I wasn't ready."

"Oh. I'm sorry, baby boy," she whispered.

"Don't. It's done. I've moved on."

He hadn't.

"And I learned from my mistakes."

That part was true.

"Okay. I'm glad. I..." Meadow took a sip of her beer, picking at the paper label on the side of it.

"What is it?" I asked, covering her hands.

"Is this fast?" Although she asked the question, she never looked at me.

I placed my bottle on the counter and moved in front of her. Taking the bottle from her, I placed it beside my own and cupped her hands. "Shade and I have shared several women before. I don't want to say a lot of women because that sounds douchey."

She laughed lightly.

"Eyes, pet," I demanded, running my thumb back and forth over her pulse point.

Her beautiful brown eyes met mine. My cock twitched. Fuck, I loved it when she listened to me.

Shade stepped up beside us, placing a hand on top of mine. That touch gave me the strength I needed to continue.

"Even though we've been doing this for years, we've never slept with the same woman more than once. We've never brought a woman home and cooked supper for her. And we've definitely never had a woman bake us dessert." I paused, my gaze dropping to our hands. Three pairs of hands. Shade's were tanned. Mine were stained from oil after working on cars for most of my adult life. And Meadow's were pale in comparison.

"Is this fast? Maybe for some," I continued. "But I know for Shade and I, it isn't fast at all. We're old fuckers and we have this beautiful, feisty as hell, hot little thing that enjoys spending time with us." I pulled a hand from her lap and pinched her chin. "You called us when you needed help. That says something, baby girl."

"It's not that big of a deal." She shrugged. "I could have called my father but that would have been brutal. Tanner would be dead or worse."

"What's worse than being dead?" Shade asked, chuckling.

"You don't know my father. Tanner would be ripped apart and spread out across the country before his crew found out." Meadow shook her head. "My dad and his friends are a little protective of me and my roommates."

"Good." I thought a moment. "I think I'd like your dad."

Meadow's gaze snapped to mine. "Uh…there is no way that is happening anytime soon."

Shade and I passed a glance.

"And why not?" I pressed, knowing I should leave well enough alone, but I wasn't always the brightest. Especially when it came to the woman in front of us.

Meadow rolled her eyes, pushing us back and jumped off the counter. "Because it's way too soon. Shade has issues from his ex. You're dealing with a psycho ex as well and I…I just…"

"What?" Shade cupped her shoulders, turning her toward him. "We're not going to hurt you."

"This is fast." Meadow pulled out of his hold and left the kitchen.

"I don't know what's going on," Shade mumbled.

"I think we fucked up by being too honest," I told him.

"For once, I actually think you're right." He scowled, following Meadow out of the room.

As much as I loved being right, this time was not one of those times.

SEVENTEEN

Meadow

IT HAD BEEN ALMOST a week since that dreadful night with Sunny and Shade. It started out well, with homemade supper and desserts but then that talk happened. I closed up completely. Sunny became even grumpier. And Shade tried being the best referee he could be. But it did nothing. So I said bye to them both, left, and hadn't seen them since.

I did get text messages every morning and every night since. They wished me a good morning and told me to sleep well when I crawled into bed. I was beginning to crave their texts and looked forward to them. But a part of me wondered if they were getting too close.

"Hey, babe."

My head popped up from the book I was trying to read when Ashton sat down beside me. He was so close, his thigh touched mine and I could smell the mint on his breath.

The hairs on the back of my neck tingled. I looked around us, half expecting Sunny to jump out of the bushes, beat his chest, and yell in broken sentences that I belonged to them. That never happened, but I wished it had, and that left a sour taste on my tongue.

I swallowed a sigh, glancing back down at my book. It was a classic fairy tale that Luna had picked up. She lent it to me that morning, knowing I needed some distracting. I wasn't much of a reader but right now, I was desperate to get these men off my mind.

"What's wrong?" Ashton wrapped his arm around my shoulders, pulling me closer.

"Nothing." The scent of his cologne wafted into my nose. It sent a flutter racing through me but not because he smelled good. No. Instead, it was...odd. I couldn't put a finger on it, but it didn't make me feel how it used to. It hadn't been that long since I let him touch me, but I almost felt...guilty.

"Hey." Ashton brushed his nose along the shell of my ear. "You're tense. I can help make you feel better."

A shiver raced down my spine. I pushed away from him and jumped from the bench. "We can't do this. It's over. You broke it off."

"We can still be friends." Ashton's brows narrowed in the center. "It's that guy. Sunny."

"And Shade," I mumbled.

"So, you really did find two men." Ashton ran two fingers along his mouth. "Interesting."

"Don't look at me like that." I pointed at him. "You've had sex with more than one woman at the same time, many times. Don't judge me."

He shrugged. "That's different. It's who I am." He leaned forward. "But it's not you."

"Are you saying it's not me because I'm a woman?"

His frown deepened. "That is not what I fucking said."

"No, but it's what you implied, Ashton. Listen." I lifted my hand when he went to speak. "I like them. They treat me well. And besides, this is my first time..." I scowled. "Why the hell am I explaining this to you?" I went to storm into the house when a gentle but firm hand caught mine. "Just let me storm away."

"I'm sorry." He wrapped his arms around my shoulders, snuggling his face into the crook of my neck. "I know I ended things, but I never actually expected it to be over. It's lame. I know. But I liked what we had."

"I wasn't the only one you were fucking, Ashton." I looked up at him then. "And I don't give a shit that I wasn't, but you can't expect me to wait for you. I like Sunny and Shade. I really do. They treat me well, even though I haven't known them for that long." Less than a month but Ashton didn't need to know that.

He cupped my shoulders, spinning me toward him. "If something happens where you're finished with them or…" He smirked. "I'll be here."

I sighed, stood on my tiptoes, and placed a soft peck on his mouth. "Go find a woman to satisfy you, Ashton. But that's no longer me."

He groaned. "I wish it was. You give the best head I've ever received."

"Right." I patted his chest. "I'm sure you tell that to all the women you've been with."

"Nah." He kissed my cheek. "I don't lie when it comes to blow jobs. The suction on those pretty lips of yours will be something I'll never forget. So, thank you for that, Meadow." He released me and headed into the house.

I blew out a slow breath, not really sure what the hell just happened but thankful that Ashton finally got the hint. Hopefully anyway.

As the night wore on, the backyard filled with people. Most of them I had seen in passing but I was always a few years younger than everyone, so I never really paid any attention.

"Meadow."

WITH US

I turned at the sound of a deep voice, finding Vincent Junior coming toward me. He was Luna's younger brother. Barely nineteen and hot as hell if you asked me. With both Italian and Japanese lineage, he got the tanned skin from his father and the deep chocolate brown eyes from his mother. My sister was a lucky lady. Although, she didn't even know it yet.

"How's it going?" I asked him, surprised that he was actually there. He couldn't drink yet, legally, so he usually stayed home. I wondered if Gigi had anything to do with him being out for the night.

"Not too bad." He shoved his hands in his pockets, then removed one and ran it through his short black hair.

"I have to say that I'm kind of surprised to see you here."

He smirked, a dimple popping in his left cheek at the movement. "I know. A couple of friends wanted to come. They heard about Gigi's parties and…"

"And she'll be here, so it'll give you an excuse to talk to her." I waggled my eyebrows.

"Right." He chuckled. "Listen, I just wanted to say that something's going on with my sister. She's holed up in her room and I don't know why. I think she got in a fight with Zach maybe."

"Oh." I smiled. "Okay, thank you. I'll be sure to check on her."

He nodded, spun on his heel, and headed back to his two friends standing on the other side of the yard.

Such a good brother, looking out for his sister. I hadn't heard that Luna and Zach were having problems. But I also hadn't been around much. My body thrummed, remembering why.

I wasn't sure what was going on between Vince and my sister either. But I noticed the way they looked at each other. Even though he was five years younger than her, you would never know it. He was well over six feet tall and had filled out this past summer. It was like as soon as he turned nineteen, the rest of his body caught up with him. But I never saw him with anyone. Even the girls who hung off of him, begging for his attention, would never get very far. He would just smile at them, give them that dimple that even *I* thought was sexy, and would continue drinking his water.

Sitting on the patio couch, I brought my knees up to my chest and was about to play on my phone when Piper and Gigi came out of the house.

"Hey." Gigi sat beside me. "We were wondering where you were."

"Have you talked to Luna?" Piper asked, sitting on the chair opposite me.

"No." Gigi pulled her hair back into a ponytail. "I think she has her hands full with Zach."

"How are things going with you and those bikers?" Piper asked me, waggling her eyebrows.

I laughed. "Good. I like that they don't make me feel like a little girl. Not that it would be an issue if they did. You know that whole Daddy Dom thing and all, but it's not really my scene." Although, Sunny spanking me because I scared him, was one of the hottest things I had ever experienced.

"Daddy Dom?" Gigi repeated, frowning.

I patted her hand. "You need to read more."

Gigi blushed. "I'm so naïve."

"Nah. You just know what you want and that's not one of them." Piper shrugged. "I wouldn't worry about it."

"I don't even know what I want." Gigi looked around her. "I feel like a dirty old woman."

"You *are* a dirty old woman," I teased.

"Is there something wrong with me?" Gigi asked softly. "Guys my own age don't do it for me. Hell, Vincent's more mature than them."

"He's only a few years younger than you," Piper pointed out. "And Luna's younger than Zach."

"That's different," Gigi muttered.

"How? Sunny and Shade are twenty years older than me." I patted my shoulder. "I'm so proud of myself right now."

The three of us erupted into laughter.

Gigi and Piper both stood at the same time, bumping their hands and knocking wine onto Piper's white dress.

"I'm so sorry." Gigi pouted. "What a waste."

"No problem." Piper patted her hand. "I was going to change anyway." She excused herself and headed into the house.

"I'm going to grab more wine," Gigi stated, staring into her empty cup. "Did you want anything?"

"No, thank you." I was still nursing my own glass of wine. Just wasn't feeling it tonight, for whatever reason.

About a half an hour later, once the party was in full swing, I had every intention of going to check on Luna like Vince suggested. But when I saw Jaron rush into the house, I thought better of it. I was lost in my own head and didn't even know he had shown up.

Following him, I saw Gigi muttering quietly to him.

"Have you seen Piper?" she asked him, looking around her. "We bumped into each other and spilled our wine. Some landed on her dress and she was going to change."

"That was half an hour ago," I added, joining them.

Jaron went back to the patio door and muttered a curse.

"Jaron?" Gigi raised an eyebrow.

He pulled his phone out of his pocket and stormed toward the hall leading to our bedrooms.

"What's going on?" Gigi followed him.

"Which room is Piper's?" he demanded, inching his way down the hall.

"Last one on the left." Her eyes were wide. "I can't find Brody."

My heart jumped. There was no way...Brody Davies had been a bit odd, but that was it. He was the mayor's son and showed up at Gigi's parties just because his father hated it. It was innocent though, wasn't it?

"Stay out here," Jaron told us as two large men came into the house.

"Who are you?" Gigi asked, jumping.

"They're with me." Jaron went down the hall, with the two men following him.

I rushed to Gigi and grabbed her hands. "You don't think something happened, do you?"

"I don't know. I mean..." She hesitated. "Brody's always been a bit off, but it's never been anything more than that. Or I never thought it was. Hell, we don't even see the guy often."

Now that he was older, he was always in the spotlight with his dad. The press ate him up because of his charm and good looks. I never thought he could actually do anything bad, especially with what his father did and who he was. None of this made any sense at all.

I moved to the end of the hall. Jaron and the other guys were nowhere to be found.

"I just told everyone they should go," Gigi said, coming up beside me. "It's getting late anyway."

It wasn't but she made a good choice, telling everyone to leave. Something told me that tonight would end up being more than just a random party.

My phone vibrated. I pulled it from my back pocket.

Shade: You still at that party?

Me: Yeah. You guys close by?

Shade: We are.

WITH US

Me: Let me guess, Sunny wanted to be close by in case I got bored.

Shade: Something like that.

A breath of relief left me. This would be one of those times where I didn't give a shit about Sunny's overprotective nature. I had a feeling I was going to need it before the night was over.

Suddenly, two cops came barreling into the house.

My heart jumped to my throat.

"Oh God." Gigi gasped.

"Someone called the police," one of the officer's stated, his brows narrowed. He had that familiar tick in his jaw that I noticed Sunny got whenever he was pissed. Which was quite often if you asked me.

"I…" Gigi's gaze flicked to mine.

"I can only assume, you want to head down that hall," I told them, pointing in the direction that Jaron and the two guys went.

The cop nodded, heading down the hall with a younger officer following him.

"What do you think happened?" Gigi asked, ringing her hands together.

I grabbed them, holding one in mine. "I don't know but I have a feeling that Piper's going to need us."

She nodded, chewing her bottom lip.

The door to Piper's room opened revealing a disheveled Jaron. Blood was splattered on his shirt, his shoulders hunched. He came down the hall with the two cops following him.

He looked up, his gaze landing on me. "Piper needs you. Take care of her."

The cops walked him out of the house.

Two more officers entered shortly after. I was vaguely aware of them talking to Gigi. I didn't know what was said. It didn't matter. Jaron was right. Piper needed us.

"The room is down there," Gigi said, pointing a finger down the hall leading to Piper's room.

"I'll talk to Piper," the female officer said.

A glance passed between Gigi and I before we went to follow the cop down the hall when we were stopped short by a scream.

A slice of fear gripped my spine.

"Oh God." Gigi clapped a hand over her mouth, her eyes welling.

The two guys who had been with Jaron, came out of the room next with Piper between them. The larger of the duo, opened another door, stepped inside and came back out into the hall a moment later.

Piper entered the room, the door shutting behind her.

The guys spoke softly between themselves and that was when I realized they were twins. Not identical but you could definitely tell they were brothers.

"Let's go." I grabbed Gigi's hand and dragged her down the hall and toward the room they had put Piper in. It was my bedroom, but she could use it for however long she needed.

When we neared the guys, I let Gigi enter the room first but stayed back. "What happened?"

The larger of the twins pulled a pack of smokes out of the inner pocket of his leather jacket. "You're Sunny and Shade's girl."

They spoke about me? "Uh…yeah, I guess I am."

"No guessing about it, kiddo." The smaller of the two, stuck out his hand. "Sammy."

"Meadow," I said, returning the handshake as the female officer entered my room to talk to Piper.

"This quiet fucker is Cyrus." He jutted his chin toward his brother. "Piper's going to need you. There's been a death."

My eyes widened. "Brody?" I whispered.

"Sure," Cyrus grunted. "His name doesn't matter. The piece of shit is dead. The cops are here. I'm sure the coroner will be here soon, and the mess will be cleaned up."

I nodded, placing a hand on the doorknob leading to my room. "You're with Hell's Harlem?"

Sammy nodded. "Yup." He clapped his brother's shoulder. They both turned and headed down the hall.

Clearly, they weren't men of many words.

Taking a deep breath, I entered my room and closed the door behind me.

Gigi was sitting on my bed with Piper, holding her and whispering to her.

The female cop was writing notes in her notepad.

"Can we have a minute with Piper?" I asked her.

She nodded.

I breathed a sigh of relief and joined my sister and Piper on the bed.

Piper's body shook as sobs wracked through her. "He's leaving me, and I only just got him back."

I joined them on the bed, unsure as to what the hell was going on. "He's not leaving you." But I didn't even know if that were true or not. I could also only assume that she was referring to Jaron. Clearly there had been something more going on between them than I had thought.

Piper looked up at me then.

I gasped. "Shit, girl. What the fuck happened?"

She had bruises and her lip was split. That was when I noticed her dress was torn.

"Brody." Bile rose to my throat.

She shook her head. "Almost."

"Jaron took care of it," I added.

She nodded.

Fucking hell.

EIGHTEEN

Meadow

AFTER GIGI AND I consoled Piper, the female police officer came to take her to the hospital. Her parents were called, and they left with her. Brody didn't get as far as he wanted to but he sure as hell tried. From the looks of Piper, it would still leave a mark on her and probably give her nightmares for some time to come.

I had texted Sunny and Shade, asking them to come over. I wasn't sure how, but I needed them to make me feel better. To distract me and help me out of my head. I knew they had been close by but wasn't sure why they never came over. They must have seen all of the cop cars.

The coroner had taken Brody's body away while the cops continued searching Piper's room for evidence. I wasn't sure what they would find. Brody tried raping her. End of story.

Knowing it would be a long while before Piper would be able to sleep in that room, I had a feeling that she would be spending the next little bit at her parents' place.

Once everyone left, I went out onto the front porch. The cops had questioned a few of us, asking if anything had been out of the ordinary. Jaron had confessed to something but none of us knew what it was.

The front door opened, and Gigi stepped out. "Piper texted and said they're home from the hospital and she's going to spend the night at her parents' place."

I nodded, pulling a joint and a lighter from my pocket. "How's she doing?"

"She's a mess." Gigi sighed. "I didn't know there was something going on between her and Jaron, but it all makes sense now. Do you remember a few summers ago when he and his parents came back to town for a dinner Mom and Dad were throwing? He was watching her. I was tempted to tell Piper, but she was always with the twins." She shook her head. "God, I'm rambling."

Sticking the joint between my lips, I lit it, and inhaled the sweet bliss. Holding it deep in my lungs, I waited a beat before blowing it out through my nose.

Gigi sat beside me, taking the joint from my fingers. "I hate rambling."

I grunted. "I think you're forgiven tonight."

Under normal circumstances, I would have said something about my sister smoking, but this wasn't normal. So I left it alone.

"Do you know what happened?" she asked, coughing and handing me back the joint.

"No." But I knew that Sunny and Shade would find out. As soon as the thought crossed my mind, two bikes rumbled up the street and turned into our driveway.

Sunny pulled his helmet off first, his dark slate eyes finding mine. He nodded.

I shivered.

Both of them turned off their bikes, kicked the kickstands out, and put their helmets on the seats of those beautiful beasts.

I made a mental note to ask them for another ride. One day. One day when I wasn't feeling so…lost.

"They good to you?" Gigi asked softly, stretching her long legs out in front of her.

I nodded again because what could I say? There were too many words to describe just how good they were to me. Men I'd only just met. Men I had let inside every part of my body. Men who had issues of their own but brought me into their little duo anyway.

Shade came toward me first. His hands were shoved in his pockets, his deep jade eyes searching my face.

"I'm going to…" Gigi stood. "I think I'm going to stay at Mom and Dad's tonight."

"Okay." I rose to my feet and gave her a hug. "If you find out anything, let me know."

"I will." She leaned back, gave me a small smile, and released me before heading back into the house.

"Meadow."

I caught Shade's gaze, let out a soft sigh, and sat back on the bench. Sticking the joint between my lips, I inhaled the delicious smoke, but it did nothing to ease the nerves racing through me.

"What's going on?" He sat beside me, pulling the joint from my mouth and sticking it between his own lips. He inhaled, the glowing ember on the end becoming even brighter. "Fuck me." He blew the smoke out in small circles. "That's some good shit, little lamb."

I smiled, leaning into him. "I only get the best."

"What happened here tonight?" he asked, wrapping an arm around my shoulders and pulling me tighter against him.

"Why didn't you come over sooner?"

"Because Jaron told us to stay put," Sunny said, coming up the steps. "We have to head to the clubhouse," he told Shade.

"I don't want..." I looked between them both. Not wanting to seem clingy but there was no way I could stay here by myself. Not with everything that had happened, and I didn't even know everything.

"What?" Sunny stood in front of us, leaning against the porch railing.

"I don't want to be alone," I confessed, looking him square in the eye.

"Good," he said gently. "Because we weren't giving you the option."

I breathed a sigh of relief, appreciating Sunny's domineering ways at the moment.

"We'll head to the clubhouse and then home." Sunny left the porch. "Or spend the night there. Either way, you don't have to worry about being alone tonight, pet."

"I don't know what happened tonight," I told them. "But I know that it's not good and that my friends will have a hard time because of it."

Shade gave me a squeeze, kissing my cheek. "We'll help them in whatever way we can."

I hoped so.

We left the porch, following Sunny to their bikes. Looked like I was going to get to ride on one sooner than I thought.

Once I reached Sunny, I threw my arms around his middle before he could even get his helmet on.

"What's going on?" he demanded, his voice rough.

I couldn't get Piper's screams out of my head. They hurt. They slid into a part of me that had never been reached before. I could feel her pain, her anguish resting heavily on my shoulders.

"Meadow." Shade ran his hand in light circles over my upper back. "Talk to us."

I grabbed his hoodie, pulling him closer to us, needing both of them. I needed them to drown out

Piper's screams. I needed them to take me far away from here. I needed them to tell me what the hell was going on.

"Meadow," Sunny barked. "Tell us."

"I don't know. Brody is dead. The cops took Jaron away and Piper had to go to the hospital. That's all I know. But her screams. God, I can't get them out of my head." I leaned my forehead against Sunny's chest, breathing him in. Leather and spice wafted into my nose. Both he and Shade smelled the same but Sunny was spicier. Almost like their personalities. Sunny was the hothead while Shade was the calm one. But I bet if you backed Shade into a corner, he would lose his temper much like his partner.

"Fucking hell." Sunny held me against him. "That must be the emergency Greyson was talking about."

"Eve is going to lose her shit." Shade straddled his bike, slipping the helmet on his head. "Drive safe. I'll follow you."

Sunny released me, placed a soft peck on my mouth, and handed me a helmet. "Hold onto me, baby girl. We'll find out what's going on. I promise you."

I nodded.

When he sat on his bike, he waited.

I swung my leg over the seat, sliding in behind him and wrapping my arms around his middle. Leaning my cheek against his back, I inhaled the sweet scent of his leather cut. The patch rubbed against my cheek, reminding me that I could quite possibly be in over my head when it came to these two. They were bikers. They skirted the law and who knew what else. A part of me wondered if I could ever be enough for them. I knew the life that most bikers lived. A lot of them weren't just one-woman men.

When we finally pulled up to the large house that the Hell's Harlem crew resided at, my eyes widened at the sight before me. I had never been to this house even after growing up with Jaron. His father was a private man and stuck to mostly having his crew over and that was it. A part of me felt sort of special that I was now here. Like I was let into a secret club that only certain people could get into.

Sunny pulled up the long driveway with Shade following behind us. Parking the bike, Sunny killed the engine and took off his helmet.

I slid from the back seat, taking off my own helmet and handing it to him.

The driveway was littered with bikes of all sizes.

"He probably has everyone here," Sunny said, his brows narrowing.

Shade pulled his bike up beside us, shut it off, and took off his helmet before jutting his chin to the house. "Think it's safe to go in there?"

"Doesn't matter if it is or not. Greyson and Eve are going to need us. Not that we can do much, especially if Jaron confessed to whatever happened." Sunny ran a hand through his hair. "You don't know anything else?" he asked me.

"No." I looked around us, crossing my arms under my chest. "Piper and Gigi had bumped into each other and some wine had spilled on Piper's dress. She went to change. I guess Brody followed her. Maybe there was a struggle and Jaron was defending himself."

"Brody is a tiny fucker." Shade came up beside Sunny, their shoulders brushing.

My stomach flipped, desire curling deep in my belly for the two men standing in front of me with only a bike between us.

Shaking my head, I rid myself of those thoughts, seeing as we had more important things to deal with at the moment.

"Come." Sunny walked around to my side of the bike and took my hand. "We'll probably be in the meeting for a bit, but you can have a beer. Have you met Bee?"

"Bee?" I repeated.

"She's Tray and Zillah's daughter," Shade explained. "She kind of reminds me of you actually."

"I never thought of that before but yeah, I agree," Sunny added. "She's definitely feisty and likes to keep her daddy on his toes."

I laughed lightly. "Definitely sounds like something I would do."

Sunny leaned down and kissed my cheek. "I know. You also like keeping this daddy on his toes too. Only difference is, I'm allowed to spank you."

A shiver raced down my spine. "Will you show me where your room is? I mean, just in case the meeting goes long. It's been a…" I wasn't tired by any means, but they had a job to do and I didn't want to get in the way.

"Of course. We actually stay in one of the guest rooms in the basement. Which means no one will be able to hear you scream." Shade winked.

I rolled my eyes, smacking him lightly in the stomach. "Now's not the time for that."

"I know but I need to lighten the mood. Even if just for a second." A shadow moved over his face. "Whatever happened to Piper…"

"Hey." Sunny cupped his shoulder. "How about you take Meadow to our room. I'll tell Greyson that you needed a moment. He'll understand."

Shade nodded and took my hand. "That good with you, little lamb?"

"It is." I looked back and forth between them. "Is everything okay?"

Sunny kissed the top of my head. "It will be."

NINETEEN

SHADE

WHAT HAPPENED TO PIPER brought me back to a dark time in my past. A past that I didn't like discussing. A past that only Sunny knew about.

With Meadow's hand in mine, we entered the large house and were greeted by the majority of the Hell's Harlem members who lived in the surrounding area. Although, some did travel a few hours, most were local.

"Wow. This house is huge," Meadow said, her eyes wide. "I had no idea Jaron grew up here."

"You've never been here before?" I asked, a little surprised that Jaron never brought his friends over. But he was also his father's kid and liked to stick to himself most of the time. He had those who were closest to him but even then, it was hard to earn his trust.

"No. I haven't. I don't even think Piper's been here."

When we were approached by a couple of our club brothers, Meadow inched closer to me.

"Well I have to say that this is new."

I turned suddenly, finding Greyson coming toward us.

He nodded toward Meadow and I. "I don't have time to threaten you if you hurt her. We have to deal with this shit first regarding my son. Meeting room. *Now*," he barked, heading in the direction of the room that sat off to the side.

Sunny gave my shoulder a squeeze and joined Greyson in the room.

Greyson peeked his head out a moment later. "Come here."

"Give me a second, okay?" I told Meadow.

"Of course." She gave me a smile in reassurance.

While the other guys went into the room, I stayed back, waiting for Greyson to chop off my balls and feed them to me.

"Listen." He ran a hand through his light brown hair. "I don't know what's going on. This isn't what's important right now but before her father catches wind of this, I just want to warn you, he's a large fucker. And he comes with navy brothers. So just be careful." He looked over his shoulder.

Sunny's head snapped up from where he was sitting at the large table. "Both of you."

Sunny saluted him.

"How did you know?" I asked him.

A short laugh escaped Greyson. "Because I'm not stupid and also, my son told me that my dogs were sniffing around her." A dark shadow passed over his face. "Doesn't matter. Listen, we need to figure out what the hell is going on and what happened tonight so I can go back and give my wife something. Anything. We need fucking answers."

I nodded, clapping his shoulder. "We're here for you, boss. Both of you. All of us are."

"I know." Greyson cupped my nape, leaned his forehead against mine, and blew out a slow breath. "I wish Butcher were here."

My chest tightened. John Butcher had been one of the original members of Hell's Harlem when Sunny and I were just prospects. He was a large beast of a man but had the kindest heart. I had always looked up to him, but never got a chance to tell him that when he was shot and killed during a raid at the clubhouse.

"Me too," I murmured.

"Alright." He gave my shoulder a squeeze before releasing me. "You joining us for the meeting?"

"I was going to show Meadow where our room is and then..." I looked at Sunny.

He nodded once.

"Sunny can fill me in," I added.

Greyson sighed. "Fine. Usually I'd argue but I'm too damn tired to do that. Go do your thing and we'll get this shit done and over with."

"Greyson?"

Both of us turned as Eve came toward us.

My heart stuttered.

Bags sat beneath her eyes, her hands wringing together in front of her.

"Eve." Greyson closed the distance between them. "I thought you were sleeping."

"I..." Her chin wobbled. "I couldn't sleep. I need to know what's going on with Jaron. Is he going to jail?"

Greyson's jaw clenched. "Yeah, I think he is, baby."

A sob escaped her as she collapsed.

"Shit." Greyson caught her, pulling her into his arms. "Catch," he bellowed.

Catch Hunter, the vice president, poked his head out of the meeting room. "Yeah, boss?"

"Start without me," Greyson demanded, his voice rough. "I need to take care of my wife." He lifted her in his arms, cradled her against his chest like a child, and headed up the stairs to their part of the house. A door slammed shut a moment later, sucking away all the air in the room.

"Fucking hell." I leaned against the wall, running a hand through my hair. Tension filled the house. It was so damn thick; a knife couldn't even cut it.

"Shade." A gentle hand landed on my shoulder.

My head snapped up. In a quick move, I pulled Meadow into my arms, crushing her against me.

She snaked her arms around my neck. "I'm here. I'm here for both of you. All of you."

My body shook.

"Hey." She leaned back, brushing her fingers down my cheek. "Show me where your room is."

I nodded, grabbed her hand and led her to a door that headed down to the basement. Black and white pictures lined the dark walls. Some were of old members of the club, people who died or retired or just decided to move on with their lives. Which didn't happen often. Once you were a member, you remained a member for life. If you were a good boy at least.

"Is that Cyrus and Sammy? The twins I met tonight?" Meadow asked, stopping in front of a picture of a woman, a large man and two small boys.

"Yeah." Sammy was sitting on his dad's shoulders while Cyrus stood in front of his mom with her arms wrapped around him. She was kissing his cheek and Greyson had caught the moment he laughed. My chest tightened. "That's Butcher and Trixie. Cyrus and Sammy's parents. They were murdered a year apart from each other when the twins were just boys."

Meadow shook her head. "That's awful."

"It was. Sunny and I were just prospects at the time. We didn't know them for long, but they were good people. Really good people."

"That's so sad." Meadow squeezed my hand. "No wonder they have that look."

"What look?" I tilted my head.

"I don't know exactly." Meadow chewed her bottom lip. "But I can feel it. It's the same thing with Aiden. Something happened and now he drinks. A lot."

"I'm not sure if the twins drink." They were almost as secretive as Jaron and his father. But I had noticed that Cyrus was smoking more and having sex was his thing. Same with his brother.

Meadow continued walking down the hall, her eyes scanning the pictures. "Hey, it's you and Sunny."

I stepped up beside her. "It is." I remembered that day like it were yesterday. "Sunny and I had just been patched in. The party was so fucking huge and lasted all weekend. I don't remember much of it."

Meadow laughed. "Sounds like a good time."

"It was." I waggled my eyebrows.

Her laugh hardened. "I can't say that I've ever partied like that before. Even with all of the parties my sister has thrown over the years. I'm not really a drinker but I do like my weed."

Our eyes locked.

My heart thumped, my body humming all of a sudden.

A sly grin spread on her face. "Take me to your room, baby boy."

My cock twitched. Fucking hell.

(Sunny)

While Greyson paced back and forth, the rest of us waited. For instructions, for what to do next, for something. Hell, anything. We needed him to guide us.

Watching one of the strongest men I knew break in front of us, set us all on edge.

"Have you heard anything from Jaron?" Catch asked, sitting on the edge of the large windowsill that looked out into the driveway in front of the house.

"Not yet. I imagine he called Piper first." Greyson rubbed the back of his neck, tilting his head from side to side. "Listen." He moved in front of the table, leaning on his knuckles and peering at the rest of us. "The mayor is going to try and eat my son alive. I talked to Cyrus and Sammy." His gaze flicked to the twins who were standing off to the side before continuing. "And was informed that it was all self-defense tonight. But you know because Brody was the son of the mayor, this shit isn't going to go away. So, whatever happens, we have to stick together. We need to be there for Jaron. For Piper." A dark shadow passed over Greyson's face. "And for my fucking wife."

Grunts and words of agreement sounded throughout the room.

"I have a feeling that Jaron is going to go away for as long as the mayor can make it happen." Greyson sighed.

"Jaron needs to try and stay safe," Catch added, leaning forward in his chair. "Some of Tanner's crew is in jail."

My stomach twisted.

"Fuck." Greyson ran a hand through his hair. "I forgot. Call everyone you fucking know. Make sure my son stays as safe as he can. He needs to keep his nose clean. If he's in jail for years, it'll kill my wife. And Piper...I don't know what's going on there but she's my son's girl. That's all I know." Greyson landed a fist hard on the table. "We need to keep him safe."

"I know one of the jail guards." One of the newest members, Twitch, stated. "I'll make a call and get him to keep an eye out. But..."

Greyson frowned. "What?"

"I just…we all know that Jaron is going to have to do shit to stay alive." Twitch paused. "It could fuck him up."

"He's right." Tray Lister ran two fingers over the gray scruff on his jaw. "You know he's right, Grey."

Greyson looked at Catch before looking at each of us. "If my son dies while in jail, I will make it my sole mission to burn this mother fucking world down. And if he dies by one of Tanner's men, there will be a war. I need to know now that you will be in this with me if it comes to that."

"Yes."

"Of course."

"You got it, boss."

More words of agreement and encouragement sounded around the room but what wasn't said was that we all hoped and prayed that it wouldn't come to that.

"He's right though," Tray said, clapping Greyson's shoulder. "Jaron is going to have to do shit to survive. He's a big guy. People are going to try and throw their weight around and also try challenging him." A dark shadow passed over his face. "But he's strong."

Greyson nodded. "Cyrus. Sammy."

The twins stood taller.

"You need to watch Piper," was all he said.

"On it," Sammy told him.

Cyrus only grunted, sticking an unlit smoke in his mouth.

"Alright." Greyson let out another hard sigh. "I need to go check on my wife."

WITH US

(Meadow)

Shade and I were sitting on the bed, watching a movie on the large TV they had mounted on the wall. The movie was old, and I wasn't really watching it, but it was distracting. Just not enough. And it wasn't what I wanted but it felt odd hinting for more from Shade when Sunny wasn't with us. Would it be considered cheating? No. Not when I told them to do their own thing whether I was with them or not.

I chewed my bottom lip, unsure as to what the rules were for this type of relationship.

"Hey." Shade pinched my chin, pulling my lip from my teeth. "What's wrong?"

"Nothing really." I leaned my head against his shoulder.

"Meadow."

"I don't know, Shade." I huffed. "I really don't know."

"Fine. I'll leave it alone for now, but you *will* talk to us."

I knew that I would. It was a given. I just didn't know how to broach the subject with them.

When Shade had brought me to the room he shared with Sunny, I was almost expecting two beds but instead, there was one large king-sized bed. He had told me they never really stayed at the clubhouse. I had assumed they just brought women here and that was it.

The door suddenly opened, revealing Sunny.

I sat up straighter. "Hey."

He didn't meet my gaze. He just closed the door, clicked the lock into place, and pulled off his jacket. Throwing it onto the chair that sat in the corner, he reached behind him and pulled a gun out of the back of his pants.

My heart jumped, not realizing he had been packing this whole time.

He placed the pistol on top of his jacket and came toward the bed.

"Sunny?" I reached out, wanting to comfort him for whatever it was going on. I wanted to help him take the edge off.

But instead, he crawled onto the bed and much to my surprise, right into my arms. He moved between my legs, spreading them more with his rough hands and laid on his stomach.

"Sunny?" I repeated, my body tingling with anticipation of what was to come next.

Resting his head against my chest, his body relaxed some, but I could still feel the tension rolling off of him in waves.

"What happened?" Shade asked, reaching out to brush his finger along Sunny's hand.

"Some of Tanner's boys are in jail. Greyson's worried they're going to try and start something with Jaron." Sunny wrapped his one arm tighter around me while linking his hand with Shade's.

Brushing my fingers through the back of his hair, I waited for him to continue.

"Sammy and Cyrus are going to watch Piper." Sunny lifted his head. "We all need to watch her but Jaron's closest with them, so I know he'll trust them more to take care of her."

Shade nodded, turning onto his side. He leaned his head against my shoulder. "Anything else?"

"The mayor has always had it out for us. I don't fucking know why either," Sunny's voice hardened. "Tanner's crew, I could understand."

"How come?" I asked softly.

WITH US

Sunny lifted his head, inching the hand Shade wasn't holding, beneath my shirt. His calloused fingers brushed over my stomach, pushing the fabric to just below my chest. "Have you heard of one-percenters?"

I nodded, my skin tingling.

"Tanner's crew is just that but while most one-percenters will do anything to make their money and gain power and control, the only thing Tanner won't do, is hurt an animal. The fucker is a walking contradiction." Sunny's brows narrowed. "He'll destroy a human's life but save an animal."

They had mentioned something to me about that before. I wondered what Tanner had been through for him to turn out that way.

"He's an odd one," Shade added. "He had to force his way to the top. Rumor is, he ripped out the previous president's tongue and broke each of his fingers and toes while two of his guys held him down. And then while he screamed in pain, Tanner fucked his wife. In front of him."

"Wow." I shook my head. "Nice guy."

They only grunted.

"So, now what?" I asked, my body buzzing at the way Sunny was looking at me.

His eyes darkened. They dropped to my waist, his tongue peeking out to lick along his bottom lip. "There's not much we can do, so right now, we wait." Sunny lifted my shirt even higher, revealing my black bra. It had tiny donuts of all different colors on it. "Donuts?"

I laughed lightly. "Yeah. My panties match too."

A slow grin spread on his face. "Show us."

My heart jumped. Pushing him back, I undid the button to my jeans and pushed them all the way down, removing them completely. Tossing them over the edge of the bed, I sat back against the headboard.

"Do you like them?" I asked, trailing my finger along the waist of my thong.

"I've never been much of a guy for sweets but this..." Sunny's nostrils flared. "This is fucking better."

I laughed.

Shade inched closer to me. "I agree with him," he murmured in my ear. "Take off your top, Little Lamb. You're going to make us feel better."

I did as I was told, throwing my shirt over the side of the bed. Spreading my legs, I waited for these men to do what they did best and use my body to give us what we all needed.

Tonight had been a shitshow. Our friends were hurting. Jaron's parents even more so.

"Use me," I told Sunny and Shade.

Sunny smirked, placing a soft peck on my bent knee.

Shade cupped my right breast. "I've never been much of a tit man but yours have definitely changed my mind."

A husky laugh escaped me.

Shade ran his hand down my stomach, slowly trailing his fingers beneath the triangle of my thong.

Sunny hooked his fingers in the sides and pulled the tiny fabric down my legs. He stuffed the thong into his jeans pocket. "For later."

I blew him a kiss.

He winked.

Shade chuckled. "Spread your legs, Meadow." He kissed my shoulder. "We're going to use you good and hard. Tell us if we get to be too much."

I cupped his cheek, placing a gentle kiss on his mouth. "I will."

He smiled against my lips. "Good girl."

My stomach tumbled at those two little words.

"You want to please your men, pet?"

I looked back at Sunny. "Yes."

"Good." He glanced at Shade, giving him a slight nod. "Kiss her."

Shade wrapped his arm around my shoulders, cupped my jaw, and crushed his mouth to mine.

Something soft, warm and wet starting stroking along my clit. It was so damn gentle, the ache growing between my thighs became more pronounced as time wore on.

I whimpered, my hips undulating against Sunny's face.

He growled, cupping my inner thighs and continuing to lick and stroke along my throbbing clit. He pushed my thighs farther apart, the scratchiness of his beard tickling my center.

Shade released my mouth with a wet smack, staring down at me. "You're fucking beautiful."

My chest rose and fell. "God, I..."

Sunny chuckled, sucking my clit between his teeth.

I yelped, a low moan following soon after.

"You like that pain, baby?" he asked, locking his eyes with mine and licking along the swollen nub.

I chewed my bottom lip, nodding.

"You a little slut for pain, pet?" Shade whispered in my ear.

I watched his fingers disappear between my legs.

"You like when he bites your clit?" He licked along the shell of my ear. "Tell me." He thrust two fingers inside of me.

"Yes," I cried out. "Yes, I like it."

"Good." He sat up, turning toward me and pumping his hand between my legs.

Sunny continued sucking on my clit, sliding two fingers into my pussy alongside Shade's.

I moaned, their fingers stretching and owning me completely.

"More," I blurted. I couldn't control this need for them. This want for everything they had to give me. I needed them to take me away. Out of my head. And to just fuck my brains out. "Please."

Sunny pulled his hand from between my legs, gave my clit a soft peck, and slid off the bed.

Shade did the same.

My body burned with the lack of release.

When both of them started undressing, they looked at each other, then back at me and grinned.

I swallowed hard.

"She wants more," Sunny said, finally standing naked before me.

"She does," Shade added, pulling off the rest of his clothes and crawling back onto the bed. "Should we give her more?" he asked, reaching for my arms and pulling me onto his lap.

"Think she's been a good girl?" Sunny knelt on the bed behind me, kissing the back of my neck. "Think she deserves it?"

"Well, if I get any say in this, I think I deserve it." I wrapped my arms around Shade's broad shoulders.

He gave me a cocky grin. "Is that so?"

Sunny unhooked my bra. "I want to fuck your pussy, baby girl. With him." He pulled the bra off me and threw it to the floor, leaving me naked between them.

When his words finally registered, my eyes widened. "Wait, you want to do what?"

Shade chuckled, laying back on the bed and gripping my hips. "We want to fuck your cunt at the same time. No condom."

"I'm down for no condom. But fucking me at the same time. Is that even possible?" I asked, my core clenching at the thought of having them both inside of me at the same time.

"It is." Sunny reached between my legs. "And I like the idea of having you bare."

Shade's eyes rolled into the back of his head. "Fuck me."

"I like that idea too." I looked down, finding Sunny's hand wrapped around his friend's cock. "Holy shit."

Sunny chuckled, the sound deep and inviting. It promised me endless hours of pleasure. "Place your hands on his chest, baby girl. This is going to fucking hurt but feel good all at the same time." He beat the head of Shade's cock against my pussy before helping me slide down the length of him.

I slapped my hands against Shade's chest, a hard moan escaping the back of my throat.

Sunny left the bed and headed into the bathroom.

Shade's grip on my hips tightened, helping me ride him.

The bed dipped behind me a moment later.

Sunny trailed his hand down the length of my spine before pushing me forward. "Just keep breathing, Meadow."

Shade wrapped his arms around me. "We got you, little lamb."

I nodded, licking along his bottom lip and crushing my mouth to his.

He groaned, deepened the kiss, and continued thrusting in and out of me.

Cool liquid suddenly dripped over my center followed by fingers thrusting inside of me alongside Shade's cock.

"Such a good girl, Meadow," Sunny whispered in my ear. "You make your daddy so proud."

I shivered, breaking the kiss.

Shade's deep green eyes locked with mine. "Tell us to stop and we will."

I nodded but I wouldn't. Not yet at least. I knew it would hurt. It wasn't like they were exactly small, but I wanted to feel them. Both of them.

"Keep breathing, pet." Sunny kissed my shoulder, lining up the tip of his dick with my center.

Shade cupped my ass, spreading me open.

Sunny's cock slid into me deeper and deeper with each thrust of his hips.

I shivered, my pussy stretching and burning. I almost expected him to slam into me. Unsure if it would help or not but this teasing was enough to drive me insane.

"Please," I blurted, gripping the blankets. "Just do it already."

Sunny chuckled, sinking his teeth into the side of my neck. "I can't, baby girl. If I do that, I'll rip you open."

"But this teasing…" I moaned when Sunny pushed farther inside me.

"I'm not going to last long." Shade's fingers gripped my ass tighter.

Sunny towered over me, resting his elbows on either side of Shade's head. "Tell me to stop and I will," he said, his voice rough.

Shade nodded.

I only panted. No words formed on my tongue as Sunny pushed and pushed. The burn of being stretched only heightened the deeper he slid into my body.

"Fucking hell." Shade's eyes rolled into the back of his head. "So damn tight."

Sunny reached beneath me, his finger stroking along my clit.

I jumped, a soft cry escaping me.

"Come on, baby girl. Let me in," Sunny coaxed, flicking his finger back and forth over the swollen nub.

My cries got louder, my body shaking between them. "Sunny."

"That's it, pet." He kissed my shoulder. "Come for us."

Shade slid a hand between us, helping Sunny rub my clit.

"God, no. Please. I can't. Holy shit." Jumbled words left my mouth, my sentences broken and incoherent. A blinding light suddenly flashed in front of my eyes, my body feeling like it was going to explode. Tingles shot up my spine when warm liquid left my body followed by a scream falling from my lips.

"That's it, baby. Squirt for your men." Sunny pushed into me in one smooth move.

Shade yelled out.

A sob escaped me.

My body felt whole and stuffed, completely and utterly filled. I couldn't move while both of them fucked my pussy.

Together.

TWENTY

SHADE

SOFT SNORES LEFT MEADOW. It was so damn sexy and adorable all at the same time. She had passed out after Sunny and I fucked her at the same time. Couldn't say I blamed her at all.

When I felt Sunny's cock sliding along mine while both of us gave her pleasure, it took every ounce of control I had not to come right away.

"I think she liked that," Sunny murmured, his voice low enough that it wouldn't wake her.

"I think she did too." I was leaning against the headboard with Sunny lying beside me while Meadow slept. He had covered us with blankets, careful not to disturb her.

"Can you have feelings for someone so soon?" I asked him, running my hand in small circles over Meadow's back.

"I think so." He pushed onto all fours. "Move forward."

I did as I was a told.

Sunny sat behind me, pulling me back against him. His cock twitched behind me, but he never took it further.

Meadow lifted her head, a small smile creeping on her face when she looked up at us. "Thank you."

"No." I lifted her until she was straddling my waist. "Thank you."

"You have feelings for me?" she asked, her hair falling down around her beautiful face.

"Uh…you heard my question?" My cheeks burned, my dick jumping beneath her ass.

She laughed, the sound husky. "Yeah."

"Well then…" I pinched her chin. "Yeah, I do."

Her smile grew. "What about you?"

Sunny shifted behind me. "What about me?"

Meadow rolled her eyes.

"Careful, pet. Just because your pussy is sore now, doesn't mean shit. I'm happy to make it worse," Sunny growled, pinching her inner thigh.

She yelped, glaring at him.

I chuckled.

"To answer your question, Meadow, yes, I have feelings for you. But I'm not one to rush into things. Clearly. But I care about you." Sunny pushed out from behind me and started getting dressed. "Will you go on a date with us?"

Meadow looked between us both. "Really? An actual date?"

"Yes. I want to take you out to dinner. I want to take you both out to dinner." Sunny frowned. He reached into the pocket of his jeans. Pulling out his phone, the buzzing of it vibrating, becoming louder. He grumbled a curse. "I…" He scowled and left the room before slamming the door shut behind him.

"What was that about?" Meadow asked.

"I'm not sure." But I had a feeling I knew who was on the other end of the phone.

(Sunny)

"You need to stop calling me."

Roxanne sniffed. "I need you, Sunny. I'm sorry for everything."

My chest tightened. Leaning against the wall, I slid down until I hit the floor with a thump. "I can't keep doing this."

"Baby, I can give you what you want. I promise I can. I'm sorry about before. I'm sorry for fighting with you. Please forgive me. The kids miss you. *I* miss you."

My stomach twisted. "Stop using your fucking kids as bait. They have nothing to do with this. This is between us and only us, Roxanne."

"Can she give you what I can?"

The hackles on the back of my neck rose. "What the hell are you talking about?" We hadn't gone out in public with Meadow. There was no way she could be seen by Roxanne or anyone else that we mutually knew.

"You know, she'll choose him over you one day. You're a moody asshole, Sunny. She won't be able to deal with that for long." The sniffling was no longer there. And instead, she became the bitch that I had been married to.

"I have no idea what you're talking about," I grumbled. "If you didn't call for a specific reason, Roxanne, I have to go."

"I'm pregnant."

I rolled my eyes. "That's not my fault. We haven't fucked in years."

She let out a frustrated scream. "You're a fucking prick. I hate you."

I stood. "Which is it? You love me or you hate me? Fucking pick one."

"I will make both of your toys regret taking you from me." Roxanne hung up, letting her words slither between us.

"Fuck." I shoved my phone back in my pocket and slammed open the door.

A soft cry shattered my heart.

Meadow cupped her nose.

"Holy shit, pet." I rushed to her. "I'm sorry. I'm so sorry, baby."

"Fucking hell, Sunny." Shade jumped off the bed, pulling Meadow away from me and leading her into the en suite bathroom.

"It was an accident," I reassured them.

"It doesn't matter what it was," Shade snapped. "You need to control your temper. Especially when it comes to her."

Meadow leaned her head back, pinching the bridge of her nose. "It's fine. I'm fine."

Ignoring Shade, I went to Meadow and turned her toward me. I placed a soft peck on her nose. "I'm sorry. You know I would never hurt you intentionally. But she…"

"Has you all wired up," Meadow added for me.

"Yeah." I ran my thumb down the bridge of her nose. "You're not bleeding."

"No. Thank God for that." She looked in the mirror, scrunching and wiggling her nose. "Tell me about this woman. You said that she's your ex-wife but clearly, there's more to it than that."

Shade sat on the toilet seat, raised an eyebrow and waited. It was like he was daring me to reveal all. Every little dark and dirty secret. Everything I had usually kept to myself but wanted to reveal at the same time.

"I..." I passed a glance at Shade. He nodded in encouragement even though I was sure he wanted to kick my ass for hurting Meadow in the first place. "She likes to make my life a living hell. I don't even know why she's calling now. It's been awhile since she's reached out." I sighed. "She got pregnant with twins after we married. She also had me convinced they were mine until I caught her cheating. I had a DNA test done and they weren't. But I still keep in contact with them since their real father has no idea they exist. I know they're not mine, it still doesn't mean that I didn't love them any less. And she's tried getting child support from me ever since." I shrugged. That was it in a nutshell.

Meadow stared at me. "Really?"

"Yeah. I always knew the kids weren't mine. I had a feeling anyway. But a part of me wanted to help her in any way that I could. Especially when babies were involved. So I did what I could. I sent her money. Bought her groceries. I had her fridge stocked for weeks on end. I made sure her children had clothing on their backs and food in their bellies, no thanks to their mother. At all."

"You did all that, for children that aren't even yours?" Meadow asked, stepping in front of me.

"It's not a big deal." I didn't do it for recognition. I did it because there was a time where I did in fact love their mother.

"I told him it *was* a big deal," Shade added. "Especially when it comes to the she-bitch from hell."

I grunted, shoving my hands in my pockets. "Well, she doesn't deserve my niceness, but those kids have nothing to do with this."

"Do you still talk to them?" Meadow asked, placing her hand on my chest.

"I do from time to time, thanks to Facebook. It's the only thing I use it for. They may not be mine, but I want to keep in touch with them. But..."

"She's using that against you." Meadow's brows narrowed. "I'm right, aren't I?"

"Yeah."

Meadow scowled. "I'll never understand women like her."

Shade grunted. "There are some men like her too."

"True." A faraway look passed over Meadow's face. Something had happened to her. She had said already that a man tried controlling her, but she was able to get away before it became worse.

"Did that man ever try contacting you again?" I asked, not wanting to be nosy but wanting to know more about the woman we were falling for just the same.

"Uh..." Meadow sat on the edge of the tub. She pulled her messy hair up into a bun, some of the tendrils falling down around her face. "No. Because I told him that I would go to the cops and tell them he was fucking a minor." Her cheeks reddened. "I wouldn't because that's not how I am. It was completely consensual. He was married, had kids. I kept my mouth shut for them. He did end up moving though, with his family. I guess he didn't trust that I wouldn't go to the authorities."

"Does anyone know about this? Your father?" If I found out my kid was sleeping with an older man when they were underage, he would be dead.

Meadow barked a laugh. "Yeah, right. No. No one knows about him. Just you two now. But my sister and those closest to me did notice a change in my attitude. I had also stopped baking for a while, so they knew something was up." She shrugged. "I wanted to talk to someone because I thought maybe it was me. He...God, I was just a kid. He tried getting me to do things and take me to clubs. I went once and…" She shivered. "He tried getting other men…"

My back stiffened.

Shade growled.

"It didn't happen," she said quickly. "I left before it could and that was how I knew that I needed to end things. I made sure to meet up with him in a public place. I was naïve when it came to the love I thought I had for him but I wasn't stupid."

"Meadow." I blew out a slow breath. "Well, if he ever comes back to this town, you can bet your beautiful ass, that I will make him disappear."

She smiled softly. "Thank you."

"I agree with him." Shade rose from the toilet seat he was sitting on. "We should go to bed. Our girl needs some rest. It's been a long fucking night."

A yawn trembled through her.

We chuckled.

"You guys go. I'm going to take a shower." I stripped as they left the bathroom and stepped into the shower. Turning on the hot water, I let it rain down over me and took several deep breaths. Tonight, was a shitshow. It was like a knife had cut into our happy little family and made all of us bleed.

Seeing Eve break like that tore at my heart. It was something I never wanted to see again but I knew that I would. It would be hard not to in the line of work we did.

The door opened.

I knew it was Shade before he spoke. I could sense him. Whenever I fell into myself, he was there to pick up the broken pieces. And what did I do for him? Nothing. I led him on and made him believe for years that there was something more when it took Meadow giving me that shove I needed.

"Sunny," came his deep voice.

"Where's Meadow?" I asked, leaning a hand against the tiled wall and dropping my head.

"In bed. She said she was going to watch a movie, but she fell asleep rather quickly." The shower door opened then. "Did you mean what you said? That you want to go on a date?"

I turned around and took a step toward Shade. "Of course."

He stood taller, his eyes widening the closer I got to him.

I grabbed his arm and pulled him into the shower before pushing him up against the wall.

His breath caught. "Sunny."

"Shut up," I demanded. "I don't know what I'm doing. I don't know what Roxanne wants besides money, but I think it's more than that." I had a gut feeling that we would find out the hard way. "But something I do know is that I like Meadow and I want more with her. But I'm...I'm in love with you." I realized then that I had never actually told him that. Even after all of these years. It had always been an *'I care about you'* but only after he told me he loved me first.

"Sunny," he repeated, gripping my hips.

"Don't." I looked away. "I just...I need to know that if this thing with Meadow becomes serious, that there's no jealousy between us. I can't handle that. I'll step away first and let you have her."

"No." He wrapped his arms around me, pulling me tighter against him. "That won't happen. She even said that you and I started first."

I leaned my forehead against his. "This is weird, you know?"

He chuckled lightly. "Yeah. I've been in love with you for years but it's like our relationship has only just started."

I sighed, running my fingers down his sides, to the waist of his jeans. "Have you heard anything about Tanner wanting Meadow to go to his club?"

"No, but I'm sure he'll contact one of us soon. Or knowing him, he'll just show up."

I grunted. "He must want something."

"He always wants something, but this is off, even for him. He hasn't been around in quite a while and now he all of a sudden is making an appearance?" Shade scoffed. "This shit doesn't make sense.

"I know," I bit out, brushing my finger over the bulge now showing in Shade's soaked jeans.

"Sunny." Shade's voice dropped an octave. "I'm not pressuring you, but you really need to stop doing that."

"Why?" I wasn't sure what was coming over me. Sure, we had done some touching already but this was something else entirely. I wanted to feel him. I wanted to make love to him like we did to Meadow. I wanted him to know that I was in this for the long run but at the same time, I was scared. What if I wasn't good enough? I knew my way around a woman's body like the back of my own hand. Better in fact. But this was different.

"Hey." Shade kissed the corner of my mouth. "We should go to bed. Check in with Greyson in the morning and then go on our date tomorrow night."

All of that sounded damn near perfect but it wasn't enough.

Before I could stop myself, I dropped to my knees, keeping my hands on his hips.

"Sunny." Shade's eyes burned into me but for fear that I would chicken out, I didn't look up at him. "You don't have to…" His voice trailed off.

I knew I didn't. It wasn't like I had ever been one to do something that I didn't want to do. I would do it for him. Because I needed to prove to him that I was his. That I was both of theirs.

WITH US

(Shade)

This was not something that I was expecting. Especially with Sunny. But when he said that he was in love with me, I knew that things between us had changed. I didn't understand why when we had been together for years. But maybe it was something that didn't need explaining. Or maybe Meadow had a hand in it without even knowing it. Either way, seeing Sunny on his knees in front of me, sparked this newfound dominance inside of me. It was a dominance I had ever only shown a woman. Not a man. And definitely not Sunny.

"I need to go slow," he told me, his voice rough. It was laced with that delicious arousal I had come to crave from him.

"You *are* in control, Sunny," I reassured him. This was all for him. As much as I loved that we were jumping over another hurdle, I didn't want to spook him and have this end before it ever began.

"I don't know if I can ever fuck you," he confessed, meeting my gaze that time. "But I want to do everything else. I want...I want to try. And maybe one day, we'll get there."

I nodded quickly, my cock jumping behind the fabric of my jeans at what he was suggesting.

"But I don't know if I can ever have you inside of me." He lifted the hem of my shirt, placing a soft peck on my hip bone. "I *do* know that I want to take this one day at a time and I want...I want you both to fuck the fear out of me."

"Fuck." I blew out a slow breath.

He chuckled, the sound making my cock jump. With nimble fingers, he pulled the fly of my jeans apart. "I want to make you feel good."

"You already have." My heart raced, knowing that we would never be able to go back from this.

"No." Sunny lowered my jeans below my ass, my cock springing free, hard and proud between us.

Before I could comprehend what was happening, he took me in his mouth.

I groaned, my head falling back against the tiled wall behind me. For someone who never gave head before, his mouth was hot, his throat tight. He sucked and pulled, devouring every inch of me. My dick was so deep inside him, he gagged, the tip bumping the back of his throat. That sound only made me harder and it took every ounce of control I had not to fuck his face.

"Sunny," I bit out through clenched teeth. "Fucking hell."

He hummed around me, sliding his hand up my torso and beneath my shirt.

I grabbed hold of it, squeezing it, and letting him hopefully know how good this was. How much I appreciated him and loved him. We would never have to take this further, as long as he loved me. That was enough for me. I just wished he could see that.

"I..." My balls tightened, the sounds of his wet mouth sucking me dry, damn near had me exploding into a billion tiny particles. "I'm going to come."

Sunny growled, released my hand, and cupped my ass instead. He pulled me away from the wall, taking me even deeper. His mouth was wide, his lips swollen. Our eyes locked.

A breathless gasp escaped me.

He winked.

I came.

Hard.

TWENTY-ONE

SUNNY

"**I WAS NOT EXPECTING** that," Shade said, pulling off his clothes and throwing them in the laundry hamper. He replaced them with a pair of dry jeans and a black t-shirt that hugged his large frame.

"I know." I leaned against the wall, watching him while Meadow's soft snores stirred through me. The black sheets hung low on her hips while she slept peacefully on her stomach. Her dark hair was a mess around her head and if we hadn't taken her already so many times this evening, I would have woken her up by shoving my cock into her mouth.

"Sunny."

My gaze flicked to Shade's. "What?"

"You good?" He came toward me.

"Yes." Before he could get another word out, I placed a hard peck on his mouth. "Stop worrying so damn much." I went to the bed and brushed Meadow's hair off her neck. "Meadow," I whispered in her ear.

She stirred, turning her head toward me. "Everything okay?"

"Now that you're sleeping in our bed, yes." I covered her mouth, slipping my tongue between her lips.

She sighed, opening to me.

I chuckled.

"You taste good." She sat up, wrapping the sheets around her. She looked between us both. "Something happened."

Fuck me, she was observant.

Shade laughed.

My cheeks burned.

Her eyes widened. "Tell me. I want to know everything."

"You're a dirty girl, pet." I shook my head.

"Did he taste good?" she asked, waggling her eyebrows.

"Yeah, Sunny." Shade chuckled. "Did I taste good?"

I sighed. "Yes, alright? I gave him a blow job and he tasted as good as your sweet pussy. Happy now?"

Meadow giggled. "You're so damn grumpy. I love it."

I scowled. "Whatever."

Shade came toward the bed and slid onto it behind Meadow. "It was so damn hot, little lamb. I never expected it." He kissed her bare shoulder.

She grinned, her gaze flicking my way. "I can't wait to watch."

My body vibrated, my cock twitching at what she was suggesting. "Yup. Definitely a dirty girl."

"I can't help it. I have two guys who are sleeping with me and who are in love with each other and…" She sighed. "I've never been the romantic type but you both…"

"What?" Shade turned her head toward him when she didn't answer. "Tell us."

"Thank you for including me in your little duo," she murmured.

My heart warmed. Sitting on the bed, I took her hand along with Shade's and held them both in mine. "Meadow, you know this isn't just a fling, right? We want you and we want to keep doing this. With you."

"You want to date me, Sir?" she asked, licking her lips.

"I already told you we want to go on a date," I reminded her.

"True." She looked between us both. "I want to date you. I want this to be official. Which is funny because I wasn't looking for a relationship. But I do just have one request."

"What's that?" Shade asked, inching his other hand beneath the sheet that was covering her.

Her breath caught, her eyes darkening. "Don't hurt me. That's all I ask."

I pinched her chin and licked along her bottom lip while Shade used his fingers to please her. "Never, pet. We will never hurt you."

"Good." She ripped the sheet off her body, revealing her naked skin to me.

My gaze fell to her lap.

Her knees were spread. Her hips moved back and forth, riding Shade's hand.

"Like that, pet?" I asked her, nipping her bottom lip.

She whimpered, her pupils dilating. "Y-Yes." She spread her legs even more, leaning her hands on the bed and throwing her head back on her shoulders. "God. So good."

Shade cupped her shoulder, picking up speed with his hand that was between her legs. "Come for me, Meadow."

She shivered. "Faster."

He did as he was told, thrusting his fingers in and out of her.

Her mouth opened on a silent scream. Before any sound could leave her, I crushed my lips to hers, swallowing her cries.

Releasing her, I wrapped an arm around her shoulders and held her against me.

Shade winked, pulling his fingers from her body and running the soaked tips over the tight little hole at her ass.

Her body trembled.

Gearing up my hand, I landed a hard blow on the cheek of her ass.

She gasped.

Shoving his fingers back inside her, he pumped once, twice before pulling them free once again. He brought them up to my mouth, running the tips along my lips.

I winked, sucking them onto my tongue.

The rest of the day ended up in a blur.

Moans. Screams. Gentle and rough demands for more.

My body ached. But with Meadow and Shade curled around me, I couldn't ask for a better way to spend an evening. It was perfect. It was needed. It was something that I could never get used to and I found that I didn't want to.

"Sleep, Sunny," Shade's deep voice whispered in my ear.

But I couldn't. My phone buzzed, vibrating on the nightstand. My thoughts raced. I was brought back to a time where I let another woman into my heart, and she ended up ripping it out in the process. No, Meadow was not her. For one, Meadow had a better head on her shoulders even though she was much younger than Roxanne.

Pulling from the clutches of Meadow and Shade, I slid off the bed and got dressed. Stopping at the door, I glanced back at the bed. Shade wrapped an arm around

Meadow and pulled her against him. She sighed, snuggling into him.

Shade opened his eyes, finding me staring at him. He nodded once.

I gave him a small smile and slipped quietly from the room.

"Sunny."

I jumped, finding Catch Hunter coming toward me. "Hey. What are you doing up?" Not that I knew what time it was. Last time I looked at the clock, it was midnight.

"Couldn't sleep." He ran a hand through his dirty blond hair. "Tonight's been..."

"Yup," I said when his voice trailed off. "Wanna get a drink?"

"Fuck yes." He clapped my shoulder. "So, I heard you have a young little thing that you and Shade are sharing."

"Word travels fast," I muttered as we headed to the kitchen.

He barked a laugh. "Can't keep anything locked up tight in this place."

Under normal circumstances, we would usually head to the bar to grab a drink, but I wasn't in the mood for socializing. The kitchen was more private, and I found that it was better. Because I needed to ask Catch how he did it.

"I can feel you staring at my pretty face," he threw at me over his shoulder while he grabbed two beers from the large fridge. He kicked the door closed and headed to the table that I was sitting at. "What's up?"

"I..." I popped the cap off the bottle and took a long swig.

"That bad?" he asked, raising an eyebrow and taking a sip of his own beer.

I placed the bottle on the table and took a deep breath. "Did you find that you were treated any differently when the guys found out you had a…a thing for Greyson and then Tray?"

Catch finished off his bottle before standing. "I think we need something stronger."

"I'm sorry. It's none of my business and I know you're with Sara now but I need to know—"

"You need to know that the guys will accept you no matter who you're fucking," he finished for me. He went to the counter and grabbed a bottle of whiskey.

"Yeah. I'm not—"

"Gay." He placed a tumbler in front of me and poured some of the amber liquid into it. "Sure. And I'm not either." He met my gaze then. "It's called bi-sexual. Say it with me, Sunny."

I rolled my eyes. "I know what bi-sexuality is."

"Do you? Are you sure?" Catch poured himself a shot and threw it back before pouring himself another one.

"Yes, I'm sure," I grumbled, lifting the glass to my lips.

"Have you ever been with a man?"

"No." I threw back the shot, the liquid burning its way down my throat until it settled deep in my gut.

"But you're with Shade. Whether it's physical or not, you're still in a relationship with him. A man."

"Yeah." I rubbed my shoulder, leaning my head from side to side, trying so damn hard to ease the tension that had rested on them since this thing with Shade had changed.

"Okay, explain to me what the issue is."

"We're bikers. We're supposed to be with women and not with men."

Catch rolled his eyes that time. "Right. You do realize that it's the twentieth century, right? More and more people are coming out. You make it sound like it's so taboo. But should I remind you that you're fucking a woman who is young enough to be your daughter. Now *that's* taboo, old man." He poured us both another shot. "There are so many different types of sexualities. What exactly is normal anymore?"

"I don't know."

"Have you been given any issues from any of us? Anyone in Hell's Harlem give you a hard time about the possibility of fucking a man? Has the woman you're sharing given you any problems?"

"Well, no." I realized then how silly I sounded. Worrying over nothing when really, I should be thankful that we had the support system we had.

"Anyone else give you a hard time?" Catch narrowed his brows when I didn't say anything. "Tell me."

"A prospect in Tanner's club. He told Shade that he should be shot and pissed on for being gay."

"What happened after that?" Catch asked, his voice coming out rough.

"Tanner broke the kid's arm." I downed my drink.

"Good." Catch clinked his glass against mine. "Your girl okay with the two of you banging?"

"That hasn't happened yet but yes, she's supportive." I swished the liquid around in the tumbler.

"Then that's all that matters." Catch shook his head. "I never pegged you for someone who cared what other people thought."

"It's not other people I worry about. It's Greyson, you, Tray, every other brother we have in this club. It's Jaron. The twins. Everyone." I stood and began pacing. "I don't want any issues. I especially don't want any issues for Shade."

"That's not going to happen."

I looked up.

Shade came into the kitchen. "Are we having a party?"

I chuckled, remembering when we first met Meadow and how she asked the same question when she found us standing outside that bar.

Shade winked, sat at the table, and poured himself a drink.

"Nah. Your boy is stressing," Catch said, leaning back in his chair.

"He does that." Shade patted the chair beside him.

I let out a hard sigh and sat.

Much to my surprise, Shade grabbed my hand. "He doesn't care. None of them do."

"I seem to recall you stressing over what our brothers thought as well," I reminded him.

"Well, I can tell you..." Catch pushed the bottle closer to me. "I don't care. As long as it's consensual between all adult parties, that's all that matters. And besides, we have more important things to worry about than what body parts you're into."

True. "Do we know anything?"

"No." Greyson took that moment to enter the kitchen. "And my wife is losing herself because of this shit."

My chest tightened.

Greyson prepared coffee, his back rigid and stiff. Once the coffee was brewing, he turned and leaned against the counter. Bags sat beneath his eyes. He looked like he had aged years in a matter of hours.

"Anything we can do?" Catch asked gently.

"Not at the moment." Greyson muttered a curse. "All we can do now is wait. The mayor has it out for him. Always has but now it's worse since he killed his son. Fuck, I don't know what Jaron was thinking. All I know is that Brody attacked Piper and Jaron stopped it." Something flashed behind Greyson's eyes, a dark shadow passing over his face. "I can't say that I'm sorry he took Brody out, but I wish he would have done it differently."

"Yeah because we all would have done it differently," Catch mumbled.

"I know." Greyson poured himself a cup of coffee. "I would have done the same thing. We all would have but it doesn't make it right. My son has a temper. He's more of a hothead than I am and that's saying something."

I grunted. "Truth."

Shade squeezed my hand, inching closer to me. "Meadow doesn't know any more, does she?"

"No." I rested our joined hands on my lap. "She doesn't. Not that she's said anyway."

"I'll ask the twins," Greyson said as Cyrus and Sammy came into the kitchen. "Speak of the devil."

Cyrus stood behind Shade and I, and reached over us for the bottle of whiskey. "We need moonshine. That shit is stronger. And this definitely calls for something stronger."

"Truth, brother." Sammy held out his hand, waiting.

Cyrus pulled a swig right from the bottle before handing it to his twin. "We don't know any more than what we've already told you," he said before Greyson had a chance to ask him.

Grey scrubbed a hand down his face. "You guys are watching Piper, right?"

"Yup." Sammy pulled back another swig from the bottle. "She's at her parents' place. We introduced ourselves to them and said we were Jaron's cousins. Her mom's a feisty little thing and her dad's a big fucker. They were just thankful that Jaron stopped it before…" Sammy cleared his throat. "Anyway. Her parents are good people."

"They are." Greyson searched the room, meeting each of our stares. "We need to keep Piper safe. Jaron is going to go through hell in jail because I can guaran-fucking-tee you that the mayor will stick his minions on him. And Tanner." He shook his head. "We need to play nice. If something happens to my son…"

"Greyson?"

All of us turned to the soft voice coming from the doorway.

Eve stood there. She chewed her bottom lip. The dark bags that were under Grey's eyes, sat beneath hers just the same.

"Hey, what are you doing up?" he asked gently, holding his arms out.

She rushed to them, wrapping herself around her husband's middle. "I couldn't sleep. I keep having nightmares that I'll never see our son again."

Grey held her against him, his eyes flicking to each of ours. "We need to find out what's going on." Before he lost his wife completely, went unsaid.

We would figure out what was going on. How long Jaron would be in jail for and anything else that we could get. It was just going to take time.

While everyone talked amongst themselves, I caught Cyrus and Sammy quietly talking to each other. My stomach twisted. Something told me that they knew more than what was being said. I just hoped they told Greyson. As gentle as he had become over the years since meeting his wife, when it came to his family, club brother or not, his wife and kid came first. It didn't matter who you were. He would take you out and ask questions later. Jaron was the exact same way and unfortunately for him, it backfired.

TWENTY-TWO

Meadow

IT HAD BEEN A few weeks and we were still no closer to finding out when Jaron's arraignment was. I understood that it took time but, in most cases, they were allowed to at least post bail. It wasn't like his parents didn't have the money. But this was different. He had been charged with involuntary manslaughter. Piper told us that he entered a guilty plea. That was a conversation I never wanted to experience again. Her cries and screams of anguish made me realize that what she and Jaron had, went far past just being a fling.

The mayor was out for blood. It didn't matter that Brody was in the wrong and deserved everything that was handed to him. I saw Piper after the fact. I saw the results of Brody's fists against her face and the aftermath of not getting what he wanted. Her torn clothes were a result of his rage.

It wasn't fair that Jaron was put away because it was self-defense and he was protecting the woman he loved.

We didn't know how long he was going to be in jail for but I just hoped that once he was out, both he and Piper could find that happiness they deserved.

It was a Friday night and Sunny and Shade allowed me to use their kitchen to get some baking done. I needed to bake a few dozen or so cookies for The Dove Project. Even though my mom had only requested the cookies, I decided to bake as much as I could. I was feeling strung out. Tanner hadn't contacted me about coming to his club and for whatever reason that bothered me. It was like when the moment was right, he would strike, and I wouldn't even see it coming. But he was right. I *was* curious and needed to know what he wanted but until he forced me to go to his club, the guys kept me within arm's length.

Ringing jarred through my thoughts.

I pulled my phone from my back pocket and saw that Piper was calling me. I hadn't talked to her since that dreaded night. I only knew how she was doing after talking to my sister.

"Hey," I answered, resting the phone between my ear and shoulder.

"Hi." Her voice was hoarse like she had been crying for hours.

My heart thumped. God, it hurt for her. "This is going to be a really stupid question but how are you doing?"

"Honestly? I don't even know. I feel numb. He saved me, Meadow. He saved me from getting…God, I can't believe Brody almost…" Her breath hitched.

My eyes welled. I wasn't an emotional person, and neither was she. I had been accused of being soulless before. Or having a black heart because nothing usually got to me. But this was different.

"I think all of us are shocked about that." I leaned against the counter. "Have you talked to Jaron?"

"Yeah." She sighed. "I was his first phone call." She laughed lightly. "It's funny because at first, I actually thought he hated me and now all of this happened."

"Girl, that man loves you." I scoffed. "I've seen the way he looks at you. Even when we were kids. Whatever you two have goes far beyond just love, Piper."

"I...yeah, I don't know. Listen, I should go though. I just wanted to keep you up to date. Or as up to date as possible anyway." She quickly said goodbye and hung up after.

I stared at my phone, my heart aching for my friends. And Jaron's parents. God, I couldn't imagine what they were going through.

When I was about to go back to prepping some more cookies, a hard knock sounded at the front door.

Hesitating, I thought of just ignoring the visitor but when a knock on the door came again followed by the doorbell, I wondered if they knew I was there.

"Meadow," a deep voice called out from the other side of the door. "I know you're in there."

Heading to the front door, I unlocked and opened it, finding my brother standing there. "Ryder? What are you doing here? And how did you find out where I was?"

"I talked to Gigi." He pushed his way inside. "You're baking?"

"Yeah." I closed the door and locked it up before following him into the kitchen. "What's going on?" As much as I loved my brother and I was happy to see him, this was random and odd, even for him. Ryder had been in the military for a while and was finally home on leave, but the military life was so ingrained in him that he was always on a schedule. And he definitely always contacted people before he made an appearance. Something was wrong.

"Ryder," I repeated. "Not that I'm not happy to see you but you're worrying me. This isn't like you to just show up before calling or at least texting."

Ryder pulled a beer from the fridge, popped the cap, and took a long swig. He finished off the whole bottle before tossing it in the recycling bin and grabbing another bottle from the fridge.

When he finished half of that one, he let out a hard sigh. "I'm sorry for just showing up. And I'm sure your guys are going to kick my ass, but something's come up and I need your help."

"My help?" I crossed my arms under my chest. "Why me? And not Dad?" It wasn't like I could do anything. "And how do you know about my guys?"

"Gigi told me." Ryder waved a hand in front of him. "It doesn't matter. It's not a huge deal but I need you to pass on something to Mom."

"What do you mean?" The sound of the front door opening a moment later, jarred through our conversation. "Stay here," I told him and headed out into the hall.

"Hey, pet." Sunny came toward me and handed me a bag of groceries. "I got a bag of sugar like you asked and some of that vegan chocolate shit. Did you know that stuff tastes disgusting?"

"Thank you." I took it from him and turned to go back to the kitchen to find out what the hell was going on with my brother when a throat clearing stopped me.

"What's wrong?"

I slowly turned to Sunny. Shade took that moment to come into the house with two bags in his own hands.

"Nothing," I muttered.

"Nothing?" Sunny closed the distance between us, pinching my chin. "You always kiss me first before anything, Meadow," he said, his voice low. "It's a routine and I don't like when routines change. Now I'll ask you again, what's wrong?"

"My brother's here," I whispered.

Shade came up to us. "Is that not a good thing?"

"He needs me to pass on something to our mom, but I don't know what that is," I explained.

"Introduce us." Sunny kissed me softly on the mouth. "Now."

"How was the meeting?" I asked, trying to delay whatever message it was that Ryder was going to give me to pass on to our mother.

"Don't try and distract us, little lamb." Shade kissed the top of my head. "Let's get this shit over with."

I sighed, leading the way into the kitchen.

Ryder stood up taller, his eyes flicking between the three of us. "Hey."

"Meadow told us once that she has a brother, but we almost didn't believe it, seeing as you've never come around. Until now," Sunny said, his deep voice taking on that rough tone I had come to learn he used whenever he was annoyed. He cupped my shoulder, keeping me safely close to him while Shade stood on the other side of me. "I have a feeling that this isn't a happy little reunion."

Ryder stiffened, his brows dropping in the center. "You let these guys control you, Meadow?"

I rolled my eyes. "Yeah. Didn't you know that I'm into men who like to control every single thing I do?" I looked up at Sunny. "Is it okay for me to think, Sir? Is that allowed?"

Sunny's lips twitched.

Shade chuckled.

"Meadow," Ryder barked. "I came to talk to you alone."

"No." I pointed at him. "If you wanted to talk to me alone, you would not be here. At my boyfriends' house. I love you, Ryder. I'm glad that you're home safe after being gone for what felt like years. But something is wrong. This is random. You don't do random. And you delaying telling us, is only going to make it more difficult for you in the long run."

Ryder crossed his arms under his chest. I noticed then how he had filled out. He had always been skinny as a kid. Both he and Gigi had that trait, while I had all the curves.

"Maybe we should give them some time alone," Shade suggested.

"Fine." Sunny leaned down to my ear, giving my shoulder a light squeeze. "Come get us if you need anything." He kissed my cheek and followed Shade out into the backyard.

"They treat you well?"

"Yes," I answered, watching Sunny and Shade. "Now what's going on?" I asked my brother who kept shifting his weight from one foot to the other.

Ryder sighed, running a hand through his hair. "I think I'm in trouble."

(Sunny)

"I don't like leaving her alone with him," Shade said, pacing back and forth in front of me.

"He's her brother." I crossed my legs at the ankles, leaning back on the patio couch we had in the backyard. I enjoyed it out here. Especially when the weather was decent. But even when it was a gloomy day, our backyard held a sort of serenity about it. It was peaceful.

"Doesn't matter. Family means shit to some." Shade finally stopped pacing and stood directly in front of me. "You don't seem bothered by this. Why is that?"

I shrugged. Truth was, I was wired. So fucking wired but I was trying to give Meadow some control she never had with her ex. The little bit she told us about him, bothered the hell out of me.

"Sunny." Shade crossed his arms under his chest. "What's going on?"

"She needs to know that she's in control," I finally confessed. "We can control her in the bedroom but other than that, her decisions are her own. As much as I like...I don't want to fuck this up before it's hardly begun."

"Huh." Shade's face broke out into a wide grin.

"What?"

"You must really like her."

I rolled my eyes. "We've already established how much I like her. And you like her as much as I do, fucker."

He chuckled, sitting beside me. "Yeah, I really like her. I like her a lot actually."

"Good."

"Have you heard anything more from Greyson?" Shade asked, pulling his phone from his pocket.

"No." We came to realize that the mayor was going to keep Jaron in jail for as long as possible. He wasn't even allowed to post bail. But Greyson had gone to see him. We were due to see him in a few weeks. I just wished we had more answers to give Eve and Piper.

"I hate waiting." Shade pinched the bridge of his nose.

I grunted. "Me too."

Shade stood and started pacing again.

The act alone was enough to drive me mad, but I got it. All of us were on edge. You would think that Jaron would get a gold fucking star for taking out a would-be rapist but instead, he got thrown behind bars. It wasn't fair. It wasn't fair at fucking all.

"This isn't fair," Shade mumbled, taking the thought right out of my head.

"Is it ever fair? The mayor hates bikers and he hates us especially." Our club hadn't always been morally sound. Hell's Harlem used to be considered one-percenters, then Greyson cleaned it up as best he could. But we still had a reputation to uphold. We never batted an eyelash when it came to protecting our own and we skirted the law half the time.

Jaron was supposed to become president after his dad retired but now that would have to wait. I was sure it wasn't the only thing on his mind anyway.

"Did you know about Piper?" Shade asked, pulling me from my thoughts.

"No." Not that Jaron was overly forthcoming with his personal life. He was private. Just like his father. But for Piper to capture his heart like she had, must have said something about her. Like most of us, we didn't want relationships. We fucked random women to curb that itch, but it never did anything. It wasn't even remotely close to satisfying the craving. Especially for Shade and I. But now that we had Meadow to share between us, it was damn near perfect. A little too perfect if you asked me.

"What's that look for?" Shade stopped in front of me again.

I frowned. "What look?" I loved him but sometimes the fact he knew me so well, pissed me off.

"That look. You're thinking or worrying. I can't decide which one."

"Fine." I crossed my arms under my chest, lifting my chin. "Do you think this is too good to be true? What we have with Meadow? She's young. Do you think this can last?"

"If you were really worried about my age, Sunny, you wouldn't keep fucking me."

My head whipped around.

Meadow was standing at the patio door, with her brother at her side. "Is that what's really bothering you? If it is, maybe you should have thought of that before you…" She snapped her mouth shut.

"Before I what, Meadow?" I stood, turning toward her.

Her jaw clenched.

"Everything good?" Shade asked, stepping in front of me.

"My brother is being dramatic. It's nothing huge but I need to relay a message to my mom. Because he's not a man and won't do it himself," she said, her voice monotonous.

"I heard that," Ryder called from inside.

"You were supposed to," she yelled back. "Anyway. It doesn't matter. I'll take care of it." She turned and headed back into the house.

We followed her but not before her brother stopped us at the patio door.

"Good luck with her." Ryder shook his head. "She takes after our mother. It took my dad forever to get her to trust him." He pointed at me. "You just made her put up another wall." He left the patio door and followed his sister back into the house.

"Good job, Sunny," Shade muttered.

Fucking hell. That was not what I wanted Meadow to walk in on. She probably thought I was worried she would leave us. Maybe I was. Our relationship with her was so damn new, these fears were normal. Or that was what I liked to tell myself anyway.

Shoving my hands in my pockets to keep myself from wringing my own neck, I followed Shade into the house.

Meadow was standing at the kitchen island while her brother sat on one of the stools. Shade moved beside her, hooking his arm around her middle and pulling her into his side.

She sighed.

"Ryder, will you excuse us a moment?" I asked, keeping my gaze locked on my target.

"Sure. I have to make a call anyway." He left the stool and went out back.

Meadow glared my way. "Have other shit to say, Sunny?"

Grabbing a stool from the kitchen island, I closed the distance between us and sat it right in front of her so we would be at eye level. And so she would realize that we were equals. Sure, I liked dominating her but that was only when she gave me her complete and utter consent.

Reaching out for her, I gripped her hips and pulled her between my spread knees.

Her breath caught.

Shade stayed close but didn't say anything as I stared her down.

"Sunny." She attempted to shove out of my grip.

"Stop." I cupped her face. "I'm going to be completely honest with you."

"Because you haven't done that yet?" Her brows narrowed. "Have you been lying to me this whole time?"

"Fuck. Meadow, seriously, woman." I shook my head, gathered my thoughts and then decided, what the hell. I was going to just go for it. "I like you. Alright? I'm an old fucker who's set in his ways, but I refuse to get hurt. I don't want to get hurt. You and Shade could break me. If something happened where the three of us parted ways, I would never be able to get over that."

Her face softened. "You...you think I'm going to hurt you?"

"I..." I sighed. "Yeah, I guess I do. Roxanne fucked me up. I know that's not an excuse but it's the same one you have because of that fucker."

Meadow looked away, chewing her bottom lip.

"He's right." Shade leaned down to her ear. "You know he's right, little lamb."

She looked between us both. "I think we need to go on that date."

I chuckled, pushing my thumb beneath the hem of her shirt and running it across her soft skin.

She shivered, giving me a small smile.

"I'm sorry, Meadow." If her brother wasn't in the backyard, I would show her just how sorry I actually was.

"I know you are." Meadow wrapped her arms around my neck. "I won't hurt you. I won't hurt either of you. I like this. I've wanted to try doing this before but the guys I've been with, were never into threesomes."

"They got weirded out?" Shade asked, placing his hand on my shoulder.

"Yeah. But you two...you're different. Besides being older, I felt safe the moment I met you. Hell, even before I knew your names." She met my gaze. "When you pulled me onto your lap, Sunny, I..."

"What?" I asked, my heart jumping at her words. Meadow wasn't a talker. I learned that rather quickly. Even though she always said what was on her mind, she never opened up to her actual feelings. So now that she was, I would take it and run with it. "Tell me."

"I liked you. Both of you." She cupped Shade's cheek. "It was instant. I've never felt that before."

My dick pushed against the fly of my jeans.

"Meadow," Ryder barked from the patio door, ruining our little moment.

Shit.

Meadow pulled away from us, the air around me suddenly becoming cold.

But as she went to walk away, I grabbed her upper arm and pulled her back against me. "We'll talk more later." I kissed the spot beneath her ear. "Because I want to know every thought and feeling running through that beautiful head of yours. And Meadow?"

"Yeah?" she asked breathlessly.

I pinched her jaw, turning her head toward me. "I felt it too."

She gave me a soft smile, placing a gentle peck on my cheek before giving Shade a kiss as well. "I want that date," she said, following her brother outside to the backyard.

"Fucking hell." Shade rubbed the back of his neck.

"Yup." I stepped in front of him, stopping him from following Meadow.

He raised an eyebrow but waited.

"I don't know about you, but I like to think I know you well enough to take a guess at it. You're falling for her." I raised my hand when he went to speak. "Trust me, I'm falling for her just the same. But neither of us have been in a relationship with the same woman before."

"If you're worried that I'm going to get jealous if I come home and find you making love to her, I won't." Shade took a step toward me. "If you think that I'm going to get upset because you want some time alone with her, I won't. Because I know, that you'll give me that time as well. But I also know that you won't want that. Sure, the three of us won't always be together. It's bound to happen. But I also can't see any of us getting jealous. In fact." Shade closed that gap between us, his gaze dropping to my mouth. "I think all of us will like it. It'll be like the anticipation of not knowing what the other two are doing."

I swallowed hard at the images he was putting in my head.

"And remember." He took a step around me. "She's not Roxanne. Roxanne didn't want me in the picture. Even after you and I started talking again." Instead of waiting for me to answer, he joined Meadow outside.

Shoving a hand through my hair, I let out a hard sigh, and made my way to the backyard.

WITH US

(Meadow)

I almost blurted something dangerous. Sunny and Shade already knew things about me that I had never shared with anyone. They unleashed this newfound awareness deep inside me and I couldn't wait to explore more with them and help them do the same. It looked like the three of us were newer at this than Sunny let on.

When he admitted to being scared that I would hurt him, my heart tore behind the walls of my rib cage. This whole time, I feared they would hurt me and here Sunny had felt the same way. I wasn't sure if Shade did as well.

"Meadow?"

My gaze flicked to Shade's.

"Hmmm?"

"Ryder asked you a question." He sat beside me. "He asked you twice actually."

"Sorry." I waved a hand in front of me. "What was your question, Ryder?"

"Uh..." He hesitated and began pacing. "I asked if you'd talked to Mom and Dad."

"Yeah." I sat forward. "Why? Is something wrong?"

"It seems that Mom has something that doesn't belong to her." Ryder stopped in front of me. "That's what I need you to get for me."

"I thought you wanted me to relay a message." I frowned.

"Kind of. I need you to find out what she has that doesn't belong to her."

"I have no idea what you're talking about." I thought a moment. "Why don't you just ask Mom for whatever it is?"

"Because I think you'll have an easier time getting it." Ryder shook his head. "Doesn't matter. I do suggest going to visit Tanner though."

My back stiffened while Shade and Sunny shifted beside me.

"What do you know about Tanner?" Sunny demanded, his voice rough.

"Not enough apparently." Ryder raked a hand through his dark hair.

"How did you meet him?" I asked, searching my brother's face. He wasn't normally nervous about things. Hell, he had been in the military for a few years now. He should be used to this kind of thing, but something had him on edge. And if Tanner was involved, I couldn't even imagine what it was. But why my mom had something to do with this, was beyond me.

"I went to his club." Ryder pinched the bridge of his nose. "Listen, I'm not trying to cause trouble. I have to keep my nose clean anyway because of my career. But I've seen things. I know things. And while we don't usually deal with the average person, sometimes we do."

"I don't know what that means." I looked at Sunny. "Do you know what he means?"

"No." Sunny looked over my head. "Do you?"

Shade shook his head, cupping the back of my neck. "No." His dark brows narrowed in the center, his eyes locking on my brother. That muscle in his jaw ticked. While he stared Ryder down, his touch remained soft. "Care to explain to us what the hell is going on and why your mom would have something that Tanner wants?"

"I don't know. I accidentally bumped into him at his club. I swear it was an accident. I was out with some of the guys and we were having a few drinks. We just wanted to go somewhere cheap. I didn't know it was Tanner's club. Next thing I know, I'm in his office and he mentions you." Ryder met my gaze then. "He told me to tell you to come to his club. He needs to chat."

"He needs to chat," I repeated. "Yeah. Right. A guy like him doesn't just chat. He wants something."

"He does but I don't know what that is. I tried hinting to Mom. I asked her if she was given something that someone else could want." Ryder pulled at the collar of his shirt. "She had no idea what I was going on about and asked me if I was feeling okay. Good thing Dad wasn't with her because he wouldn't have let me leave until I told him everything."

That was an understatement. If something was off and Dad felt that his wife and kids were in any sort of danger, he didn't let up until he got the information he was looking for.

It was how all of our fathers were wired. I couldn't blame them. And now I was dating two men who were exactly the same.

"Meadow." Sunny cupped my knee. "I don't want you going there alone."

"I know." I stood. I didn't take Tanner's requests lightly. I liked to pretend that he didn't scare me, but I wasn't stupid. He did. He terrified the hell out of me. "Let's go."

TWENTY-THREE

Meadow

I **WAS ALMOST EXPECTING** Sunny and Shade to argue with me. But when I stood from the bench and went into the house, they followed. They didn't utter a single word. They didn't say anything even as we drove to Tanner's club. They didn't tell me I was crazy for wanting to speak to him and for actually listening to his demands. They stood at my side as we walked into his club. And they remained back when I found him coming toward us.

"Ah, Meadow. It's nice to be listened to. I see that you talked to your brother." Tanner nodded once, glancing over my head.

"What do you want, Tanner, and why the hell does my mom have something to do with this?" I demanded, not caring in the least that we were out in the open. I didn't care that we weren't alone. I wanted answers and when it came to my family, just like the guys I was dating, I would do anything to get the answers I was looking for.

Tanner turned on his heel. "Follow me."

When I went to take a step forward, a heavy hand landed on my shoulder, stopping me.

"Be careful, little lamb," Shade whispered in my ear. "He's an evil bastard who will do anything to stay at the top."

"I don't care," I told Shade. "If this has something to do with my mom, then Tanner will see just how evil *I* can be. My dad was in the U.S. Navy," I reminded him. "And someone I consider an uncle, was a sniper." I kissed his cheek and started following Tanner. But I heeded to Shade's warning. Tanner made me nervous. He acted nice but once you crossed him, he would never forget. I had a feeling that he had many notches on his bedpost and it wasn't from sleeping with people. There was an eerie feeling about him. It was like looking into dead eyes even though his heart still beat inside him. He was soulless.

Standing up taller, I took a deep breath and walked down the long hall that Tanner had gone down.

With Sunny and Shade behind me, I gathered the strength I needed to see this through. I didn't know what my mom had done or why she was involved in whatever mess Ryder had gotten himself into. Either way, Tanner better hope my mom stayed safe because he would have to deal with my father if she didn't.

"You're probably wondering why I've asked for you to come here," Tanner said, finally stopping at a door.

"No," I said, drawing out the word. "I just assumed we were here for tea."

Tanner's mouth twitched. "Funny." All humor left his dark cold eyes. He unlocked the door and pushed it open. "After you, Meadow."

I swallowed hard, walked past him, and entered the room.

"Not happening."

I turned.

Tanner was standing in the doorway, stopping Sunny and Shade from joining me in the room. "This is between Meadow and I."

I opened my mouth to argue when Tanner shut the door and clicked the lock into place. Crossing my arms under my chest, I lifted my chin. I refused to let him see that he made me nervous. And I especially refused to let him see that he got to me. I didn't know what he wanted. I wouldn't have cared either but when he brought my family into this, nothing else mattered.

"What are you wanting, Tanner?" I demanded, taking in the office I was standing in. It was large. Bookshelves lined the one far wall and a large oak desk sat by another. My gaze dropped to a dark stain on the floor. My stomach twisted, not wanting to know what that was from.

"To chat." Tanner leaned against the door, crossing his arms under his chest and mirroring my pose.

"About what?" The office reminded me of the owner himself. It was dark, cold and sent a tremor of unease racing through me. I didn't want to be there but at the same time, felt I had no other choice. Whatever my mom did, my dad was going to lose his shit.

"Your mom has something that I want."

"How do you even know my mom? And what the hell did Ryder do to get caught up in this shit?"

"Wrong place, wrong time. It's not my fault he bumped into me." Tanner shrugged, which was odd in a way for someone so damn big. "Listen, it doesn't matter. I just want something that your mom has."

"My mom doesn't even know you." Not that I really knew if she did or not, but Tanner didn't need to know that.

"Come on, Meadow. You're not stupid." He pushed away from the door he was leaning against and took a step toward me. "You will get what I want."

"How do I even know that my mom has something that belongs to you?" I backed up until I hit the wall. "You could be lying. I've heard about you and your ways."

Tanner chuckled, running two fingers along his mouth. His dark eyes roamed down the length of me before meeting my gaze. "You know...you are beautiful. I don't usually go for young ones, but I'd make an exception for you."

"Well aren't I lucky," I said dryly.

His laugh deepened. Something flashed behind his eyes. Tanner Horsch wasn't your typical man. Whatever happened to him had fucked him up. He had seen things. Bad things. Evil things that only happened in nightmares. Something haunted his dreams. I knew because I had seen that same look in the men I grew up with. While they were older and had practice dealing with their demons, Tanner was younger and let that shit eat him up.

"You're staring, Meadow."

My cheeks burned. "Just wondering what happened to make you this way."

"Wanting to fix me, little one?" Before I knew what was happening, he stood right in front of me. Placing his hands on the wall on either side of my head, he leaned down to my ear. "No one will ever be able to fix me. I'm unfixable."

I felt sorry for whoever fell for him. If that could ever happen in the first place. "Sunny and Shade won't like that you're so close to me," I murmured, unable to step away from him.

"Don't care." He caged me in, the scent of spice invading my nose.

"Tanner." I stared up at him. "What do you want?"

"Your pussy wrapped around my cock would be a good start."

My heart jumped at what he was suggesting. "Sorry, buddy. You don't do it for me." Sunny and Shade were going to kick his ass. Or worse.

Tanner tilted his head, giving me a cocky smirk. "I do it for everyone."

"You're too young for me." I ducked under his arm and moved across the room, getting far away from him before he did something stupid. Not that I cared if Sunny and Shade did anything to him, but this place was packed with bikers. I didn't need them to get hurt.

"Interesting." Tanner nodded once. "They must have magic cocks if you're turning me down."

"This is not the reason I came here. Tell me what the hell my mom has to do with this shit or else I'm leaving, and I'll tell Sunny and Shade what just happened."

Tanner chuckled. "You're going to tell them anyway, so that threat doesn't work with me." He moved behind the large oak desk sitting by the one wall and lowered into the leather chair. He leaned back in it, tenting his fingers under his chin. His dark eyes locked with mine, his jaw clenching.

A shiver raced down my spine.

"You will get me what I'm looking for."

"How the hell am I supposed to confront my mom about this if I don't know what you're wanting?" This didn't make sense. Not one bit.

"Tell her that Tyler Bones gave her something. A long time ago. She'll know what you're talking about." Tanner wiggled the mouse and started clicking away on the computer sitting on the desk in front of him.

"Tyler Bones…" I frowned. "Are you related to him?"

"You ask a lot of questions." Tanner turned the computer screen toward me, showing me a picture of a woman and a man.

My eyes widened when I realized who I was looking at.

My mom stared back at me, a smile on her face but that same smile never reached her eyes. She was young in the photo. Maybe my age or even younger.

The man standing with her was wearing a leather vest. It said vice president on the left breast. He had his arm around my mom's shoulders. This man was not my father. This man looked outright mean. He had a smirk on his face and the resemblance to Tanner was uncanny.

"You *are* related to him," I stated, my heart thumping hard. "Who is he?"

"He *was* my father." Tanner turned the screen back around toward him. "Died when I was just a boy." He met my gaze. "By someone you know actually."

"He...he was murdered?" Oh God. This was not good. Not good at all.

"It seems my father didn't want your mother to be happy and your dad got in the way. Your typical shit."

I shook my head. "What does this have to do with me or even you and how do you know all of this?"

"My dad had a big mouth." Tanner shrugged. "He told my mother this shit." His gaze hardened. "And she died because of it."

My mouth went dry. "I...I don't know what you want."

"I want you to go to your mother and tell her that Tanner Horsch wants something that she has. Something that doesn't belong to her."

"Why can't you go to her yourself?" I suddenly felt small. The longer he stared at me, the harder my chest tightened. My heart thumped. My palms became sweaty.

Tanner sat forward. "Numbers, Meadow. I want numbers. It's an account number. A number to a safety deposit box. I don't know. But I know that my dad gave them to your mom." He turned toward his computer. "You can leave."

"I think you've seen one too many movies," I mumbled. "Or your dad did." Just as I was about to turn and head to the door, knowing there was no point in trying to get more information from the guy, a large shadow loomed over me. Ice cold fear froze me in place.

"I don't suggest making jokes, Meadow. I don't give a shit who you're fucking." A heavy fist captured my hair, ripping my head back.

I cried out, strands of hair pulling free from my head.

The door suddenly crashed open, revealing a red-faced Sunny with Shade standing beside him.

"Get your fucking hands off our girl," Sunny seethed, his fists clenching at his sides.

Tanner tugged my hair, forcing me back a step.

I winced, reaching up to try and pull his hands off me but he was too strong.

Sunny and Shade came farther into the room, followed by some of Tanner's men. They had their guns drawn, aiming them at Sunny and Shade but neither of them seemed to notice.

"Now boys, we wouldn't want any issues." Tanner wrapped his other arm around my shoulders. "Would we, Meadow?"

"Just let me go and I'll get you what you're looking for." Not that I knew if my mom would have any idea what numbers he was going on about, but it would be worth a shot.

"Nah. You see." Tanner kissed my cheek, earning him a growl from Shade. "I'm enjoying this actually. I'm not really into voyeurism but it would be hot as fuck if they watched."

Bile rose to my throat, my eyes widened. He wouldn't. There was no way that Tanner could be that evil. Hell, he broke his prospect's arm for insulting Shade over being bi-sexual. But then I remembered the story that Shade had told me about Tanner, and I realized right then and there that I had no idea how we were going to get out of this. If he had fucked that guy's wife in front of him, who even knew if it had been consensual on her part.

"You wouldn't," I said, my voice shaky. Sunny and Shade had warned me about him and his club. Even though Tanner stopped people from holding dog fighting rings, he didn't care about humanity. Especially women. "Please, Tanner. Just let me go."

"Nope. Not happening." Tanner kept a firm hold on my hair, pulling my head back even more. "My boys leaving you alone?"

I opened my mouth to answer when Shade responded.

"Yeah, for now," Shade growled, taking a step toward us.

Sunny cupped his shoulder, stopping him.

"Good." Tanner leaned down to my ear. "How long do you think it would take before they snapped? What do you think I would have to do to you to make them break, little one? Think they would care?" His lips brushed along the shell of my ear. "With my men here, I could probably get away with a hell of a lot, couldn't I?"

I swallowed past the bile threatening to burn my throat. "No," I croaked.

"No?" Tanner chuckled, the sound cold and evil much like the man holding me. "Are you sure about that?" His hand moved to my stomach, sliding up to just beneath my left breast. "I know your boys are smart. They wouldn't want to start a war. And they would also let me do anything to you as long as that never happened. You know I'm right."

While Tanner spoke, I kept my eyes on Sunny and Shade. Both of them looked like they were holding themselves back from charging for Tanner. But he was right. If they did anything stupid, Tanner's men could shoot them, and I didn't want that. So instead, I stood there and waited.

(Shade)

I was brought back to my first experience with a guy who never took no for an answer. He touched me in places I had longed to be touched but never by him. I had thought I wanted it at first, but he had moved too fast for me. After that night, I swore off men completely until Sunny finally started opening up to me. But now, watching Tanner touch Meadow, something that didn't belong to him, red clouded my vision.

Sunny shifted from foot to foot beside me. The air became thick between us.

Meadow's eyes pleaded for us to save her but with the guns at our backs, there was nothing we could do but wait.

"What do you want?" Sunny demanded, taking a step toward them.

Tanner smirked, whispering in Meadow's ear.

Her eyes widened even more but her mouth remained closed. She didn't utter a single word which pissed me off even more. She always said what was on her mind. No matter who was involved. And she never let Tanner know in the beginning that he scared her but now, that fear rolled off her in waves.

"We have to do something," I muttered.

"I know," Sunny growled.

Both of us watched them.

We were helpless. Absolutely utterly fucking helpless. With another man's hands on Meadow, I knew that this could possibly hurt her in ways that Sunny and I weren't prepared for. She already had issues with another man trying to take from her what she never consented to, but this was somehow…worse.

"I'll call my mom," Meadow finally said, her voice rough like she had just gargled with broken glass.

Tanner kept his arm around her waist and handed her a phone. "I don't suggest doing anything stupid. My boys have been itching for blood for a while now. I'd hate to see them take that out on Sunny and Shade."

As if he needed his point made, the guys behind us cocked their guns.

After a few click of the keys, Meadow put the phone to her ear. "Hey, Mom…I—"

The phone was suddenly snatched from her. Tanner shoved her to her knees. "You think I'm stupid, don't you?"

My heart jumped.

Tanner pressed a button.

"Your call could not be reached. Please hang up and try again."

"Shit, pet," Sunny murmured.

Meadow's jaw clenched; her gaze hard. "I'll get you what you want but I'm not calling her. If I did that, my dad would know something was wrong." She shoved to her feet, much to Tanner's surprise. "I don't give a shit what you do to me but if you hurt them, I'll unleash more firepower on you and your little club than you've ever seen, asshole."

Just when I thought Tanner was going to hit her, he threw his head back and laughed.

Taking that as my chance, I went to her and pulled her away from him, not caring in the least that guns were aimed at us. I needed her in my arms and to let her know that we would do anything to get her out of this.

Her body was stiff, but she latched onto me. "Get me out of here. Please."

I didn't like the desperate tone of her voice. Pushing her into Sunny's arms, I took a step toward Tanner.

His laughter died, his gaze hard and determined. "Get me what I'm looking for or next time I won't be so nice." He snapped his fingers and went back around to the other side of his desk.

The men moved away from the door, letting us leave.

Not arguing, I led the way.

Sunny kept Meadow's hand in his and followed me.

My bones were tense beneath my skin. The tiny hairs on my body tingled. My heart beat so damn hard, it was like it was trying to escape the walls of my rib cage.

Once we reached the SUV and Sunny tucked Meadow safely into the back seat, I joined her. Pulling her against me, I pushed my face into the crook of her neck. I took a deep inhale and then another, needing every ounce of her to make me feel better.

I was vaguely aware of the driver's side door opening and the engine starting. Instead, I was focused solely on the woman invading my senses.

"Shade," she whispered, inching her hands beneath my shirt.

When her fingers came into contact with my skin, a growl escaped me.

My teeth found the side of her neck, earning me a soft gasp.

Her hands ran around to my back and higher beneath my shirt, holding me against her. "I'm fine. We're fine, baby."

Fisting her hair, I held her head and stared intensely into her eyes. "We're fine."

She gave me a soft smile, cupping my cheek. "We are."

With her other hand, she trailed it beneath my shirt and up to my chest. "Shade, your heart's racing."

"Give him a minute, pet," Sunny said from the front seat.

"It's adrenaline," I told her, my voice husky. It took everything I was made of not to erase Tanner's touch with my own. It could have been worse. So much worse but the fact that he even touched her in the first place, made me crave her skin against mine more so now than ever before.

I turned my head, locking eyes with Sunny's in the rearview mirror.

He nodded once.

I blew out a slow breath. "I just need a second." When Meadow went to pull away from me, I caught her arm. "Not happening, little lamb."

"I was just going to put on my seat belt," she explained, snuggling into my side.

I did up the seat belt for her, keeping her in my arms. To think that tonight could have gone so much worse than it already had. "What did he say to you?"

"You heard what he said." She looked away.

"No, when we couldn't hear him. What did he say?" I cupped her jaw when she didn't answer. "Tell me, Meadow. I need to know. We need to know so we can replace those vile words with our sweet ones."

She looked up at me then, giving me her beautiful dark eyes. "He told me he wanted you to watch him fuck me."

"Turn around," I demanded.

"No." Sunny lifted a hand. "I am not turning around so you can go barging in there and shoot up the place. I need you alive. And so does Meadow. Hell, our club needs you as well. So before you start arguing with me,

I'd quit while you're ahead. Besides..." Sunny turned down a dark street. "It's my job to lose my temper and go in with guns blazing."

"Fucking fuck." He was right. Not that I told him that though. I turned back to Meadow and brushed my fingers down her jaw. "You sure you're good?"

"Yeah but I really need out of these clothes. I didn't like the way he was touching me. I just..." She shivered, looking away.

"I know, Meadow." I kissed her temple. "I know."

TWENTY-FOUR

Meadow

YOU WOULD THINK I just grew a tail by the way Sunny and Shade were watching me.

They were on edge. I could feel the intensity rolling off of them in waves. I also knew that whatever they had in store for me tonight, would be nothing like I had experienced already with them.

We needed to go to my parents' place so I could confront my mom and find out what the hell Tanner was looking for but first, we headed back to the guys' place. While I took a shower, they stayed in the bathroom and waited.

"You guys don't have to be in here with me," I told them, running my hands through my hair as the hot water rained down over me.

"Yes, we do, pet." Sunny pulled back the curtain. "Shade's damn near vibrating out of his skin. You done yet?"

"Oh." I turned off the water. "I am now."

"Good. Come here." Sunny held out a towel.

I went to him, letting him wrap me up in the soft terrycloth.

He picked me up off my feet, holding me against him like a child. "Bedroom."

Wrapping my arms around his shoulders, I glanced at Shade. He stood off to the side with his hands in his pockets. A dark shadow passed over his face.

"Put me down," I whispered.

Sunny kissed my forehead and did as I asked.

I pulled off the towel, leaving me naked between them. Taking a step toward Shade, the air crackled between us. He needed something but I wasn't sure what. Sex? To fight it out? Whatever it was, he was losing control and even though I hadn't known the guys for long, I knew that it pissed Shade off.

Instead of saying anything, I moved directly in front of him and placed my hand on his chest just above his heart. The muscle was beating fast.

In a quick move, Shade wrapped his hand around my wrist.

I swallowed a gasp, locking eyes with him.

He leaned forward, brushing his mouth along the shell of my ear. "I'm having a hard time, Meadow."

My stomach tumbled as his deep gravelly voice washed over me.

"I'm having a really hard time." Shade pulled me flush against him, snaking his arm around my middle. "I want to tell you how proud I am that you stood up to Tanner but at the same time, I want to spank your ass for letting your mouth get in the way."

"I'm sorry." And I realized that I actually *was* sorry. I didn't want them mad at me, but Tanner pissed me off. As much as he terrified me and it was obviously stupid on my part, I needed to show him that he couldn't take whatever he wanted and not pay the consequences.

"Are you, Meadow? Are you really sorry?" Shade's deep voice washed over me, kissing every inch of my skin.

"Yes," I whispered, licking my lips.

"I have a confession." His mouth brushed along the line of my jaw before kissing the corner of my lips. "I'm falling for you."

My breath caught in my throat.

"I don't give a shit that we haven't known each other for long. I don't give a shit that we're old enough to be your fathers." While he let his words sink in, he brushed his hand down the length of my back before dipping his fingers between the crack of my ass. "I don't care that this is new for all of us." His finger dipped lower, brushing over the spot that had been theirs from the very beginning. "I don't care at all. About anything."

"What do you want?" I asked Shade, lost in this moment with him.

I was vaguely aware of Sunny moving around the room. I didn't know what he was doing but I did know that I was safe. I was finally safe. My heart. My body. My soul. All of me was safe because of these men.

Most had a hard time finding one man to fulfill their needs. To love, to hold, and to cherish. But I had two. To love? Was I in love with them? Could that happen over only a matter of weeks?

I stared up into Shade's eyes.

With his finger brushing lazily back and forth over my center, I searched his face. "Don't hurt me, Shade."

"Never, baby." He leaned his forehead against mine. "Never. But I'm asking you not to do the same."

"Never, baby," I said, repeating his words.

He blew out a slow breath.

"Are you better?" I asked, leaning back but keeping my hand on his cheek.

He pushed his face into my palm. "I am now."

"Good." I pulled away from him and went to the bed. Sunny was leaning against the dresser with his arms crossed. "I need you both. Right now. Inside me." I knelt on the bed and shuffled forward at the same time Sunny came toward me. "Please."

Sunny leaned his head from side to side. "Thank fuck."

I laughed when suddenly, both of them were on me.

(Sunny)

I was thankful that Meadow wanted us because Shade and I were wound up tight. I didn't want to go to her parents' place on the verge of snapping. Because I knew that it would get to the point where Shade and I would fuck her anywhere and we didn't need to deal with her father because of that.

When Meadow's moans slid into my ears, I knew that this was where I should be. Her body moved between Shade and I. She rode his cock while I was deep in her ass. She was tight. It was slow. It was perfect.

Shade kept a firm grip on her hips, helping her bounce for him.

At first, I wanted fast but now that we were in this position, I craved the ecstasy that the slow movements could bring.

"God." Meadow arched against me, digging her nails into Shade's chest.

When I met his gaze, he gave me a smirk.

I love you, he mouthed.

I love you too, I mouthed back.

He nodded his head toward Meadow.

I nodded back.

His smirk grew.

Pulling her back against me, I cupped her throat and sunk my teeth into her shoulder.

She moaned.

"Spread your legs, pet," I growled against the side of her neck.

She did as she was told. Such a good little pet.

Before she could even guess what we were about to do, my palm connected with her pussy.

She gasped, her eyes popping open.

I repeated the movement.

Shade picked up speed with his hips.

And I slapped her pretty little pussy. Again.

Slap. Slap. Slap.

She cried out, her eyes rolling into the back of her head.

Shade nodded, silently telling me to do it again and again. To take our little pet and shove her over that delicious edge of ecstasy.

Slap. Slap. Slap.

Meadow's pupils dilated.

Her body tightened on our cocks.

Shade groaned. "Again," he barked.

I slapped her again when a gush of liquid flowed between us followed by a soul shattering scream.

Meadow shook, falling back against me.

"Come again, pet." I kept a firm hold on her jaw, pumping my hips and fucking her sweet little body. "You like that, don't you?"

She moaned, her eyes fluttering closed.

I landed my palm against her pussy once again before all of us fell.

(Meadow)

A finger brushed along my lips, pushing a tiny hard object onto my tongue. It was sweet. I chewed it, realizing that it was chocolate.

"Thank you." I sighed, rolling over onto my stomach.

"You're welcome, little lamb." A soft peck landed on my cheek.

My muscles twitched. My bones vibrated beneath my skin, but I felt better. Lighter. Much better than I did an hour ago. Or maybe it had been longer. I couldn't tell. Time was lost to me as I curled up in the blankets and wrapped myself in the scent of our sex.

Opening my eyes, I lifted my head and looked around me. I was alone but still in Sunny and Shade's bed.

Sliding off the bed, I threw on my clothes, fixed my messy hair as best I could and made my way out into the hall. Faint voices sounded from the living room. Once I reached it, I found Sunny and Shade sitting on the couch.

"I don't know what he could want," a deep voice said, coming from the phone in Sunny's hand. "But it must be important if he's willing to go to all this trouble for it."

I recognized it as Greyson's voice. It sounded strained. Like he had been up for days. He probably had been. He had his wife to take care of and a son who was in jail for protecting the woman he loved.

Life wasn't fair if you asked me.

"He wants a set of numbers." Sunny caught my gaze then. "Not sure what they're for. We're going to

Meadow's parents' place to see if we can get some answers, but we needed…"

"We needed a moment," Shade finished for him.

I moved to the spot between them and sat, wrapping my hands around Shade's arm and leaning my head against his shoulder.

"I get that. I need lots of fucking moments," Greyson grumbled. "Listen, whatever you find out, let me know."

"Will do." Sunny ran his hand over my upper back in circles.

"You good?" Shade asked me, his voice low.

"I am now." I gave him a small smile. "Someone fed me chocolate."

"I did." He kissed my forehead. "Your blood sugar would have been low," he explained while Sunny and Greyson continued talking.

"Oh. Really? How come?" I shivered when Sunny's hand inched beneath my shirt and cupped my breast. Always touching me and never taking it further until I gave the go ahead. "I didn't know that was a thing."

"We fucked you good and hard. It's like going for a run without having any water after," Shade explained.

"That makes sense." I realized that I hadn't eaten much that day either, so I was thankful for the chocolate.

Shade smirked, his gaze dropping to my chest. He lifted my shirt, watching Sunny's thumb push its way inside the cup of my bra. "I like seeing his hands on you."

My breath caught.

His gaze snapped to mine. "Thank you, Meadow."

"For what?" It wasn't like I had done anything. Really, it had been all them. They brought me back to their place and made me feel better. Tanner bothered me in ways I had never known before. My ex was a sadistic bastard, but Tanner was outright evil. And he didn't care. There was no moral bone in his body. Even though he brought down a dog fighting ring, I had a feeling that it was a ruse. Sure, he liked animals more than he liked humans but if what the guys said was true, there was an ulterior motive to Tanner's ways.

Shade only gave me a soft smile instead of answering.

"Alright, boss. I'll let you know what we find out," Sunny told Greyson. They said their goodbyes and Sunny disconnected the phone.

"What time is it?" I asked, wishing I didn't have to confront my mom about this. I just wanted Sunny and Shade to take me away, so we could get to know each other better. Maybe in time we could. And we still needed to go on that date.

"Almost nine," Sunny answered, slipping his fingers beneath the cup of my bra. "We should go before it gets too late." But even though he said the words, he never released me.

"We should." But I unhooked my bra instead.

"Take this off so I can touch you whenever I want," Sunny grumbled, kissing the side of my neck.

"Already ahead of you, Sir." I placed a soft peck on his cheek. Pulling my arm back inside my shirt, I slipped the bra off of me through one of the arm holes and readjusted the shirt.

"It's like magic," Shade said, staring at me in awe.

I gave him a small smile and handed him the bra. "As much as I want to continue this though, we should really head to my parents' place."

Both of them sighed.

"If we must." Sunny gave my nipple a pinch before releasing me completely.

"We really need to go." I stood from the couch and began pacing.

"Meadow," the guys said at the same time.

I spun on them. "We need to go because I want to get this over with so we can spend the night in your bed. I need…" I wrapped my arms around myself.

"Hey." Sunny came toward me, followed by Shade. "Whatever you need, pet, we're here." He cupped my cheek, brushing his thumb along my bottom lip. "You hear me?"

"Yeah." I sighed. "I do."

"Good." His dark eyes roamed down the length of me. "We need to get this shit over with so I can spend the night inside you."

Usually I would have given him a smart remark but instead, I wrapped my arms around his thick neck and pulled him against me. The hug told him more than my words ever could. I cared for him. I cared for both of them. And I knew why. Hell, I had known it all along. But Sunny had been right. I was young. I had my life ahead of me. But none of that mattered. I wanted my life to be with them. Sunny and Shade. Two men who had loved each other for years but only just started exploring those feelings more.

"Meadow." Sunny's deep voice rumbled through me, his mouth finding the side of my neck.

"Tonight scared you," I told him. "Didn't it?" I asked, leaning back.

"Yeah." He searched my face. "It did."

"And it scared you too," I told Shade as he came up to us.

"It did because I knew that I would have done anything to keep you safe." Shade rubbed a hand over his head. "If Tanner would have taken it further than what he already did, I don't know what I would have done."

I swallowed hard. "I know." I shivered at the thought. "But enough of that, we're going to be talking about him with my mom anyway. But before that, I just…I want you both to know…" I looked between them. Two very different men. Sunny's beard had grown in more while Shade's eyes held wrinkles at the corners. Both had graying hair, and both cared for me in ways I never even knew was possible.

"What is it, pet?" Sunny tilted his head. "Tell us."

My heart raced, thumping so damn hard, I was surprised they couldn't hear it themselves. "I'm falling in love with you. I know we haven't been together for long, but I don't care about that. Which is funny because I never believed in love at first sight but you two—"

A hot mouth crushed mine in a toe-curling kiss.

I sighed, my eyes fluttering closed.

"I'm falling in love with you too, pet," Sunny whispered against my mouth.

My eyes popped open, landing on his handsome face.

He smirked.

Shade had a goofy grin on his face. He pulled me away from Sunny. "And I'm in love with you too, little lamb." He brushed his nose along the length of my neck. "So fucking in love with you."

"Really?" My eyes welled. I wasn't normally a crier, but this deserved all of the happy tears.

"Yes." Shade kissed the side of my head. "We'll celebrate later but right now, let's go to your parents' place and get this over with."

"I agree with him." Sunny pinched my chin and placed a soft peck on my mouth. "Until later."

(Sunny)

She loved us. And we loved her. The confession sparked something inside of me. It was a feral need to claim her as ours. To make her my ultimate pet. To put a damn collar around her beautiful throat. But that would come in time. For now, we would take this one day at a time. I still had Roxanne to worry about.

While I drove us to Meadow's parents' place, her and Shade sat in the back. He would meet my gaze in the reflection of the rearview mirror every now and again. He gave me a small smile every so often, followed by a contented sigh and I would grip the steering wheel. Truth was, I was on edge. The sex hadn't curbed the itch to completely consume Meadow.

"Sunny."

My eyes snapped to the mirror.

Meadow was staring at me. "We got this." She cupped my arm, running her hand up and down it soothingly.

I sighed. "I know but I don't like that Tanner touched you. I don't like that he brought you into this shit and I also don't like that he's bringing your mom into this either."

"I know." Meadow sat back. "I don't know much about my mom's younger days. They're hush hush about that shit. They want to protect us. Apparently, there was some issues with my aunt."

"Aunt?" Shade repeated.

"Yeah. My mom's twin." Meadow shrugged. "I haven't seen my Aunt Violet in years. She was taken when she was my age. Maybe even younger. And she was sold." A shiver tremored through her. "I don't know much but I know whoever took her, also took her finger. These people are disgusting."

"Shit, baby girl. I had no idea." I shook my head.

"My mom doesn't like talking about it. She was almost taken from my dad herself, so it's a sore spot for them." Meadow looked out the window, chewing her bottom lip. "I just want all of this to end. But I know it won't. That's why the center was built. I'm not there much but it means everything to me." When she looked my way, her gaze was hard and determined. "I'm not sure if Tanner is into this shit as well but either way, we need to find out what's going on and why he thinks my mom can get him what he wants."

"We'll find that out, little lamb." Shade pulled her into his side. "I promise you."

Once we pulled in front of her parents' place, they left the back seat of the SUV. While I hoped Shade's promise held true, there was no way of knowing what was going to go down once Tanner got the information he was looking for.

Shade and Meadow waited for me. To snap? To do something else? I wasn't sure. But what I did know was my feelings for her. For him. For us. We were a trio. There was not one or two but three of us. While it wasn't normal for most, it was normal for us.

But as happy as I was, there was still that nagging little feeling deep inside of me. The calm before the storm. As cliché as it sounded, something else was going to happen. Something worse. And I wasn't sure if any of us was strong enough to come back from it.

TWENTY-FIVE

Meadow

I **WALKED UP THE** sidewalk with Sunny and Shade on either side of me. A part of me wanted to hold their hands but I also didn't want my dad to pitch a fit. I had to ease him into this situation, especially when I was about to confront my mom over…hell, I didn't even know what I was going to ask her.

Hey, mom, do you know a Tanner Horsch? No? Well he sure knows you.

My father was protective when it came to us. But he was almost overbearing where my mom was concerned. I wasn't sure why, but I had a feeling that it had to do with something that happened long before my siblings and I were born.

While the guys remained silent, I took the steps leading up to the front door of my parents' house and knocked. It had felt like years since I had been home, even though it had only been weeks. If that. Truth was, I didn't go home much or as often as I would have liked. There was no reason for it, but I wasn't like my brother or sister. They had their career paths laid out for them.

Even though Gigi's took a different turn than she would have liked, she still had her own business.

And me? I baked for a local business when I could but that was it. It wasn't enough to support myself. I realized then that I was in a rut and I had no idea how to get out of it.

"Meadow." Sunny's deep voice graced my ears. "You got this, baby girl. And once we're done here, we'll go home and take care of you."

"What about giving Tanner what he wants?" I asked him, staring up into his dark eyes that held me captive every damn time I looked into them.

"We can meet up with him tomorrow." Sunny's voice was final, leaving no room for question.

Not that I would anyway. Tanner creeped me out and I would be happy if I never had to see him ever again.

Before I could respond, the door opened.

"Meadow." My mom smiled down at me. "How are you?"

Instead of answering, I threw my arms around her middle.

"Meadow." Mom wrapped herself around me, returning the embrace. "Not that I'm not happy to see you but what's wrong?"

"How do you know something's wrong?" I asked, even though I already knew the answer. She was a mom. Mom's always knew when something was wrong with their kids. It was in the mom handbook.

"Because you haven't been by in a while and the last time you were here…"

I leaned back when her voice trailed off, remembering that I had stopped by when Ashton and I had started sleeping together. I was confused and wanted to ask my mom her thoughts on the matter. But it never got very far when my dad overheard and threatened to kill the boy who broke his baby girl's heart. But Ashton never broke my heart. No, I broke his instead because he wasn't enough for me. It wasn't his fault. It wasn't mine. We were just never meant to be.

"I'm fine." I pulled from her grip and stepped back between Sunny and Shade.

Mom's eyes flicked between them. "Friends of yours?"

I choked back a laugh. "Something like that."

"Well, please come in." Mom turned and went back down the hall she had come from.

"What was that about?" Sunny asked.

"I broke a boy's heart," I muttered, entering the home I grew up in.

"Really?" Shade followed me.

"No." I turned toward them. "But he wanted more, and I couldn't give that to him. Also, I was looking for something else."

"What were you looking for?" Sunny reached out and brushed the back of his fingers down my cheek.

"I was looking for both of you," I told him, my heart stuttering at the soft touch.

He grinned.

Shade stood up taller. "I am pretty awesome."

I laughed, shaking my head. "Yeah, you are."

"Meadow?"

My smile fell when I heard my father's deep voice. "Uh…" I turned back around, giving him a small wave. "Hey, Daddy."

His back stiffened. "What's going on?"

"Um…" I took a deep breath. I had never brought a guy home before, so this was new for me. And Sunny and Shade weren't just random guys. They were more. So much more. They were everything I had been looking for without even realizing it.

"You got this, baby girl," Sunny whispered.

I cleared my throat and took a deep breath. "Dad, this is Sunny. Sunny, my father, Angel."

Sunny stuck his hand out.

Dad returned the handshake.

"And this is Shade." I cupped Shade's arm.

"The name is Roy, but I go by Shade." Shade linked his fingers in mine, giving me the strength I needed to face my father over the fact that I was with, not one, but two men.

Dad released Sunny's hand and crossed his arms under his chest. His dark eyes that mirrored my own, dropped to my joined hand with Shade's.

Sunny stepped closer to me.

I never thought I would see the day where I would bring home two men to meet my parents. How could you even approach your father with that?

Hey, Daddy. So, I'm fucking two guys. K? K.

"I'm not sure what's going on right now," Dad muttered as my mom stepped up beside him.

"Why don't we go into the living room and we can talk because I'm assuming you didn't just come here for a visit, did you?" she asked me.

"No." I sighed. "I didn't." When I went to take a step forward, dad raised his hand, stopping me.

"I need to know one thing first." His dark eyes flicked back and forth between Sunny and Shade. "You treating my girl well?"

"Yes, sir," Sunny answered, which was almost funny in a way seeing as they were closer to my dad's age than my own.

"Dad." I stepped between him and the guys. "Whatever you're thinking, I'm sure it's not as bad as what's really going on." Not that I knew what he was thinking of course but I could tell by the deep frown between his brows that he assumed the guys forced me into this. It was a typical fatherly trait. It was always the man's fault. No matter how kinky their daughter was. Not that he knew my kinks. God, I was losing my mind. My cheeks burned. Sunny and Shade had me all over the place. And after our confession, it only seemed to get worse.

"You have no idea what I'm thinking, Meadow," he growled, his jaw ticking.

"Angel," Mom said gently, taking his hand in hers. "She's happy. Finally. You can see it."

"Will you give us a moment please?" I asked the guys. "You can head out back."

They mumbled a response and went out into the backyard.

"Daddy," I said once we were alone.

"You're with two men." Dad searched my face. "Aren't you?"

"I know it's not what most would consider normal, but it is becoming more of a thing. And besides, two of your navy brothers are with the same woman," I reminded him, knowing Piper's Aunt was happy with the two men she had met years ago.

"That's different." Dad started pacing.

"How is that different?" I demanded, not needing to talk about this at the moment when Tanner's request was looming over my head.

"It's different because you are my baby. My little girl. My youngest. Those men are old enough to be your father. They're my age, Meadow." Dad rubbed the back of his neck, dropped his arm to his side and rubbed his neck again.

"Well, technically they're only in their forties," I blurted.

Dad stopped suddenly, glaring my way.

"Angel." Mom stepped in front of him.

"She's with two men, princess." He cupped her cheek. "Two of them."

"I know." Mom gave him a cheeky grin. "Two men...Hmm..."

Dad's face reddened. "Oh, hell no. Woman, you get that thought out of your fucking head. I'm all the man you'll ever need."

Both of us laughed while Dad looked like his head was about to explode.

"Trust me, baby. That's not my thing," Mom said between laughs.

Dad pinched the bridge of his nose, took a deep breath and let it out slowly. "You women are going to put me into an early grave."

My laugh got louder. I stepped toward him and wrapped my arms around his hard middle. For someone who was in his fifties, he kept in good shape. "I'm happy, Daddy. I promise you. But we're not here because of that."

"I figured," he mumbled. "Who do I have to kill?"

I stepped away from him and headed to the patio door. "No one yet." I signaled for Sunny and Shade to come back inside.

"Everything good, pet?" Sunny asked, pinching my chin.

My heart skipped a beat at being touched by him in front of my parents. Not that I was ashamed or anything, but this was new. So damn new and exciting. Definitely exciting.

"Answer him," Shade said, his voice firm and final.

"God." I shivered, cleared my throat, and walked away from them before I got caught doing something I shouldn't and especially in front of my parents.

They chuckled, following me into the house.

"Now, tell us why you're really here," Dad said, leaning against the wall by the TV.

"I met someone who knows someone you did," I told my mother.

Her perfectly arched brows narrowed in the center. "Who?"

"Tanner Horsch." I waited for any sort of recognition to dawn on her face.

"I don't know a Tanner..." she said, her voice trailing off.

"Apparently Tanner is the son of someone you used to know," I said gently.

"Really?" Mom hesitated. "Who?"

"I don't know. I don't remember his name, but he showed me a picture of you with him and he had his arm around you. You looked young and he was wearing a vest."

"I don't..." Mom's face paled. "No." A shaky laugh left her. "There's no way."

"What?" I looked between her and Dad.

"I grew up around bikers," she reminded me. You know that. It could have been anyone."

I tapped my chin. "Well, he looked young. Like your age."

"Hold on." Mom rushed down the hall. A few minutes later, she came back holding a small shoebox. She placed it on the dining room table and started rooting through it. "Was this the guy you saw in the picture?" She held out a small photograph.

I leaned forward, scanning the picture. "Yes. That was him."

"Shit." Mom threw the picture back in the box. "That's Tyler."

Dad's head whipped around. "The fuck?"

"But I didn't know he had a son." Mom placed her hands on her hips, staring at the box.

"You didn't know?" Dad asked her.

"No." She scowled. "How the hell would I know that? I broke up with him and hadn't seen him until I started dating you."

"You didn't know about Tanner. At all," Dad repeated.

"No." She glared at him. "What are you accusing me of, Angel?"

I almost laughed, knowing that I got my fiery energy from my mom.

"Nothing. Fuck, woman. The guy is dead and he's still causing shit. I'm going to get a beer." He stormed away, stomping into the kitchen.

"Mom." I went to her side. "I'm sorry. I didn't realize...I just...I'm sorry."

"It's not your fault." She sighed, giving me a small smile. "You may be the baby but you're definitely not a baby anymore, are you?"

"No, I'm not." I nodded toward Sunny and Shade. "They love me."

"And you love them." She took my hands in hers.

"I do. I would have told you about them sooner to kind of ease you into this, but things happened fast and now Tanner wants information. I don't know what he wants though. He said you have numbers. He wasn't making sense. I'm not even sure he knows what he's talking about. But I know it's bad. He's scary, Mom, and he's not a good guy. At all." I took a breath, waiting for her to tell me that I was imagining things.

"I figured. Being Tyler's kid, it doesn't surprise me that he would be just as bad as him. If not worse." She shivered. "I don't know what Tanner could want though."

"He seems to think that you have something of his," Sunny said, sitting on the couch. "Did Tyler ever give you anything?"

"A couple of black eyes. Some broken ribs. Heartache." Mom shrugged. "The usual."

"Mom." I squeezed her hands. "I had no idea."

"We don't like talking about what happened before you kids were born. All of us had it hard. Even when we had perfect childhoods, something still happened to fuck us up." Mom's gaze flicked to where Dad went into the kitchen. "Your dad is my life and I wouldn't change what I have with him for anything but sometimes, he can be an asshole. He won't admit it anymore but he's still jealous of Tyler. Even though he's dead and gone."

"I heard that he kidnapped someone, and she took him out," Shade said. "But no one will say who it was."

A faraway look passed over her face. "Max shot him, and he ended up in jail. She saved my life. I was pregnant with your sister. She saved us both from him." She pulled away from me and I knew when not to press for more. Max, Piper's mom, may have shot the fucker but it was someone else who actually killed him. I knew when to leave well enough alone, so I thought of something else. Anything that could get us the answers we were looking for.

"I had no idea." I wondered if Piper even knew what her mom had done.

"Of course you wouldn't." Mom cupped my cheek. "We wanted to keep all of you safe from our past, but secrets can only stay secret for so long before they're revealed." Her gaze flicked over my head. "I promise whatever you're thinking, it's not true."

I followed her stare, finding my dad standing behind the couch Sunny and Shade were sitting on.

"What did Tanner say?" he asked me, ignoring my mom.

My heart gave a start. "Uh...he said for me to ask mom about a set of numbers and showed me a picture of her and Tyler." I thought a moment. "I'm not...I'm not related to Tanner, am I?"

Mom's eyes widened. "What? No! God no!" She shook her head. "Is that what you thought?" she asked, going up to my dad.

"I don't know what to think." He shoved his hands in the pockets of his jeans.

"Angel." Mom placed her hand on his chest. "I love you and I promise that Tanner isn't mine. If that's what you're thinking or worried about. I never had Tyler's kid. My babies are yours. That's it."

Dad pulled her against him, wrapping his arms her. He murmured into her hair, something that only she could hear.

A light laugh followed, setting the tension resting on my shoulders at ease.

"I'm sorry, baby," he whispered.

"Don't be. Tyler was a fucker and even dead, he's still a…" She leaned back, cupping her husband's face. "Fucker."

Dad smirked.

I joined Sunny and Shade on the couch, dropping my head in my hands. Tanner wanted something but even my mom had no idea what it was.

"There's no set of numbers or anything that Tyler could have given you?" Sunny asked, running his hand in circles over my back.

"I'm not sure." She went back to the box and started looking through the items in it. "There's not much in here. I have some pictures. Old movie stubs. A guitar pick. A ring."

I went up to her and tried helping as best I could, but it was hard when I had no idea what Tanner could want either. I picked up the ring. "This is pretty," I murmured.

"Why the hell do you still have that shit?" Dad demanded.

"Before you get all alpha male on me and demand why I still have this, I kept it because it reminds me of how far I've come."

Dad only grunted.

Mom sighed, nodding toward the ring. "He had that inscribed with numbers. Maybe that's what Tanner's looking for. Not sure what the numbers are for though. I tried asking Tyler, but he never told me." She shrugged and brought a picture out of the box. "Oh this is of me and you." She handed it to Dad. "It must have gotten accidentally put in here."

"It was after we went on our first date." Dad beamed, standing up taller.

While they continued reminiscing about their date, I read the inscription on the inside of the ring. Mom was right. There was a set of numbers. "This might be what Tanner wants," I said, turning the gold ring back and forth. It was beautiful with a single red diamond in the shape of a heart clasped inside four claws. "Thank you. I just hope we can get this situation under control and that Tanner leaves us alone."

"I can make a call," Dad said, cracking his knuckles.

"I'm sure you could but I wouldn't want anything to happen." I pulled away from my mom as Sunny and Shade came up behind us.

"Tanner's crew isn't like ours," Sunny explained. "Greyson has been trying to clean up Hell's Harlem's mess for years but Tanner? He just doesn't care."

"What crew is he with?" Dad asked, wrapping an arm around Mom's shoulders.

"He's the president of Devil's Rejects," Shade answered, crossing his arms under his broad chest.

"Shit." Dad shook his head. "I've heard of them. Your dad's crew had issues with them in the past, did they not?" he asked my mom.

"Yeah." Mom pulled me back into a hug. "You be safe," she murmured into my hair. "You hear me, Meadow? I know you're strong. You are so damn strong but it's okay to ask for help."

"I know, Mama," I whispered.

She leaned back, cupping my face. "I love you."

I covered her hand with mine. "I love you too."

(Shade)

I expected Angel to rip off our balls and feed them to us but for whatever reason, he didn't. It was almost like he was okay with both Sunny and I dating his daughter. But Greyson had been right. He was a huge fucker. Even though he was older and probably well into his fifties, he kept in good shape. There was no extra weight around his middle from what I could tell.

Get it together, Shade. Now you're checking out your girl's father.

I shook my head.

"Hey." A heavy hand landed on my shoulder.

I was met with slate eyes, eyes that had grown cold over the years but warmed whenever they landed on Meadow and I.

"You good?" Sunny asked, tilting his head.

I stepped closer to him, needing his strength. "I don't know. Something's wrong." I couldn't shake this feeling that the issue with Tanner was just a cover-up for something worse that was about to happen. It didn't make sense. Sunny and I were finally talking. We were on the same page after years of skirting around the truth. We had Meadow who loved us and put up with our lack of communication with each other. She taught us to explore these feelings we had for one another and we gave her everything in return. I could never thank her enough for what she had done for us.

While we stood by the SUV and waited for Meadow to join us, we were silent. I let the events of the evening rush over me.

Tanner touching our girl. Him threatening her. Him being the fucking bastard that he was. Him wanting something.

I was thankful that we were able to get it, if in fact it was what he wanted. The numbers on Meadow's mom's ring could have also meant nothing.

Pulling a pack of smokes from the inside of my leather jacket, I lit one up. I didn't smoke often. Only when I was stressed. But this called for a smoke. And a drink. A hard fucking drink.

The door of Meadow's parents' place opened, revealing Meadow and her mom. She gave her another hug and started walking toward us.

My body stirred. Everything inside of me came alive the closer she got to us.

"I think we should meet up with Tanner and give him this ring," she suggested once she stood in front of us. "I just want this over with."

I nodded, butting the smoke out on the bottom of my Shit-Kicker and moved around to the back door of the SUV.

"As much as I don't want to, you're probably right," Sunny said, heading to the driver's side door. "He just better keep his hands to himself this time."

Meadow shivered. "I hope so."

"Let's go." I slid into the back seat. My nerves were shot. Something was coming. Something big. And I knew that none of us were prepared for it. "Maybe we should call Greyson."

"He has enough shit to deal with." Sunny started up the engine.

I huffed, crossing my arms under my chest and looking out the window.

"What if Tanner does something stupid though?" Meadow asked, doing up her seat belt. "Maybe calling Greyson or one of the other guys, isn't such a bad idea. We may need backup." She shook her head. "Is that even a thing? Do you guys ever call each other for backup? I'm so new."

She was nervous. I learned rather quickly that random things would leave her lips whenever she was rattled.

Sitting forward, I grabbed her hand and brought it up to my lips. "It is a thing," I told her, brushing my mouth along her knuckles. "We'll definitely call the guys and tell them to meet us at Tanner's clubhouse. But Greyson needs to worry about his wife and son."

Sunny nodded, gripping the steering wheel tight.

"Do you think I can give Tanner the ring and that will be it?" Meadow shook her head. "There's no way he would just let me go after that. If what happened earlier tonight is any indication."

I agreed with her but never said it.

I was vaguely aware of Meadow calling Tanner and choosing another place to meet up. It was somewhere public which would be safer than meeting him at his club.

As we drove to the meeting point, the three of us remained silent. Something was eating at me and I couldn't figure out what it was.

"What's wrong?"

My gaze snapped to Sunny's. "What do you mean?"

Meadow looked between us both.

"I mean that you're on edge. I understand why, with this Tanner shit and all, but there's something else," he said, his eyes searching my face. "Isn't there?"

"I don't know." I looked out the window, watching the world pass us by. The closer we got to the café we were meeting him at, the more on edge I felt. My nerves were shot. Maybe it wouldn't have been so bad if we had just gone into this with Meadow as something fun. But now that we had fallen in love with her, it made it almost…worse. Like we would do anything to protect her and not care in the least who we had to go through to make sure she was safe.

"Something isn't sitting right with me," Meadow murmured, voicing my thoughts.

Sunny grunted.

I didn't respond.

Why would I? There was no point. I wasn't one to get nervous often, but I was man enough to admit it. Tanner Horsch set me on edge. He was the epitome of evil. There had been many times I wanted to ask him why and what happened to make him that way. But I knew that it was a conversation that not very many had with him. If anyone ever at all.

I had a feeling that we would find out just how deep his depravity went before the night was over.

I just prayed that we would survive it.

TWENTY-SIX

Meadow

I COULD FEEL THE tension rolling off of Sunny and Shade in waves.

They had decided that it would be best to meet up with Tanner somewhere else rather than at his club. So I had called him and gave him a meeting point. Surprisingly, Tanner had agreed and met us outside of a local coffee shop in the downtown area of our city. It wasn't overly busy with people or traffic, but it was safer than going to his club.

Even though it was later in the night, people still milled about. It was one thing I loved about our town. People still sat outside, enjoying their cups of coffee, no matter the weather and time. Piper had told me it reminded her of Europe in a way.

"I'm assuming I should go by myself," I said, finding Tanner sitting at a table just outside of the café.

"As much as I don't like it, yeah, you probably should." Sunny killed the engine and turned toward me. "If Shade and I go, it might spook him. But we'll be right here."

I took a deep breath and left the SUV.

Tanner looked my way.

Knowing that Sunny and Shade were close by, gave me all the strength I needed to confront him.

As I neared the table, the hairs on the back of my neck tingled. My stomach twisted, my heart racing the closer I got to Tanner.

"I won't hurt you," Tanner said as I sat across from him.

"Isn't that what the villain usually says before they kill their victim?"

Tanner searched my face. "Doesn't matter if you believe me or not. Doesn't matter if anyone believes me or not."

"Good because I don't." I looked around me, finding nothing out of the ordinary but still feeling like we were being watched just the same. Besides Sunny and Shade being close, I had a feeling that some of Tanner's crew were around as well. The backup from Hell's Harlem hadn't shown up yet and that fact alone, set my nerves on edge.

"Did you get what I asked for?" Tanner asked, picking up the small mug and taking a sip of whatever drink he had decided on.

"You never asked but yeah, I got it." I pulled the ring from my pocket. "I'm not sure if this is what you want though. My mom had no idea what you were talking about."

Tanner took the ring from me and read the inside of it. "I'm not sure either."

I frowned. "What do you mean?"

"My dad was a twisted individual." He squinted as he read the inscription.

"Why didn't you ask my mom yourself?"

Tanner's gaze met mine. "Have you met your father? He's a scary fucker. I've toyed with death before but even I'm not stupid enough to cross his path."

"Do you know my father?" Even though I didn't like Tanner, for whatever reason I found him intriguing. He had an air about him where it was like he just didn't care.

"Not personally, no. I've tried to stay away. Cause you know, I'm in Hell's Harlem territory and all." He winked.

I rolled my eyes. "This place is away from their clubhouse, so I think you're good."

"Listen, what happened before..." He hesitated.

My eyebrows rose. Was Tanner Horsch actually going to apologize to me?

"I'm a bastard and I'd rather deal with animals than humans but that...anyway, thanks." He stood from the table.

"Wait." I rose to my full height. "That's it?"

"What more do you want?" Tanner demanded. "I suggest leaving before what happened earlier tonight is the least of your worries."

"I just..." I shook my head. "This doesn't make sense."

"Meadow."

My head whipped around.

Sunny came toward us.

"Please, tell me why you would go through all of this trouble just for those numbers," I said quickly.

"You ask way too many questions." Tanner stuffed the ring into his pocket. "Leave it alone, Meadow."

"He's right." Sunny grabbed my hand. "Let's go."

"No." I stepped around the table, blocking Tanner's path. "Why demand for me to get this from my mom? What's in it for you?"

Tanner glanced over my head. "You need to put a muzzle on your pet."

Before I could stop myself, I shoved him. "I want answers."

A wicked grin spread on his face. "Listen here, little girl. I'd be very careful who you demand answers from. My crew is not as nice as Hell's Harlem. Although, I seem to recall a time that they were actually much worse than my club." He chuckled. "Those were the days."

"Tanner." I clenched my hands into fists at my sides. "How did you know that my mom had that ring or even those numbers you were looking for?"

"Because it was in my dad's will," Tanner finally confessed.

My eyes widened. "What?"

"If you must know, when my dad died, he had stipulations in his will that it be read at a certain time and on a certain date."

"I think he saw one too many action movies," I muttered.

"That date has come and gone already," Tanner said, ignoring my comment. "His lawyer called me and told me, but I didn't have these numbers then. I almost didn't believe it myself."

"I don't care what the numbers get you but why do I feel like there's a catch?" I asked, staring up at him. "You can't just want those numbers and be on your merry way."

"And why not?" Tanner turned back around. "You'll learn to leave well enough alone, Meadow. Don't make me change my mind." When he started walking away, a breath escaped me like he had sucked the very air from my lungs.

"This doesn't make sense." I spun on my heel and walked past Sunny toward their SUV. Shade had stayed back, leaning against the large black vehicle. I just wanted to go home and for them to spend the night holding me. "This doesn't make sense at all," I added.

"Why does it have to make sense?" Sunny asked, rushing to catch up to me.

"Because he's a biker. If he's so scary like you guys suggest he is, then I feel like..." I huffed when the guys just stared down at me. "Whatever. I know what I mean. Maybe I'm just being paranoid. Maybe..." Maybe I expected something to take place and was disappointed when it didn't. Could that happen? It would be like watching an action movie and it building up to the big explosion scene and then...nothing. God, I should get it together and be thankful that—

A loud bang sounded.

I jumped when a heavy body hit mine, pushing me to the ground. I landed on the hard cement beneath me with an oomph, all the weight being knocked from my lungs.

Bangs continued, popping in my ears and making them ring.

My heart jumped to my throat. I tried struggling out from beneath the heavy weight on top of me, but the body kept me close.

"Stop."

I stilled at the deep voice. "Sunny? What's going on?"

He grunted, the popping continuing.

It was followed by shouts, women screaming and men yelling. It all happened so damn fast; I couldn't make out what was being said.

"Sunny, what's going on?" I asked, my voice shaking.

Suddenly the popping stopped, followed by sirens sounding off in the distance. As time wore on, they only became louder and louder.

"Sunny." I tried pushing him off me. "Baby, you're too heavy." I pushed him again, but he wouldn't budge. His hot breath fanned the side of my face.

"I'm sorry," he wheezed.

My eyes widened. "Sunny." I shook him. My hand landed against something sticky. Pulling it back, I saw that it was coated in something. A dark liquid. My stomach sunk. "No. Shade!" I screamed. "Shade! I need you." I gently nudged Sunny. "Please, Sunny. Sir. Please." My eyes welled, my throat working over the hard lump suddenly lodged in it.

"I love you, baby." Sunny wrapped himself around me. "Take care of him. Take care of my boy." He coughed, his body shaking with ragged breaths. "Take care of him."

I squeezed my eyes shut, shaking my head and praying with everything in me for this not to be happening. For us to go back to that morning. For us to have gone on our damn date instead. We should have met up with Tanner tomorrow like Sunny had suggested earlier but then changed his mind, so we could get this over with.

But now…

Sunny's rising back, slowed until his breathing became even.

A sob escaped me.

I knew. God did I know.

That date would never happen.

With Sunny wrapped around me, protecting me, keeping me safe, he whispered his final breath.

TWENTY-SEVEN

SHADE

THE HORROR SURROUNDING US was like it came right out of an action film. Gunshots had fired, Tanner's men blew up the damn parking lot. But of course, Tanner had been nowhere to be found. I wasn't sure if he set this up. If he had, that meant war and a war was what he was going to get.

While Meadow had gone to give Tanner the ring, Sunny and I stayed back. When he got what he wanted, he went into the café and that was when the gunshots started.

It had happened so damn fast. At one moment, Sunny and Meadow were coming toward me and the next, they were on the ground.

Sirens sounded, police cars barreling down the road as the red and blue lights flashed. They indicated their arrival and while I would have breathed a sigh of relief at seeing them, I was focused solely on the bundled heap laying on the ground by Sunny's SUV.

As quickly as I wanted to go to them, my feet were stuck. It was as if I were in quicksand and couldn't move. Time seemed to stand still the longer I stared.

Voices shouted, someone grabbed my shoulders and shook me.

A cop. A cop was shouting in my face.

Why couldn't I hear him?

He released me and disappeared into the mess spread out around us.

Sunny. Meadow.

My feet finally moved.

One step. Two. Three.

Several more before I reached the pile.

"Shade." Meadow. She sounded so far away. Her voice was small. Helpless. Blood splattered her face and the pieces of clothing I could see. "Please. Sunny."

That snapped me out of it. When I reached them, I fell to my knees, shoving Sunny back a few inches so Meadow could move out from beneath him. When his eyes didn't open, I knew. When he didn't demand for answers with that gravelly voice of his, I knew. When he didn't tell me that he loved me and that everything would be fine, fuck, I knew. But I still needed to hear the words.

"Meadow," I croaked, pushing Sunny off of her completely and gently turning him onto his back. When I pressed two fingers to his pulse point at the side of his neck and felt nothing, a muffled sob left me.

Through blurred vision, I tilted his head back and started giving him CPR. I would do anything to give my life for him. To breathe into his lungs and make his heart beat again.

I placed two fingers at his sternum, then put the heel of my other hand next to them and started chest compressions. "Please, Sunny. Wake the fuck up. You need to wake up. I need you."

"Shade," came Meadow's muffled sob.

"Please." Tears rolled down my cheeks, dripping off my chin and onto his leather cut.

"Shade." Meadow hiccupped. She placed her hands on top of mine. "He's gone."

"No," I shouted. "He can't die on me." Not when we were finally getting somewhere. After being together for fifteen years, we were finally starting to feel like a normal couple. "No. Sunny." I stopped the compressions and beat my fists against his chest instead. But it did nothing. Sunny laid there, still and unmoving, and Meadow cried.

She threw her arms around my neck, muttering over and over how sorry she was but it did nothing to curb this ache. This agony that threatened to consume me completely.

"Say it," I demanded, holding her against me.

She shook against me.

"Say. It," I repeated.

Meadow lifted her head, staring at me. "He's…he's dead."

Screams shattered from my lips, tearing my throat to shreds. It was like death himself had ripped my heart from my chest only to crush it in his very hands all the while laughing in my face.

"Sunny Harrison."

I stood stock still, staring up into the grayest eyes I had ever seen. I wasn't new to being attracted to the same sex, so these feelings weren't unnatural for me, but I had never run into someone who looked like…well…Sunny. He looked to be about my age, with dark hair that was cut short at the sides, leaving the strands a little longer on top. He had a full beard on his strong jaw, but it was his eyes that drew me in.

He cocked his head to the side, raising an eyebrow. "Something on my face?"

I chuckled, my cheeks burning. Sticking out my hand, I gave him a smirk. "Roy Allen."

Sunny slipped his fingers in mine. "Nice to meet you."

As soon as our fingers touched, a shock of electricity ran through me. I wasn't sure if Sunny was into men or not, but I knew right then and there that I was attracted to him. But as deep as that attraction went, I could see the walls he had put up. And I was determined to break through them. Even if it took me years.

This couldn't be happening. There was no way that Sunny could be dead.

"Shade."

My name was said but I couldn't make out who was saying it. My mind was in a fog. My stomach lurched, threatening to spew everything I had consumed that day on the ground in front of me.

"Shade," my name was repeated, firmer that time.

Meadow held me against her, but I never returned the embrace. It wasn't her fault. None of this was her fault and yet, I still placed the blame. On her? On myself? On Tanner? I didn't know who killed Sunny, but I would avenge him and make them pay for taking him from us.

Much to my dismay, Meadow was pulled from my arms and placed in the SUV that Sunny and I had owned together. Although he had been the only one to ever drive it, both of our names were on the ownership. I realized then that he had truly loved me. In his own way. Even though it took a while for him to come out and say those words, it was the small things. We owned a house together. After he moved in originally when he had been with Roxanne, he invited me to move in with him instead. She had never been happy about that fact, knowing that even when Sunny and I fought, it was him and me. It was always us. No one else. Until Meadow came along, it was just the two of us.

"Shade." Greyson ran toward me. His gaze dropped to Sunny laying on the ground at my knees. "Fucking hell." He put a phone to his ear and started barking orders, but I couldn't make out what was being said. All I could focus on was the fact that Sunny was dead. He was gone. It was like my soul was ripped from my very chest. I couldn't do this. Leaning over Sunny, I brushed my fingers over his eyes and kissed his forehead.

"I love you, Sunny," I whispered, tasting my tears on my tongue. "I will always love you."

I could almost hear him say, *Take care of our girl.*

"I will," I promised him. "I will take care of her."

But she would have to take care of me just the same. Sunny had always been the strong one in our relationship but now it was my turn. I didn't want it to be my turn. I wanted Sunny. He was all I ever wanted. I wasn't ready to live life without him. We were supposed to grow old together. Before we met Meadow, we had made plans to travel once we retired. Now that would never happen.

"You need to go to the hospital with Meadow." A heavy hand cupped my nape, pulling me from my thoughts. "Shade."

I looked up, finding Greyson staring down at me.

"You need to go with Meadow. We'll take care of Sunny," he said, his voice thick.

I only stared at him, wondering how he did it. He had lost members years ago when Sunny and I were both just prospects. But he seemed to move on even though I was sure it had been hard.

"How do you do it?" I asked him, my voice rough and thick with the excruciating pain burning through me.

Greyson's jaw ticked. "What do you mean?"

"All this death. How?"

His face softened. "I have my wife. She helps me."

"I can't do this." My eyes welled all over again. This pain was something I had never felt before. It grated over my bones, dug into my flesh, and ripped my heart into tiny little pieces.

"You can." Greyson cupped my shoulders, staring intently into my eyes. "Listen, you two joined the club together. You were prospects at the time and drove me fucking crazy. You were hotheads much like myself. Eve said it's why we butted heads most days."

I looked away, remembering the many arguments we had but in reality, it was all in fun. We respected the hell out of Greyson.

"I need him," I whispered.

"I know." Grey slid his hand to the back of my neck, leaning his forehead against mine. "I promise you that you will get through this. But as much as I want to continue this conversation, you need to go. Take care of your girl, Shade. She needs you."

I pulled away from Greyson and kissed Sunny one last time, not caring in the least who was watching.

"Shade?"

I looked up at Meadow sitting in the back seat of the SUV. The door was open, and her arms were out like she was waiting for me to run into them. To run into her safety and suck whatever strength it was that she was willing to offer me.

Greyson gave my shoulder a final squeeze before he started rounding up the guys to follow us to the hospital and to speak with the coroner about putting Sunny's body away for safekeeping until we could bury him.

Pushing away from Sunny, I trudged toward Meadow.

She caught my shirt in her hands before I could touch her myself. Pulling me into the back seat, she threw her arms around my shoulders and cried into the crook of my neck.

I pulled her onto my lap, held her tight, and shut the door.

Cyrus slid into the driver's seat, followed by Sammy joining him in the passenger seat. Cyrus caught my gaze in the rearview mirror and nodded once.

Blowing out a slow breath, I let my eyes close and held Meadow while she cried.

Once we were cleared to leave by the police, Cyrus and Sammy drove Meadow and I to the hospital themselves. The EMT had checked her out but I wanted to be thorough, knowing that it was what Sunny would have wanted as well.

As much as I just wanted to go home, I knew that Meadow needed to be checked out. Sunny had pushed her out of the way but also landed on her quite hard. They were both knocked to the ground and even though Meadow hadn't complained about being in pain, the adrenaline could have masked that.

Meadow lifted her head, sniffing and wiping under her eyes. "I…"

"Shhh…" I wrapped my hand up in her hair and kissed her forehead. Letting my lips linger, I inhaled the sweet scent of her skin. Running my thumb along her cheek, I breathed her in. Her scent calmed me. It eased some of the pain rushing through the soul of my very being. I knew in time we could get through this but getting over it?

Never.

With shaky hands, I pulled a pack of smokes out of the inner pocket of my leather jacket. I attempted to light a cigarette, but the lighter wouldn't spark.

"Hey." Cyrus grabbed the smoke. "Let me." He took the smoke from me and stuck it between his lips, lit the tip, and inhaled. The sweet smoke billowed around us. He handed it back to me and stretched out his long legs in front of him.

"Thank you," I murmured, taking a deep inhale of the sustenance that I needed. "I thought you quit."

"I did." He nodded toward his brother who paced in front of us. "He's the smoker. I'd rather have liquor. And you were struggling, so I wanted to help."

I let out a hard sigh and puffed on the smoke between my lips. "I don't know what to do," I said after a couple of minutes of silence fell between us.

"You will," Cyrus said gently. "Maybe not now. Maybe not even tomorrow. But you will figure out what to do. With Meadow there to help you, both of you will get through this."

"You don't know that," I said, my voice rough.

"Nope." Sammy stopped pacing. "He doesn't but we can tell you from experience that it will get easier. Some days are harder than others. You could see things that remind you of him. Or smell something. Or even just seeing Meadow could remind you."

I swallowed hard, looked away, and butted out the smoke on the sidewalk beneath us.

"You're strong, Shade. Both of you are." Cyrus nodded toward Sammy. "Hell, I don't know what I would have done without this fucker."

Sammy grinned, patting his own back. "I am pretty spectacular."

I chuckled.

They laughed along with me.

I let out a heavy sigh. "Thank you."

"Anytime, brother." Cyrus cupped my shoulder. "You should get in there though. I'm sure they're done checking on Meadow."

I nodded. I wanted to stay with her, but she had insisted that I take a breather.

Rising to my feet, I brushed off my jeans and stared up at the large building in front of us. General Hospital sat in big red letters on the tallest part of the building. I hadn't been there often. Last time was when Sunny had a cold that turned out to be the flu. He refused medication, so it only got worse and to the point where it ended up being pneumonia.

A shuddered breath left me as the memory slid into my mind.

Making my way into the building, I headed to the room that Meadow was staying in. As I reached the floor she was on, I walked down the long white hall. As soon as I stood outside her room, two words came from inside the room. Two words that I never thought I would ever hear. Not when it came to someone I was in love with.

"What did you just say?" I heard Meadow ask, her voice soft and unsure.

The doctor cleared her throat. "You're pregnant."

(Meadow)

My mind was numb. I didn't care about anything but at the same time, I did. It was confusing. I was confused. The tears no longer fell. I hadn't known Sunny for long but for the time that I did, I fell in love with him hard. The three of us balanced each other out. While Shade submitted to me, Sunny dominated me and gave me everything that I needed. He was my Sir. My Daddy. While some wouldn't find it normal, it was our normal. It made us up, as individuals and as a trio. And now it was just Shade and I. If he still wanted to be with me.

My eyes burned, the tears threatening to escape once again. It hurt. Every inch of me hurt. Physically. Emotionally. Fucking mentally. I missed him. God, I missed him. He was taken from me far too soon. And Shade, I had no idea how we would get through this.

My chest tightened, the air escaping my lungs, burning through me.

WITH US

After everything that happened outside the café, the police questioned everyone who was in the vicinity and surrounding area. They had shown up at the hospital, asking both Shade and I questions. But of course, no one had any answers. Bottom line, either Tanner or one of his crew shot up the place and we lost Sunny because of it.

Hell's Harlem made an appearance, the police asked everyone questions, cleared us to leave and now I was at the hospital. Truth was, I couldn't remember much of the night. I had passed out in Shade's arms. Under normal circumstances, I was sure an ambulance would have taken me away, but these biker clubs liked to do things their own way. So, they drove me to the hospital themselves.

"You're pregnant."

I broke down into tears when the doctor told me that I was carrying a baby. I hadn't even known Sunny and Shade for that long. It didn't make sense.

"Condoms aren't foolproof," the doctor said gently, giving me a small smile.

We did the math and estimated that I was just over a month along.

It had felt like I had known them for much longer when really, it had been almost two months. I couldn't believe I was carrying Sunny and Shade's baby. But I didn't know where Shade was. Maybe I would never see him again. Maybe this was it. Maybe Sunny's death broke us. I had told him to take a breather but maybe he left for good. Maybe he was only with me in the first place because of Sunny himself.

No, that wasn't the case. Shade loved me.

The sound of the door opening followed by heavy footsteps rang through me but I couldn't look to see who it was. Even though I knew. I could smell him before he got close enough. I could feel him. Taste him.

The bed dipped beside me.

A sob lodged its way into my throat. He never left.

Shade pushed his face into the crook of my neck, wrapping his arm around my middle. His body shook with silent but rough cries. He lost a piece of himself. A man he had been in love with since he was young. A man he gave his complete self to. A man who took and gave him everything in return. A man I could never compete with.

"Don't leave me."

My head whipped around. I stared up into Shade's red-rimmed eyes. "What?" I croaked.

"Don't leave me," he repeated, leaning his forehead against mine. "I couldn't handle it if you did."

"Never." I cupped his cheek, his thick beard tickling my fingers. He had grown it in some once he realized how much I liked it. "I thought you would leave me. I thought it was us three. And that's it. Now that it's just us two...I...I just..." Tears fell, rolling down my cheeks and dripping off my chin. "I'm sorry."

"Don't." Shade pulled me against him, crushing me into a deep hug. "It's not your fault," he said, his voice shaking. "I'm not leaving you. Never, Meadow."

"I should have done something. I shouldn't have called Tanner on like that. I should..." A sob tore through me, crushing every bone in my body with the weight of my anguish.

"Baby." Shade wrapped his hands in my hair, holding me tight and crying along with me.

"It should have been me," I sobbed, tugging him tighter against me. My hold on him was so damn tight, it was like I was trying to burrow beneath his skin. Maybe I was. I wanted him to take the pain away and I would do the same for him.

"Don't say that," he pleaded, his voice thick.

"If you wouldn't have met me..."

"Don't." He leaned back, staring down at me. "We met you because we were supposed to. You helped Sunny and I become closer. You helped him confess his love for me and I…" He swallowed hard. "The same."

"But he was taken from you. Because of me."

"No." Shade cupped my face. "He saved you."

"But he died because of that," I cried, shoving from his grip. I tried pulling away. Even though I was in a hospital bed and hooked up to an IV, I still tried to get as far away from him as possible.

"Don't, little lamb." Shade sat behind me and pulled me back against him. "Please don't pull away from me. I need you. I can't do this alone."

My shoulders slumped with defeat. All the weight of what happened tonight, came down hard on my body. "I want him back."

"I know." Shade cupped my stomach. "The doctor said that you're pregnant."

I nodded, fresh tears rolling down my cheeks.

"Sunny died for you and his baby. My baby."

I covered Shade's hand. "*Our* baby."

"I'm so sorry, Meadow." Shade kissed the side of my head. "I promise you that I will be the best father I can be. I'll never be able to replace what you had with Sunny but I'm here. I'm always here."

I looked up at him then. "I was thinking the same thing."

Shade cupped the side of my neck. "What do you mean?"

"I can't replace what you had with Sunny either." I kissed him softly on the mouth. "I'm sorry for your loss, Shade. I'm so sorry."

Shade leaned his forehead against mine. "I'm sorry for yours."

I had gone into this wanting to fulfill a fantasy and instead, I fell in love with two men at the same time. While Sunny was taken from us, this baby would be a way for us to heal. But I knew the only way that Shade and I could truly heal was by being there for each other. No matter what happened.

"We never got a chance to go on our date," I murmured.

Shade sighed. "I know."

Not that it was important but Sunny had been determined to prove to the world that this was right. That poly relationships happened. He let on like he didn't care what people thought but he did. He was worried that Shade would leave him because of other people's opinions over what they shared. Over what *we* shared.

"This isn't weird for you?" Shade asked a little while later. His fingers were in mine, his calloused thumb rubbing back and forth over my palm.

"What do you mean?" I really wanted to go home but the doctor insisted I stay overnight for observation. Especially since I hit my head pretty hard, add to the fact that I was pregnant. My heart jumped. I still couldn't believe I was carrying Sunny and Shade's baby.

"Well I know you wanted a relationship with two men. And you're pregnant. It could be either mine or Sunny's or..."

"Or?" I looked up at him.

His usually bright green eyes were no longer green but a shade of gray. They reminded me of Sunny's slate eyes. Eyes that I had looked into for what felt like an eternity when really, it hadn't been that long at all.

"You were with someone else before us." Shade shook his head. "I'm not accusing you of anything." He sat up, pushing out from behind me and sliding off the bed. He started pacing. "I'm sorry."

"Hey." I held my arms out. "Come here."

Shade stopped and turned to me. "We can get a DNA test."

"No." I patted the spot in front of me. "Sit. Please."

Shade came back toward me and sat. "I won't be upset."

"Listen to me." I wrapped an arm around his shoulders and kissed his cheek. "I love you. I love you and Sunny. And while he's gone, he will always live on with this baby." I grabbed Shade's hand and brought it to my stomach. "Our baby. I know it's either yours or Sunny's. Not the other guy's. The math doesn't add up and I had my period right before I met you both."

Shade's body relaxed at that.

I ran my hand down his chest. "Whatever this is…I felt like it was right with you two. All along I knew it was where I needed to be and who I needed to be with. I don't believe in fate but…"

"I know." Shade kissed my forehead. "I felt it too. All along. The whole damn time."

"This baby belongs to both you and Sunny. And we'll raise them to understand that they have two daddies. Even though Sunny is…" I swallowed hard.

"Meadow." Shade threw himself around me. "You're fucking incredible."

"I'm really not," I said, hugging him back.

"You are." He fisted my hair, staring intently into my eyes. "I love you."

"I love you too," I murmured. "More than I can ever tell you."

TWENTY-EIGHT

Meddow

SHADE AND I STOOD hand in hand, both of us staring as the casket was lowered into the grave. I had never lost someone. My grandfather passed away a couple of years ago but other than that, I had never experienced this sort of loss. This pain that felt like someone was stabbing me constantly with a knife. It ripped into my heart, turned and twisted until all I felt was agony shredding my damn soul.

Members of Hell's Harlem from all over had shown up to the funeral. They offered their condolences, the air around them thick and tense. While they offered their gentle words to me, they told Shade they would help him avenge Sunny. He would only nod or grunt in response but never took his hand from mine.

Our friends and family had been beyond supportive. My brother apologized. I could sense the guilt resting on him, weighing him down constantly when really, this had nothing to do with him. He was just in the wrong place at the wrong time. Everyone offered their condolences but never asked us how we were doing. Why would they? It was obvious how we were doing. We were hurting. But it was harder for Shade. Not that our pain could be compared to one another, but he had been with Sunny longer than I had.

Shade tugged my hand.

I looked up at him.

He gave me a small smile.

My heart stuttered. Maybe we could get through this. One day at a time. One step at a time. As long as we had each other, we could get through anything. It was as if I could hear Sunny whispering those words to me himself.

We hadn't told anyone that I was pregnant. We wanted to spend some time, keeping that piece of information to ourselves. At least for a little bit.

After Sunny was buried, I gave Shade some time alone with him and went up to my parents.

My mother's head turned around, her gaze catching mine. Her face softened.

I rushed up to her and threw my arms around her middle.

"Oh, baby." She enveloped me in a hug, kissing the top of my head. "I'm so sorry."

Dad hugged us both, muttering his own condolences.

"I can't do this," I finally said, my voice thick.

"Yes." Dad spun me toward him. "You can." He cupped my face. "I promise you that you will get through this. Together. It'll be hard. I'm not going to lie and say it isn't. But together, you and Shade will heal."

I nodded, blinking back tears at my dad's words.

I caught Gigi, Luna, and Piper coming toward us.

Dad released me.

The girls picked up their steps until they reached me. They wrapped me in a group hug, crying along with me.

"I'm so sorry."

"I can't imagine what you both are going through."

"We're here. Whatever you need."

I wasn't sure who was saying what, but I didn't care. I needed them. My friends. Who I also hoped would one day be Shade's friends just the same.

"Meadow."

My head snapped up, finding Aiden and Ashton standing near us. They mirrored each other's poses with their hands shoved in their pockets. A solemn look was on both of their faces.

I released the girls and went up to the twins.

"I'm sorry." Aiden wrapped me up in a tight hug. He gave me one final squeeze before gently pushing me into his brother's arms.

Ashton's hug lasted a little longer than what was deemed appropriate.

"Fucker shouldn't be touching what belongs to us."

A laugh mixed with a sob, escaped me.

Ashton only hugged me tighter.

"Meadow, tell him to keep his hands to himself."

I pulled away from Ashton.

He frowned.

"I'm sorry." I wiped my face, letting out a harsh breath. "I could hear him grumbling like he was actually here. I know it doesn't make sense."

Ashton tilted his head. "Did he say for me to stop touching you?"

I laughed lightly, thankful that he didn't think I was going crazy. "Something like that."

Ashton gave me a small smile. "I'll keep my hands to myself, Meadow. I promise. I know when I'm no longer needed."

I stared up at him.

He gave me a small smile, his shoulders lifting with a slight shrug.

"Thank you for taking care of me," I told him as a large shadow came up behind me.

Ashton stood taller, his gaze flicking over my head. "We haven't officially met." He stuck out his hand. "Ashton Donovan. I wish it were under better circumstances."

Shade returned the handshake. "Roy Allen but everyone calls me Shade."

Ashton nodded. "Your girl and I go way back. You got a good one."

Shade reached for my hand.

I took it, holding it tight and trying with everything in me to suck all the strength he had and wrap it around me. "I have a good one as well."

Ashton took a step toward me, cupped my shoulder, and placed a soft peck on my cheek. "Take care of each other, Meadow." He gave my shoulder a light squeeze before he left us and rejoined his brother who was now standing with the girls and my parents.

"Meadow."

I looked up at Shade but not before I caught a woman standing by one of the cars a few feet away. "Do you know who that is?"

Shade followed my gaze. "Yeah. That's Roxanne."

"Oh." I swallowed hard but took a deep breath. With Shade's hand in mine, I led us toward her.

"Meadow." He tugged my hand. "We don't have to do this."

"I know." But I was being the bigger person.

When we stood in front of Roxanne, I released Shade's hand and wrapped my arms around her middle.

She gasped, her body stiffening.

"I'm sorry for your loss." I gave her a final squeeze before releasing her and moving to Shade's side.

"I…" She pulled at the collar of her tailored suit jacket. She wore all black, the pencil skirt hugging her figure. Her dark hair was around her shoulders in waves.

Her full red lips pressing into a thin line. "I don't even know what to say."

"Well…" I looked around her. "Sunny said he kept in contact with your kids. Are they not here?"

"They're in school," she said, as if that were a good enough reason for them not to show up to a funeral for someone who they were apparently close with.

"Meadow," Shade said gently. "We need to meet with Greyson and the guys."

"Oh. Okay." I looked back at Roxanne. "Well, it was nice meeting you. I wish it could have been under better circumstances."

She snorted. "Right. I'm sure you do." She gave me a curt nod. "Shade." And with that, she spun on her heel and headed back toward her car.

"Well that was odd," I muttered.

"Yeah, she's never been a fan of mine." Shade cupped my shoulders and spun me around until I faced him. "But enough about her. We have to meet with Greyson. It's about Sunny."

(Shade)

Greyson didn't want to meet so soon. Especially when we'd just buried Sunny. But Meadow and I both needed answers so we could try and move on. It would still be difficult, no matter what information we got but Sunny deserved justice.

After we left the graveyard, we told Meadow's parents that we would be by later that evening. Thankfully they understood. It helped when Meadow's father was a hothead and would have gone through hell first to get the answers he was needing if someone he loved died.

Sunny would definitely understand because I knew that he would have done the same thing if the roles were reversed.

"I'm nervous," Meadow said, pulling me from my thoughts.

"I know, baby. So am I." I pulled the SUV into the large driveway sitting in front of the Hell's Harlem clubhouse. This would be the first time that I had ever stepped foot into the building without Sunny.

My heart jumped to my throat.

I inhaled a shaky breath.

"Let's get this done and over with." Meadow's voice was soft. So damn soft, I almost didn't hear her.

I nodded and left the vehicle.

Trudging around to her side, I opened the door and leaned in before she could exit. "I love you." I cupped her face. "Whatever we find out, we are in this together. I'm not leaving you. Not for anything."

She covered my hand. "I'm not leaving you either."

"Good." I kissed her softly on the forehead and grabbed her hand, helping her leave the SUV.

When we made our way inside the house, we were greeted with friendly but sad smiles, hugs, condolences, and more hugs. But while that went on, my hand always remained connected with Meadow's. I wasn't letting her go. Ever. I knew that at first, she was concerned that I would leave her because we had gone into this as a ménage. A trio. But none of that mattered to me. I loved her. I meant that. Sunny wouldn't want us to end things just because he was no longer around. It wasn't how we worked. Once we loved, we loved hard and we remained faithful. It was why I had waited so damn long for Sunny. I knew he would come around. It would have only been a matter of time before he got his head out of his ass.

I just wished he could be there for when our baby was born. He loved kids. Even when they weren't his own.

"Alright, let's give them the information we know, so they can have some time alone." Greyson's booming voice left no room for question.

With Meadow's hand in mine, I led her to the meeting room. Non-club members weren't usually allowed in the room, but this was an exception.

"Shade." Greyson stepped in front of me. His gray eyes locked on mine. Much to my surprise, he pulled me in for a hug. "I'm so sorry, brother. So fucking sorry. I know you loved him."

My eyes welled, that damn lump burning in my throat again.

"I'm proud of you though."

I leaned back, wiping under my eyes. "What do you mean?"

Tray and Catch came up on either side of him.

"You didn't go in guns blazing when you found Sunny," Greyson explained. "You went to the hospital to be with your girl and let the police do their job."

I shrugged. "It's not a big deal."

Meadow squeezed my hand, giving me a small smile.

Tray clapped my shoulders. "Yeah, brother, it is. It means you're stronger than you think you are."

Maybe so but I sure as hell didn't feel like it.

Tray let me go, nodding toward an empty chair by the head of the table. I sat in it, pulling Meadow onto my lap.

Greyson moved to the president's chair while the rest of the crew rolled in. He took a breath, scrubbed a hand down his face and then took another breath. "First, Sunny wouldn't want us wallowing. The fucker hated this shit."

I grunted, knowing for a fact that he was right.

"But it doesn't mean that we aren't allowed to grieve." Grey met my gaze. "Especially both of you."

I nodded.

Meadow hooked her arm around my shoulders and kissed my cheek.

"What have you found out?" I asked, knowing it couldn't be much since Sunny died only a few days ago.

"Well..." Greyson met my gaze.

I shifted in my seat. "What?"

"What all do you know about Roxanne Wilson?"

A look passed between Meadow and I before she started talking, "She's Sunny's ex-wife. They had some problems. He tried helping her and her kids, but she was using him. She was there today."

"Of course she was," Grey muttered. "Some of our boys stayed behind after the police left and both of you went to the hospital." He stood and started pacing. "It sounds like Roxanne has been busy."

"What do you mean?" I asked, his pacing making me nervous.

"I have a feeling that Tanner has nothing to do with this," Greyson said, rubbing his jaw.

"What?" Meadow sat forward. "But he was there. He...he touched me. He's..."

"Hey." I pulled her back against me. "Shhh..." I whispered, cupping her cheek.

"But it's true." Her body shook.

"Listen." Greyson stopped, his brows narrowing. "I know he's an evil fucker. Trust me, I've seen that shit firsthand. For someone so damn young...hell, he's my son's age." Grey shook his head. "Doesn't matter. After the twins took you to the hospital, we tried to confront Tanner and find out what the hell happened."

"And? Did you find out anything?" I demanded, needing some answers. Just something. Anything to hold onto so we could heal.

"Shade," Grey said gently. "Tanner disappeared."

Meadow gasped.

Bodies shifted around us.

I just sat there.

The doors suddenly opened.

Catch and Tray held a young man between them. Prospect was written on a patch on his leather cut. His face was badly beaten while blood had matted his bangs to his forehead.

"Let me go," he demanded but his voice came out shaky.

"What's going on?" Meadow asked, curling against me.

"Tell them," Greyson demanded.

Catch pushed the prospect until he was bent over the edge of the table. "Tell them," he repeated.

The prospect looked squarely at me. "Roxanne set you up. It was supposed to be you who died. Not Sunny."

"The fuck?" I gently pushed Meadow off of me and stood. "What are you talking about?"

Catch cupped the prospect's nape, pushing his face into the table. "Answer his damn question."

"I don't know all of the details. I'm only a prospect," he said quickly. "But I overheard a few of the guys talking about taking over the club and kicking Tanner out. That's why he disappeared. He found out there was a mole. They want him dead. I don't know why or any more than that."

"What does Roxanne have to do with this?" I grit out.

"She started dating one of the guys. I didn't see them when they were talking. I swear I didn't. I'm new. Please believe me. She wanted Sunny back. That's why she was trying to take you out. But the guy she's dating doesn't know this."

"Then, how do you?"

"Because she was talking to someone else and I overheard them."

"Wow." Meadow blew out a slow breath. "I knew she was crazy, but I didn't think she'd go this far."

"You and me both, Meadow," I mumbled.

"Where's Roxanne now?" Greyson asked the prospect.

"I don't know. She left after Tanner did." The prospect struggled beneath Catch's weight. "Please, let me try and get answers. I'll do what I can. I can find Tanner as well."

Greyson raised an eyebrow. "Take him to the basement. I'll be there in a moment."

Tray and Catch pulled him away from the table and out of the room, his screams following behind them.

"We'll find out answers," Grey finally said. "You said Roxanne was at the graveyard today. So she can't be far. I promise you we will find out what the hell is going on. But I think you should act like you know nothing. Text Roxanne. Try and contact her in some way and let her know how sorry you are for her loss. Whatever shit you want to say. Maybe she'll cave eventually and come forward."

Unlikely. But I only nodded.

The rest of the meeting ended up in a blur. The guys promised to take care of things and get answers. I texted Roxanne, letting her know everything I knew which wasn't much. When she called me, that was not a conversation I wanted to repeat. She had been off at the funeral, not how I expected her to react. But hearing her sobs on the phone, tore at my heart. As much as I didn't like her, I knew that somewhere deep down inside of her, she did in fact love Sunny.

I was still trying to wrap my head around the fact that she had tried to take me out so she could be with Sunny herself.

"Did you call Roxanne's kids?" Meadow asked later that night when we were finally alone.

"I did." That wasn't a conversation I wanted to repeat either. I had called them before Sunny was buried but couldn't get ahold of them. It seemed Sunny made things seem better than what they were. Roxanne had them believe Sunny was their dad. I wasn't sure how that was possible but since Sunny was never around, it made him look like a deadbeat father. All because of a woman who couldn't let go.

My chest ached, my heart hurting for a man who could no longer defend himself. I did my best to clear the air but that only did so much.

Time was what they needed.

It was what we all needed.

TWENTY-NINE

Meadow

I WOKE TO A heavy body wrapped around me. Shade's hot breath scorched the side of my face. His breathing was deep and even. His hand was beneath my shirt, cupping my breast. Brushing his thumb back and forth over my nipple, it sparked a need inside of me, but I didn't hint for more. I needed Shade to want it on his own time. It had felt like weeks since we buried Sunny when really it had only been a matter of days. Was it more? I wished it were more. Maybe then, it wouldn't hurt so much.

I tried with everything in me not to forget his voice or his face. Shade had shown me pictures of him when they were younger. It seemed Hell's Harlem kept photo albums around. I had come to learn that Greyson liked things old-school. He would rather write letters instead of texting and he kept physical copies of pictures. Rumor had it, he even had negatives of some of the pictures as well.

As Shade showed me images that sparked up memories of their past together, I realized that I never got a picture of him. Of us. After that, I broke down into a fit of tears.

"I did."

"What?" I looked at him through my tears.

"I did get a picture," he said, showing me his phone. There was a photo of Sunny and I smiling at each other.

My eyes welled all over again. "How?"

"Neither of you were paying attention." Shade shrugged. "I also have this one." He swiped a finger across the screen before showing me it. It was of the three of us.

As Shade continued showing me more pictures, I cried silently in his arms. We made a promise to frame each picture and place them in photo albums as well. It wasn't enough. It would never be enough, but it would have to do.

There were so many things I wished I could have done differently. I didn't know Sunny for long. I envied Shade for that fact but felt sorry for him just the same. The agony was written in the hard lines of his face.

We started sleeping in Shade's bedroom, knowing the one we shared, the three of us, was too hard and the pain was too raw. I wasn't sure if we would ever be able to sleep in that bed again. Maybe we would eventually, but for now we spent our time in Shade's room instead.

I rolled over onto my side, fresh tears welling in my eyes.

"You up, Meadow?" Shade asked, his voice rough. Both of us had been crying ourselves to sleep. We were told that this would get easier, but I wasn't sure how.

"I am," I whispered but I never turned back around.

"I keep thinking about what Roxanne was trying to do," he murmured.

"Me too." Truth was, I was terrified. She already had Sunny killed. Even if he wasn't the one who was meant to die. It still happened. So now, would she have Shade killed just out of spite?

"I'm not going anywhere, baby," he said, his voice thick with sleep.

"You can't promise me that." I swallowed hard.

Shade pulled me tighter against him. "I can and I will. I'm not going anywhere. I know we don't have all of our answers yet but one thing we do have, is each other." He kissed the side of my neck, pushing his waist into the seat of my ass.

I bit back a gasp. His large erection pressed up against me. A sob lodged its way into my throat. It had felt like so long since we had been together, but I knew he needed time and that I needed patience.

"I'm sorry," Shade murmured, his mouth finding the side of my throat. "I was dreaming about you. About us. And I woke up…"

"Don't be sorry." I turned around this time, facing him. Cupping his cheek, I placed a soft peck on his mouth.

Shade pulled away from me, turned on the lamp sitting on top of the nightstand, and lay back down beside me. "It's been awhile but as much as I want you, I feel like it's too soon."

I nodded. "I know. And we've…"

"We've never been together." Shade kissed my forehead. "Alone."

I nodded again, wrapping my arm around his waist. Sliding my hand up his strong back, I reveled in the way his muscles jumped beneath my touch. "I miss you."

"I know, baby." He kissed my nose. "I'm so sorry for pushing you away."

"You haven't. It's only been a few days since we…since Sunny." My voice cracked. I moved my hand to his chest, feeling his heart beat beneath my open palm. "I'll wait a lifetime for you."

His breath caught. "Sunny wouldn't want this. He'd go on a rampage, trying to figure out..." His voice became thick. "He wouldn't want us wallowing."

I laughed lightly even though the humor was never there. "I can almost hear him telling you to do what you're good at."

Shade smirked, placing a soft peck on my mouth. "Same."

Brushing my fingers through his beard, I ran my thumb over his bottom lip. "I'm here. For whenever you're ready. There's no rush on anything."

"I know." His dark eyes met mine. They were pleading, begging for me to take away the pain that he was trying to run away from. Could he ever truly run away from it? No, because I couldn't either. But I could run beside him.

Taking a chance because I wasn't exactly sure what he needed, I kissed him again.

Much to my surprise, he cupped the back of my head and pressed his mouth against mine harder.

Slipping his tongue between my lips, it slid and danced along with mine. He spoke to me through that kiss alone. It was a quiet apology for pushing me away when he knew I needed him most. But it was also a cry for help. To take him out of his head. To help him heal. To give him something to focus on besides the pain tearing at his heart.

"Shade," I whispered against his lips.

His mouth trailed down my jaw and back up before covering mine once again. The kiss picked up speed. It bordered on desperate. It was a need to erase all the heartache the last week and a bit had brought us.

Shade slid his hand down my side, sending a shiver of goosebumps along with it. He cupped my rear, squeezing and massaging his fingers into it. "Sunny loved your ass."

I whimpered, breaking the kiss.

Our chests rose and fell.

Licking along my swollen lips, I stared into the eyes of the man I was trying to heal. "I love you," I told him.

Shade slid his fingers around to my front, brushing lightly over my abdomen. "I love you too. And this baby. So damn much." He pushed his hand beneath the fabric of my shirt and spread his fingers over my belly. "I think we should turn Sunny's room into a nursery."

My stomach tumbled. "Really?"

"I know it's hard, but I like to think that he would be watching over our baby. It would be a way for our son or daughter to be close to him."

My throat burned. "I like that idea."

"I'm glad." Shade placed a soft peck on my stomach. "I want you, Meadow. But..."

"It's weird without him," I answered for him.

He nodded.

"We don't have to do anything. We can just take this one second at a time and see what happens."

Shade nodded again, his fingers running along the edge of my sweatpants. "Kiss me."

I did at the same time he pushed his hand into the waist of my bottoms. A moan lodged its way into my throat when Shade slipped his fingers through the folds of my pussy.

He grunted his approval, knowing that no matter what happened, my body would always react to him. I couldn't help it. Both he and Sunny had given me everything I had ever needed. And now that it was just Shade and I, both of us had to try and fill that empty hole that Sunny left behind.

Shade slipped a finger inside me, followed by another and another. He swallowed my gasp, my sounds of pleasure getting lost between us. Sliding his other arm beneath my head, he deepened the kiss.

Hooking my fingers into the waist of my pants, I pushed them down my legs and kicked them off my feet.

His hand picked up speed, shoving all three fingers inside of me.

I grabbed his free hand, gripping the blankets beneath me with the other one.

He had never been overly dominant but this...this was his. I would do anything to help him feel better.

Shade's mouth slowed, kissing me softly while he fingered my lower body.

My thighs shook, that familiar tingle starting in my toes.

He broke the kiss, holding my hand against the bed beside my head and stared down at me. "Come for me, pet."

My eyes welled at the term of endearment he had used.

"Come," he repeated, stroking his thumb along my swollen clit.

My body broke, a hard cry leaving my lips at the release slamming through me.

Shade crushed his mouth to mine, swallowing the rest of my cries. He released my hand and moved to the spot between my knees but kept his fingers inside of me.

He reached between us, replacing his fingers with the tip of his cock. Pushing into me slowly, he filled me to the hilt and swallowed my gasp.

This was the first time without Sunny.

It was our first time as a couple. Just Shade and I.

The revelation hit me.

Sunny was actually gone.

A sob escaped me.

Shade broke the kiss, leaning his forehead against mine and brushing a hand over my head. "I know, baby. I know," he said, his voice thick.

Wrapping my legs around him, I held him tight.

We made love and cried. God, did we cry. Our tears mixed with the sounds of our pleasure opened up this newfound awareness that neither of us could have ever expected. My love for Shade became deeper at that point.

"I love you, little one," Shade told my stomach later that night. "And I promise that we will tell you who your second Daddy is. He would have loved you. So much." Shade rested his head on my lap, his dark eyes meeting mine.

I ran my fingers through his hair, my throat working through a hard lump.

One day we'll meet again, Sunny.

Whether you believed in that or not, I needed to believe. I needed to know that Sunny would come back to us. I didn't get enough time with him, but I would make up for that with Shade and our baby. And all the future babies we shared. Sunny would never be forgotten. No matter how much time passed.

I went into this wanting to fulfill a fantasy and ended up falling in love instead. As much as it hurt, I never regretted it for a second.

For that, I would forever be thankful to both Sunny and Shade.

I also knew, even years later, that Sunny would always be in our hearts and...

...with us.

Always.

EPILOGUE

Meadow

A YEAR HAD PASSED, and it still wasn't easier. To deal with the pain. The loss. To not have him by my side. To not hear his deep voice telling me what to do and how to please him or seeing his gray eyes light up whenever they landed on both Shade and I.

But I liked to think that Sunny was looking down on us, encouraging us to take it one day at a time. If it weren't for Shade, I knew that I would have fallen into myself, never to return. And I was sure that if it weren't for me, Shade would have done the same.

Having Sunny's room done up as the nursery helped us heal. It wasn't much but it was a start. Somehow, him being gone made Shade and I stronger. Individually and as a couple. But I could still hear him cry himself to sleep when he thought I wasn't listening. I could also hear him talk to himself, like he was having a conversation with Sunny whenever he looked at our son.

Andrew was our life and because of him, we were able to get through each day.

"What are we going to name him?" I asked Shade as I stared down at our newborn baby. A son. God, we had a son.

"Andrew," Shade said, his voice thick. "That was Sunny's middle name."

My eyes welled. I nodded. "It's perfect." I cupped Shade's cheek and placed a soft peck on his mouth. "Absolutely perfect."

And it had been. Andrew was the perfect baby. He never cried but instead, cooed and giggled, talking to us in his baby babble. It was funny in a way how much he reminded me of Sunny already. With his deep blue eyes and his constant chatter, he was always telling both Shade and I what to do in his own way.

A warm body stepped up behind me, followed by a hot mouth landing on my neck. Shade growled. "You smell good."

I laughed, turning in his arms. "I had a shower and I don't smell like baby puke anymore."

Shade chuckled, his eyes roaming down the length of me. "Andrew's down for a nap."

"Oh?" I raised an eyebrow, placing my hands on his chest. "He must have passed out after I fed him because it's not his nap time."

"Don't care." Shade crouched.

"What are you—" He had me over his shoulder before I could finish my question. My laughter followed us into our bedroom.

"It's been awhile." Shade threw me on the bed, gripping my hips and pulling me to the edge of the bed.

"It hasn't been that long." Truth was, it had been weeks, but I was always so damn tired, I didn't feel like showering much less having sex. It had also been hard since Sunny died. Neither of us cared to admit it though. I thought I had been the glue for both Sunny and Shade when really, it had been Sunny all along.

Shade kissed the spot between my breasts. "You good?"

I smiled, running my fingers through his dark hair. "I am. I am really good."

After Shade fucked me good and hard like we both needed, I was leaning against the headboard with him lying on his stomach. His head rested against my chest. It had been a signature move for us even if we hadn't had sex. He would lay on top of me. I would run my fingers through his hair. He would fall asleep. And I would breathe a sigh of relief and hope that he had happy dreams.

We still hadn't heard from Tanner, but Greyson had found out that he had gone into hiding. Looked like his club had turned on him after all. A part of me felt bad for him but at the same time, if I ever saw him again, I would kick his ass.

Greyson would call every so often and fill Shade in on club business but other than that, he never expected Shade to show up. He needed time. We both did.

I had nightmares every so often about Sunny dying on top of me. Some of those dreams, would follow with Shade dying instead. I would always wake up in a cold sweat with my screams silent on my tongue. Shade would calm me down and I would fall back asleep in his arms. It was hard. It was so damn hard. But with each day, each step, we got through it.

Death wasn't something you could get over though.

Especially not in this case.

But together, Shade and I were learning to heal.

Ever since Andrew was born, our worries and fears, fantasies and thoughts, were focused solely on him.

He was the reason we got through each day.

He was the reason we survived the nightmares from our minds.

I saw Sunny in him and I also saw Shade. We didn't know whose DNA ran through him, but we didn't care.

He wasn't Sunny's.

He wasn't Shade's.
He was *ours*.

THE END

Add Before Us (Next Generation, #3), a novella, to your
TBR list:

Goodreads -
https://www.goodreads.com/book/show/52760653-
before-us

ACKNOWLEDGEMENTS

This is my very first ménage. I'm nervous but so excited
about it all at the same time. So if you've read this far,
thank you for taking a chance on my little trio!
First off, thank you to my team of ladies! I couldn't do
this without you.
My Alpha reader, Angie, and my beta readers, Christina
and Jennifer. You girls have been through book after
book with me and I will never be able to thank you
enough for all of your help.
Joanne, my editor and friend! Thank you for helping me
make my books better.
Jennifer, again because now you're my PA! Thank you as
always for your never-ending help. And thank you for
letting me bounce my super random ideas off of you and
for just being there whenever I need a reason to kill off a
character.
J.M.'s Jems: I couldn't do any of this without you. You all
are my rocks!
Bloggers and fellow authors: Thank you for taking a
chance and for reading my stories!
My readers. You are the reason I get to do what I do. I
can't thank you enough.
I started writing the parents' books a few years ago and I
can't believe we're already the second book into The
Next Generation. This series is everything and holds all
the things we love about romance!

ABOUT

J.M. Walker is an Amazon bestselling author who also hit USA Today with Wanted: An Outlaw Anthology. She loves all things books, pigs and lip gloss. She is happily married to the man who inspires all of her Heroes and continues to make her weak in the knees every single day.

"Above all, be the HEROINE of your own life..." ~ Nora Ephron

Website: http://www.aboutjmwalker.com/
Facebook: https://www.facebook.com/jm.walker.author
Reader
Group: https://www.facebook.com/groups/JMsJems/
Twitter: https://twitter.com/jmwlkr
Instagram: https://www.instagram.com/jmwlkr/
Goodreads: https://www.goodreads.com/author/show/5132 169.J_M_Walker
BookBub: https://www.bookbub.com/authors/j-m-walker
Amazon: https://tinyurl.com/y7dpjkud
Newsletter: https://tinyurl.com/ya9hycak

Want more? Head on over to my website for my complete backlist!
https://www.aboutjmwalker.com/books